He stepped into the dark.

"Honey, I'm home," the man singsonged as his hands reached up for the flashlight he'd left on a hook on the right side of the wall. "Did you miss me?"

He stepped into the room and paused to light the candles on the makeshift dresser that stood along one wall. "I missed you all day, sweetheart. I couldn't think about anything or anyone except you." He knelt down next to the bed. "About being here with you, just like this."

She struggled against the restraints, her eyes wide with fear, her cries muffled by the gag that protruded from her mouth. The sounds she made were choked, incoherent.

He chuckled and pulled the gag from her mouth.

"Now, sweetheart, you know that—"

She spat in his face.

At first he froze, then he laughed. "Well, well, we still have a little fight in us, do we? Baby, you ought to know there's nothing that turns me on more than a little bit of fight."

Books published by The Random House Publishing Group
are available at quantity discounts on bulk purchases for
premium, educational, fund-raising, and special sales use.
For details, please call 1-800-733-3000.

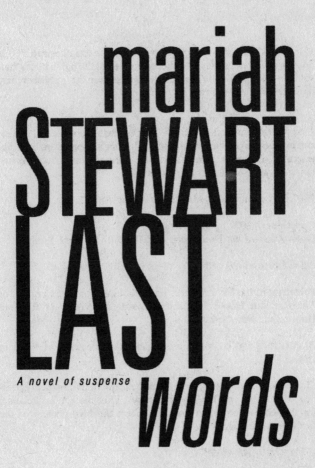

mariah
STEWART
LAST

A novel of suspense

words

BALLANTINE BOOKS • NEW YORK

2007 Ballantine Books Mass Market Original

Copyright © 2007 by Marti Robb
Excerpt from *Last Breath* copyright © 2007 by Marti Robb

Published in the United States by Ballantine Books, an imprint of The Random House Publishing Group, a division of Random House, Inc., New York.

BALLANTINE and colophon are registered trademarks of Random House, Inc.

This book contains an excerpt from the forthcoming hardcover edition of *Last Breath* by Mariah Stewart. This excerpt has been set for this edition only and may not reflect the final content of the forthcoming edition.

ISBN 978-0-345-49223-4

Cover design: Tony Greco
Cover image: Jupiterimages (woman)

Printed in the United States of America

www.ballantinebooks.com

OPM   9   8   7   6   5   4   3   2

For Laurie, self-proclaimed stalker/fan,
and Elsie, her sister, who tries to keep her in line

Acknowledgments

Many thanks to C. J. Lyons, M.D. (and author of medical suspense novels), for so patiently answering all my questions about the decomposition of the human body under extraordinary conditions.

Prologue

He leaned a little closer to the mirror, checking for signs of five o'clock shadow, tilting his head this way and that to satisfy himself there was no stubble to sully his image. He washed his hands and dried them on the beige hand towel his wife had hung on the bar that morning, then adjusted the collar of his polo shirt and straightened his shoulders.

He did look fine.

"Honey?" His wife called from the hall. "Are you watching the time?"

"Not closely enough, apparently." He called back, taking one more glance in the mirror before snapping off the bathroom light.

"Don't forget to say good night to the kids," she called over her shoulder.

"I won't." He fought to keep the touch of annoyance from his voice. As if he'd forget.

God, but she was annoying sometimes.

He poked his head into the kids' rooms. If he'd been an honest man, he'd have admitted that the delay was more to let the excitement within him continue to build than to have an extra ten minutes with his children. But he was far from honest, and so divided the time equally between them before reminding both to finish their homework and say their prayers before they turned off their lights at bedtime.

"See you at breakfast," he promised as he headed downstairs.

"I wish your out-of-town clients could show up during normal business hours," his wife complained when he came into the kitchen. She was rinsing the dinner dishes before stacking them methodically in the dishwasher and didn't bother to turn around when he came into the room. He fought an almost overwhelming urge to bash in the back of her skull with a heavy object. Which fortunately—or unfortunately, depending—was not within reach.

"What's the big deal?" He patted her on the butt with what he hoped would pass for affection, "It's barely seven. And you know very well it's not unusual to see clients in the early evening hours."

"Well, it just seems you're out more and more in the evenings." She turned to him. "But I guess I should be grateful you get home every night to have dinner."

"You know how strongly I feel about families sitting down at the table together at the end of the day." He opened his briefcase and pretended to be looking for something. "And I probably don't need to remind you that you work through dinner more often than I do."

"Not my idea," she protested.

"Not the point." He closed his briefcase with a snap.

"I don't get to set my own hours," she reminded him.

"I'm aware of that. I'm not finding fault. I'm just saying that sometimes if I leave work early to spend time with the kids, I have to make up that time later, which is what I'm doing tonight. It's a trade-off, that's all. I know you don't have that luxury." He checked his watch. "I've got to get going. I'll try not to be too late."

He kissed her cheek and walked out the door that led to the garage. On the way, he took a deep, healthy breath of fresh air. It smelled of lavender and late summer roses, and underneath it all it smelled of freedom. Of promise. Of something wicked and yet oh-so-fulfilling.

He drove carefully through town, stopping at the stop sign at the end of his street, and waving casually to a neighbor. He made a left at the first light and went on to his office, where he parked his car and went inside. Leaving the lights on inside—anyone passing by would think he was working late, as he often did—he slipped out the back door and walked to his destination. It took him a while, and he was mildly winded by the time he arrived.

Unlocking the padlock he'd installed after his last visitor had almost departed on her own, he stepped into the dark.

"Honey, I'm home." He singsonged as his hands reached up for the flashlight he'd left on a hook on the right side of the wall. "Did you miss me?"

His footsteps echoed on the wooden floor and he walked slowly, following the stream of light deeper into the building, letting the anticipation build in him—and the fear in her. He stopped when he came to a doorway, and stood still, sniffing the air, as a dog might, seeking the scent that a woman gave off when she was terrified.

There, there it was.

Lovely.

He stepped into the room and paused to light the candles on the makeshift dresser that stood along one wall. Inside, her clothes were folded and stacked. She would no longer have a need for them but he didn't have the heart to toss them out, so he'd washed them and put them away neatly.

"I missed you all day, sweetheart. I couldn't think about anything or anyone except you." He knelt down next to the bed. "About being here with you, just like this."

She struggled against the restraints, her eyes wide with fear, her cries muffled by the gag that protruded from her mouth.

"Oh, look at you." He tsk-tsked softly. "You've soiled yourself again. What am I going to do with you?"

He left the room for several moments, then returned with the garden hose.

"We're just going to have to give you a little shower, aren't we?" He smiled. "Can't have you getting all snuggly with your man, looking like that."

He unlocked the shackles on her ankles, then

one of the restraints that tied her wrists to the bed-post. Forcing her to stand on unsteady legs, he moved her as far away from the bed as he could, stretching the arm that was still attached to the bed as far as it would stretch. When he realized that he couldn't hose her down without getting the mattress wet, he debated momentarily before releasing her other arm. He knew her legs wouldn't support her even if she had the strength to try to get away—which she obviously wasn't about to do—and led her several feet to the right before turning on the nozzle.

The first blast of cold water hit her right in the middle, and she cried out, raising her arms to shield her eyes as best she could.

"Now, now, sweetheart, this will just take a minute." He turned her around to hose off her back and the backs of her thighs. "And you know, if you hadn't been such a naughty girl, this wouldn't be necessary."

He walked around her with the hose, enjoying her efforts to avoid getting the harsh spray in her face. When he was done, he dried her off with one of several towels he kept there for this purpose.

He noted the red welts all over her body. "The mosquitoes have really been feasting on you this week, haven't they? Maybe if you're nice to me, I'll bring something to put on those bites. They really are unattractive, you know."

He forced her stiff legs to carry her back to the bed. Tiny tears rolled down her face as she submitted to the humiliation of having her arms locked above her head once again. The shackles were not, however, re-fastened to her legs.

He stood and took off his polo shirt in one motion and placed it on the back of the chair he'd brought here when he first decided to feather his love nest. His shoes were next, then his pants, which were also carefully folded and then laid on top of the shirt.

"Like what you see, sugar?" He leaned down and touched the face of the woman on the bed. "I know you do, baby. And it's all yours. All for you . . ."

He eased himself down on top of her, his breathing coming faster now.

"And if you're a good girl, after I'm finished with you, maybe I'll give you some water. Would you like that?"

The woman struggled inside her bonds. The sounds she made were choked, incoherent.

"Yes, I know you would. Now, are you going to be a good girl?"

She nodded her head with as much vigor as she could muster.

He chuckled and pulled the gag from her mouth.

"Now, sweetheart, you know that—"

She spat in his face.

At first he froze, then he laughed. "Well, well, we still have a little fight in us, do we? Baby, you ought to know there's nothing that turns me on more than a little bit of fight."

He shoved the gag back into her protesting mouth. Before he forced himself inside her, he reached under the bed, seeking the recorder he kept there. Once located, it was activated with the touch of a finger.

"Later, baby," he whispered over her muted cries. "We'll have plenty of time to talk later. . . ."

1

Two years later

The sun was just rising, hot and round, tentacles of color wrapping around the early morning sky like fingers around an orange. From his kitchen window, Gabriel Beck watched the pinks turn coral then red.

Red sky at morning, sailors take warning.

"Oh, yeah," he grumbled under his breath. "This sailor's taking warning . . ."

The coffeepot beeped to announce its brew was ready, and he poured into the waiting St. Dennis Chamber of Commerce *DISCOVER SAINT DENNIS!* mug. He unlocked the back door then stepped onto the small deck and inhaled deeply. Early June in a bay town had scents all its own, and he loved every one of them. Wild roses mixed with salt air, peonies, and whatever the tide deposited on the narrow stretch of coarse sand that passed as beach overnight. It was heady, and along with the coffee he sipped, was all he really needed to start his day off right.

His cell phone rang and he patted his pocket for it, then remembered he'd left it on the kitchen counter. He went back inside, the screen door slamming behind him.

"Beck."

"Chief, I hate to do this to you so early in the morning, but we have a two-vehicle tangle out on Route 33," Police Sergeant Lisa Singer reported.

"Injuries?"

"One of the drivers is complaining of back pain. We're waiting for the ambulance. Traffic's really light right now, but if we can't get these cars out of here within the hour, we're going to have a mess. I've got Duncan directing traffic around the accident but it's going to get hairy here before too much longer."

"Christ, the Harbor Festival." So much for starting the day off right. "I'll call Hal and see if he can come in a little early today."

Beck tossed back the rest of the coffee and set the mug in the sink. "You called Krauser's for a tow truck?"

"Yeah, but I didn't get an answer. I called the service and asked them to page Frank, but I haven't heard back yet."

"I'll have Hal stop by on his way in, see if he can shake someone loose. Chances are Frank left his pager on the front seat of his car and he and the boys are outside shooting the shit and no one's opened the office yet."

"That's pretty much what I was thinking."

"I'll see what I can do."

Beck turned off the coffeepot and the kitchen light, then headed out to his Jeep, his phone in his hand. Once behind the wheel, he punched in the speed-dial for Hal Garrity as he backed out of his driveway. Hal, one-time chief of police in St. Dennis, Maryland, was now happily retired but always agreeable to working part-time hours in the summer when the tourists invaded the small town on the Chesapeake Bay. At sixty-five, he was still in fine shape, still took pride in being a good cop, and had no problem taking direction from his successor. After all, he'd been instrumental in hiring Beck.

Hal answered on the first ring. He was already on his way in to the station, but was just as happy to head out to the accident scene, and wouldn't mind a stop at Krauser's Auto Body to check up on that tow truck. Beck smiled when the call ended. As much as Hal loved retirement, he sure did love playing cop now and then.

The narrow streets of St. Dennis were waist-high in an eerie mist that had yet to be burned off by the still rising sun. Wisps of white, caught in the headlights, were tossed about by Beck's old Jeep, the ragged pieces floating across Charles Street, the main road that ran through the village, from the highway straight on out to the bridge over the inlet that led to Cannonball Island. Here in the center of town all was unbroken silence. No other cars were on the street, no shops opened, no pedestrians passed by. All was still. Peaceful.

This was the St. Dennis Beck loved, the one he remembered when he thought about moving back two years ago. But, with all the renovations, and every available building being bought up and fixed up and turned into one fancy shop or another, the St. Dennis he'd known would someday be little more than a fond memory. Now, though, in the early morning hours, before the tourists came out and the shop lights went on, the village was his home again. Peaceful, the way it was supposed to be.

Except for that damned traffic accident out on the highway, and knowing that by nine this morning the first of the tourists would arrive. They would be eager to spend their money in the picturesque boutiques and crowd his peaceful streets as they did every day starting in the middle of April and going strong right on through till Christmas. Today would be especially lively.

Beck checked the time. It was not quite six. The third annual Harbor Festival officially began at two that afternoon, but soon the first cars would begin to pull into the free parking lots across from the municipal building, and the early arrivals would descend on one of the three eateries in town that opened for breakfast.

He made a left onto Kelly's Point Road and eased slowly down the narrow stretch to the municipal building. He parked in front of the sign that read RESERVED: G. BECK and got out of his car. The tightly compacted crushed clam and oyster shells that covered the parking lot and served as fill crackled under his feet as he walked toward the building.

Beck entered his department through double glass doors off the lobby and was greeted by the dispatcher.

"Morning, Chief."

"Morning, Garland. You're in early. Who was on night dispatch?"

"Bill Mason. He had an asthma attack around five and called me to come in."

"Mason called you at five and asked you to come in?" Beck frowned.

"I didn't mind. I was already awake. He filled in for me when my car died in Baltimore a few weeks back."

"Glad you guys get along."

"Two peas in a pod," Garland replied before turning all business. "You heard about the accident out on thirty-three?"

"Lisa called a while ago. She's out there with Duncan. Hal should be out there by now, too." Beck looked through a short stack of phone messages that had come in overnight. "Give Lisa a call and tell her to come on in. And tell Duncan to make sure he's back in town before nine. I want him on foot patrol. By then, Hal ought to have the accident scene cleaned up, and we can put him on parking."

"Will do." Garland Hess, a thirty-five-year-old transplant from Boston three years earlier, went to work.

A long hall separated the quarters assigned to the police department exactly in two. Beck's office was at the end of the hall, and ran the width of their end of the building. On the opposite side of the lobby were the town's administrative offices, and a combination of meeting rooms and conference rooms, with storage on the second floor. The basement was a damp black hole that invited mold to grow on anything placed down there, and the attic was hot in summer and cold in winter. Some old police files and council meeting records going back decades were packed away in fading boxes tucked under the eaves, though no one ever ventured up there. Beck suspected that if examined, many of the boxes would be found to have been gnawed on by mice or covered with bat droppings.

Every once in a while Beck thought about climbing the open stairwell to the third floor to see just what-all had accumulated up there over the years, but he hadn't made it yet, and wasn't likely to any time soon. The "archives," as Hal liked to refer to the stored files, would have to wait until the tourist season had come and gone. This weekend's Harbor Festival, slated to run from Friday through Sunday night, was just one of many weekends planned by the mayor and the Chamber of Commerce to bring in crowds and revenue. The merchants, understandably, all thought it was swell. The old-timers, like Hal and some others, thought it was all a pain in the butt.

"These narrow little streets weren't designed for so much traffic," Hal complained to Beck when he made it back to the station after having directed traffic out on the highway for two hours.

"That's why the powers that be had those parking lots put in behind the shops on Charles Street." Beck said, and took the opportunity to remind him, "Rumor has it that you were one of the powers who thought it was a good idea."

"That was six years ago. Harbor Day was barely a gleam in the mayor's eye back then." Hal shook his head. "Who'da figured this sleepy little town was about to wake up?"

"It has done that," Beck muttered, and leaned across his desk to pick up the ringing phone. At the same time, he motioned to Hal to take a seat in one of the empty chairs.

Beck's call was short and he hung up just as Lisa poked her head in the door.

"First of the onslaught is just starting," she told the chief. "What do you want to do about traffic control?"

"Put Duncan out on the highway till eleven"—Beck pulled his chair up to his desk and sat—"then call Phil in and ask him to take over out there until two. Things should have eased up a lot by then."

"What about here in town?"

"I expect the only real problem will be where Kelly's Point runs into Charles Street, there at the crosswalk," Beck said.

"I'll take that until noon," Hal told him.

"Then I'll take over from you from twelve to four," Lisa offered.

"Aren't you supposed to be off today?" Beck frowned and searched his in-bin for the schedule.

"Monday and Tuesday." Lisa leaned against the door jamb.

"I'd have thought you'd be down at the boatyard to give your husband a hand." Hal smiled. "Bound to be some foot traffic, all those people down on the docks. Someone's going to want to look at a boat. Singer's Boatyard is the only show in town."

Lisa smiled back. "The boatyard's Todd's baby. He does his job, I do mine. His sister took the kids to the beach for the weekend, so we're both doing our own thing today. But yeah, we're hoping that a few folks in the crowd will be looking to pick up a boat this weekend. He's put a few on sale, so we'll see."

"Well, if you want to take the lot down nearest the dock, that's okay by me. We can put Sue on bike patrol," Beck said, "just to have a presence on the street. Discourage pickpockets, find lost kids, lost parents. Give directions, that sort of thing."

"Sue just came in at eight," Lisa told him. "I'll let her know she's on bike today."

"I'll do a little foot patrol from time to time during the day," Beck said. "Tomorrow, Lisa, you can take bike. I expect people will be leaving at different times throughout the day, so I don't think we're going to have the mess we'll have today."

"So who's going to be minding the fort back here?" Hal asked after Lisa left to find Sue, the only other woman on the force.

"Me," Beck told him. "I'll be in and out all day. Frankly, I don't expect much. This isn't a biker convention—it's not much more than a bunch of yuppies out to put a few miles on their Docksiders, looking to see how much money they can spend in a single weekend. Buy some cool artsy stuff at Rocky's gallery, maybe some antique something at Nita's, grab an ice-cream cone at Steffie's after they eat crabs out at the pier or over at Lola's. Then maybe they'll spend a few hours down at the harbor watching the boats, maybe even wander into Singer's and buy one of those fancy boats Lisa's old man has sitting in his showroom. I'm thinking the most action we might see will be the parking tickets Duncan writes. A fender bender or two, maybe, since people will be traveling on foot most of the time, once they come into town and park."

Beck leaned his arms on his desk and grinned.

"And like I said, this isn't exactly a party crowd."

"You're probably right." Hal hoisted himself out of his seat. "I'm going to head on down to Charles Street. Guess I'll see you around at some point during the day."

"Thanks, Hal." Beck stood as the older man started toward the door.

"For what?"

"For coming back to help out."

"My pleasure. Truly, it is. I don't mind traffic. Never did." He stood in the doorway, half in, half out. "Even when I sat where you're sitting, I never minded traffic patrol."

"You just wanted to see what was going on in town. Who was driving what. Who was going where with whom," Beck teased.

"Damn right. Part of the job." Hal was still talking even as he left Beck's office. "Chief of police has to know what's doin' in his town. Only way to know for sure is to get out there and keep an eye on folks."

Beck could hear Hal at the end of the hall, talking to Garland and flirting harmlessly with Sue, who was twenty-five and good-natured enough to flirt back.

Well, there was no denying Hal was in his element here, Beck thought as he returned to the pile of mail that had yet to be answered. He figured today would be a good day to get to that. The building would be all but empty for most of the day, and by noon he should have all the mail caught up.

He glanced out the window behind his desk and noted that cars were starting to pull into the lot across the road from his building. Beyond the lot he could see the New River, and beyond that the Chesapeake Bay. Off to his right and hidden from his view was the small, shallow harbor and the docks. He knew from past experience that by noon the town would be filled to near capacity. The latecomers would be looking for parking out on the side of the road leading out of town and walking back to the center of things. Like they say, the early bird gets the best parking space.

Beck turned on his computer and quickly scanned his e-mail. One message stood out.

MISSING WOMAN read the subject. Beck opened it and read the note from his fellow chief of police up in Ballard, a town about four miles away.

The e-mail contained a photo of a pretty young woman with light brown hair and gold-brown eyes. She laughed into the camera, as a large black dog climbed into her lap. The e-mail identified her as Colleen Preston, of Ballard. Twenty-two years old, last seen on June 26. Beck glanced at the calendar. She'd been missing for two weeks now. He knew what the chances were they'd find her alive.

He tapped his fingers on the side of his keyboard. Hadn't there been a similar e-mail from another police department just a few weeks back?

He checked his old mail. There it was, from Chief Meyer, over in Cameron. He opened the e-mail and read it through, then printed out both that notice and the one from today. He placed the pictures side by side. The two women couldn't have been more different. Colleen Preston was five feet nine inches tall. Twenty-year-old Mindy Kenneher, from Cameron, was five two and had short blond hair. The only similarity appeared to be that they'd both left home one morning to go to work, and never came back.

Beck got up and walked to the end of the hall, taking both printouts with him. At the bulletin board, he pinned the two pictures up, side by side. On his way back to his office, it occurred to him that Cameron was about seven miles from St. Dennis. Which made it only three miles from Ballard. Way too close to St. Dennis for comfort.

He wondered if either of the girls had turned up. If the investigations had led to any leads. If Meyer in Cameron had been in touch with Chief Daley in Ballard. If they'd traded notes. That's what he'd do, if it happened in his town.

God forbid, he thought as walked back to his office.

The photo of Mindy Kelleher was still on his computer screen. Pretty girl, he thought as he closed the e-mail. As the image faded away, a solid chill went up his spine. It gave him pause for just a moment. Then he turned off the computer and headed down the hall.

"I'll be on foot for a while," Beck told Garland as he passed by and left through the front door.

He walked swiftly to the path that led from the building to Kelly's Point Road. From there it was a short walk to the center of town. It was a path he'd walked more times than he could count. Today he couldn't seem to walk fast enough.

Like Hal said, the chief of police should know what was going on, and today was as good a day as any to see what folks were up to, and who was walking the streets of his town.

2

"So what was the final tally?"

Vanessa Keaton, Beck's sister, slid into the booth across from her brother, then plunked her large designer handbag on the seat next to her.

"Is that thing alive?" Beck asked.

"Is what thing alive?" Vanessa frowned.

"That . . . whatever it was you just tossed onto the seat there." He pretended to crane his neck to see over the table. " 'Cause you know, this is a nice restaurant. They don't allow animals in here."

"Very funny." She held up the bag, which was a patchwork leather number trimmed in faux fur. "Isn't it darling? I get them from a designer in Baltimore. And for your information, it's fake fur. I wouldn't sell anything with real fur. And I sold eight of these little babies this weekend. I'm going to have to order more."

"So I take it your shop is doing well?"

"Please. It's a boutique." She fluttered her eyelashes and tossed her long black hair over her shoulders. "And quite the froufrou boutique it is, too."

"Yeah, froufrou. Whatever," Beck said and signaled for the waitress.

Vanessa laughed. Beck tried not to.

"So you didn't answer my question." She opened

her menu and began to scan the specials. "What was the final tally for the weekend?"

"Four fender benders, sixteen parking tickets, three lost kids, six lost parents, one pedestrian knocked down by a bicycle—fortunately, not a bike ridden by one of my officers—three stolen purses, and a couple of lost credit cards." He sipped the beer he'd ordered before she arrived. "All in all, not so bad, given the size of the crowd we had."

"How's the pedestrian?"

"She's fine." Beck looked up as Shirley, the waitress, approached. "I'll have the soft-shells tonight, Shirl."

"Good choice. They're perfect." She made a note on her order pad. "Salad dressing, Chief?"

"Blue cheese."

"Same for you, Vanessa?" the woman asked.

"Ah, you mean, crustaceans cooked in garlicky butter in their allegedly edible little shells?" She wrinkled her nose. "I think not. I'll have the flounder special. Balsamic dressing on the greens."

"You'll never be mistaken for a native, you keep talking like that," Beck teased.

"I don't have a problem with that." She shook her head firmly. "I never pretended to be a native of the Eastern Shore, bro. And therefore I am exempt from having to eat those floppy little crabs."

"Those floppy little crabs are damned tasty."

"I just can't get past the fact that they're caught while they're *molting*, for Christ's sake. Scooped up when they're most vulnerable, sold to the highest bidder, and slapped into a pan of butter and herbs. . . ."

She faked a shiver. "Inhuman, I say. Sneaky and un-derhanded, even."

"But damned tasty," Beck repeated.

"So you say."

"And what was your tally this weekend?" he asked as their salads were served.

"I did so well, Beck." Vanessa's eyes shone with pleasure. "My best sales ever. It was just wonderful. All those customers, oohing and aahing over all the pretty things. It was just the way I always dreamed it would be, having my own little shop."

Beck cleared his throat.

"*Boutique*, that is," she corrected herself with a grin. "Lots of customers lined up at the cash register all day long. It was just . . . perfect."

"Now, you know that every weekend isn't likely to be as busy," he reminded her.

"I know it won't always be this good," she said, nodding, "but I think St. Dennis is going to continue to attract crowds, right on through to the fall. And the Chamber of Commerce has all those wonderful plans for Christmas; the brochures were given out all weekend. I was handing them out to the customers and a number of people said they'd be back."

"I'm just saying take it as it comes, Ness. I don't want you to be disappointed."

"I appreciate that, but I think it's going to be a great season. I think all the advertising has paid off. I saw Jonah on my way over here, and he said his inn is booked straight into September."

"You're kidding."

"No. I'm telling you, St. Dennis is the new hot spot on the Eastern Shore."

"Swell," he said, half under his breath.

"It is swell. For us merchants, anyway." She poked at her salad happily. "For you . . . well, maybe not so much. Maybe you need to think about hiring a few more officers."

"There's nothing in the town budget for that. I'm lucky to have Hal and Phil even part-time this year."

"Well, with all the extra money the town is going to bring in over the next few months in parking revenue alone, you should be able to get maybe one more cop out of the town council, don't you think?"

"We'll see." He speared a chunk of cucumber. It wasn't just the salary, he could have told her, it was benefits, uniforms, another car, higher insurance, but Beck was tired from the long weekend and wasn't up to giving his sister a lesson in municipal finance.

"Anyway, I'm glad you had a great weekend, Ness."

"I had a super weekend." She grinned, her eyes sparkling.

"Something else happen?"

"I got asked out to dinner for tomorrow night." She wiggled her eyebrows. "As in a date."

"Who?" He frowned. "Who asked you out?"

"Mickey Forbes."

"Forbes?" Beck's frown deepened. "He's married with kids."

"No, he's not. They're getting divorced." She ignored his disapproval. "Where have you been? She left him months ago."

"Still . . ."

Vanessa tossed her hair back, and the image of Colleen Preston flashed through Beck's mind.

"How well do you know him?"

"Beck." She put her fork down. "It's dinner. *Dinner*. That's all. What's the big deal?"

He hesitated, not sure what to say.

"Look, it's really sweet of you to want to be the big brother. I kinda like it sometimes, especially since I didn't have that growing up, you know?" She tried to laugh. "And God knows, I could have used some brotherly guidance, back then."

"Ness . . ." His face darkened with regret.

"Hey, not your fault. That wasn't meant as anything other than a statement of fact." She reached across the table and patted his hand. "And you've more than made up for it this past year. There's no way I can ever repay you for helping me set up the shop and finding the apartment for me and—"

He waved her words away.

"Just be careful who you go out with, where you go, keep your doors locked, that's all I'm saying."

"Do you know something I don't know?" Her eyes narrowed.

"Little sister, I know lots of things you don't know." He tried to interject a little humor into the conversation but it fell flat.

"Admitted, but right now we're talking about Mickey Forbes. Is there something you know about him that I should know?"

"No, nothing. I just didn't know he was getting divorced, that's all. Wouldn't want to see you step into a mess."

"I appreciate that, Beck. I really do."

Their dinners arrived and the conversation ceased for a moment as each concentrated on their meal.

"There is one thing," he said after a few minutes of near silence. "I got alerts from the chiefs of police in two nearby towns. One from Cameron, which is about seven miles south of here, and the other from Ballard, which is—"

"I know Ballard. The stable where I ride is in Ballard." Vanessa nodded. "What was the alert about?"

"Each town has a young woman missing. Cameron a little over a month ago, Ballard two weeks ago."

"And they haven't been found?"

"Not as far as I know."

"But they haven't been found dead, either, right?"

"Right."

"So they could just have run away or left town or be off on a binge someplace? Couldn't it just be a co-incidence that there are two of them?"

"It's possible. I don't know enough about either case right now to say, but I guess when someone's missing, those are all possibilities. Earlier today I called both Daley and Meyer, but I haven't heard back yet. Of course, I was out of the office all day. I expect I'll learn more once I've been able to catch up with them. But in the meantime . . ."

"I hear you, and I understand what you're saying." She nodded slowly. "And I promise not to do anything stupid or go anyplace alone. Though God knows St. Dennis is probably the safest place I've ever lived."

"There's no place that's entirely safe from everything, Ness." He cut his soft-shell crab with his fork and raised the fork to his mouth.

"Oh, man, that is one ugly thing you're eating." She visibly shivered.

Beck waved the fork at her, relieved to have the diversion. The two young women had been heavy on his mind ever since he'd read those e-mails yesterday morning. Vanessa's comments were right on. Either or both of them could have returned home by now, or contacted their parents to let them know their whereabouts. Or they could have run away from home.

Or they could be dead.

He shook off the last thought. If he didn't hear back from someone by tomorrow noon, he'd try Warren Daley again. Maybe he'd have some news that he hadn't gotten around to sharing with the surrounding departments yet.

Maybe then that cold spike Beck got up the back of his neck every time he thought of Colleen Preston or Mindy Kenneher might go away for good.

They finished their entrées and talked quietly while Vanessa polished off a huge serving of strawberry shortcake and two cups of coffee. Shirley returned twice to the table with the coffeepot in her hand.

"You sure, Chief?" She asked when he declined a second cup.

"I'm sure," he told her. "I'm up with the sun again tomorrow. Any more caffeine and I'll still be awake come dawn."

"Which would make him very cranky," Vanessa stage-whispered.

"Well, we couldn't have that, now, could we?" Shirley placed the check on the table. "Whenever you're ready, Chief."

"That's mine." Vanessa reached for the check. "And don't argue with me. I had a very good day."

"So you said." He leaned against the back of the booth and smiled. "And I'm not arguing."

"Good, 'cause it wouldn't do you any good." She placed several bills on the table and looked across at her brother. "You ready?"

"I am."

They both stood at the same time and headed for the door, Beck stopping at this table and that to have a word here and there. While he did so, Vanessa waited patiently, watching her brother shake a hand or pat a back, always with a smile on his face.

"You're in your element here," she said when he joined her at the door.

"Seems so." He pushed the door open and nodded to the couple coming in as he and Vanessa went out.

"I'm glad. It was a long time coming."

He didn't bother to respond. There was nothing to be said.

"You're almost happy here, aren't you?"

"Almost."

"I guess that's something." She touched his arm lightly to acknowledge his admission, then pointed to the end of the street. "My car's down there. Where's yours?"

"I let Hal take the patrol car. He spent too much

time on his feet today. I figured I could walk home, walk in to the station in the morning."

"Walk me down to my car, then, and I'll drive you home."

"Sure."

They strolled along the newly cobbled sidewalk, renovated in the early spring when the final colonial touches were made to the town to play up its revolutionary war heritage and hopefully, bring in some tourist money. Vanessa's heels tapped on the stones as they walked the two blocks to her car.

"I got a postcard from Mom," Vanessa told him when they'd gone half a block. "She's in North Dakota."

When Beck didn't respond, she said, "She's remarried. A sheep farmer this time."

"Did she invite you to come to see her?"

"No."

"Did she say she'd come to see you?"

"No."

"Did she apologize for—"

"Stop it." Vanessa had reached her car and stood at the door, her key in her right hand. "Just . . . stop."

"Then stop telling me about her. I don't care where she is and I don't want to know what she's doing."

Vanessa unlocked the door. "Get in. I'll drop you off."

"I think I'll walk."

"Don't be mad at me, Beck. I just thought you'd want to know—"

"Know what? That Maggie's alive and well and living large out West? Fine. You told me." He exhaled a long, deep breath. "I'm not angry with you. I swear I'm not. I just don't want to hear about it, okay?"

"Okay." Vanessa nodded. "You sure about the ride?"

"Positive. I really feel like walking, but thanks anyway. And thanks for dinner."

Vanessa saluted and got into her car. Beck stood on the sidewalk and watched until the sedan disappeared around the corner at Gull Lane, then began to walk home. It was hardly late—barely ten o'clock—but already St. Dennis had turned in for the night. Many of the houses were closed up, with lamplight or the blue haze of a TV in the occasional window. Almost everyone in town had participated in some way over the weekend, and everyone who had done so was tired from their efforts. Beck's long legs covered a lot of ground in a short amount of time, and within five minutes he was home. He unlocked the front door and stepped into the dark house, snapping on a lamp in the living room as he passed through to the kitchen, where he poured himself a glass of water and tried not to think about the fact that he now knew where his mother was. Life was so much easier when he didn't know. Not knowing relieved him of the responsibility of having contact with her.

Yeah, right, he snorted. Like anyone in this family has ever really been responsible for anyone else.

Not true, he reminded himself. He'd made himself responsible for Vanessa the day she walked into his life and announced, "Hi. I'm your little sister. Mom said it was about time we met . . ."

So typical of Maggie. That was just the way she'd

dumped Beck on his unsuspecting father. Just as Beck had had no idea he had a sister, his father had had no idea he had a son.

Beck figured that, in the long run, he'd gotten the best of the bargain. Maggie had done only two things for Beck that really counted in his life: she'd dumped him on his father's front door when he was fourteen, and she'd sent him a sister. Twenty-six years old at the time and newly divorced from an abusive husband— her second—and as different from Beck as the sun is from the moon, Vanessa had quickly been welcomed by not only her brother, but by his father as well. They certainly made an odd trio, he mused as he turned off the lamp he'd switched on earlier. The craggy old man, the beautiful, leggy young woman who looked like a fashion model, and the cop who'd taken a lifetime to find himself.

He was about to climb the steps to the second floor when he noticed the blinking light on his answering machine. He hit the play button and leaned against the wall while the message played.

"Beck, Warren Daley over here in Ballard. I got your message but this is the first chance I've had to return the call. Listen, all hell's breaking loose over here, so call me as soon as you get this. I'm hoping to God you called me because you have something that will help make some sense out of this, because I sure as hell don't understand it. Never seen anything like this in my life. Call my cell . . . doesn't matter what time. God knows I'll be up . . ."

Warren Daley repeated his cell phone number twice, and Beck made a note of it. Whatever was going on in Ballard did not sound good. Beck dialed the number and identified himself when Daley answered the phone. He listened carefully as the police chief told him what they'd found in Ballard earlier that evening.

"Where are you now?" Beck asked.

"Still at the scene. I expect we'll be here for a while."

"Mind if I drive down there?"

"I wish you would, buddy. I really wish you would. It's the last house on Crawford, where it dead ends."

Beck hung up and went right out the front door. In his haste he'd forgotten he did not have his patrol car and had to go back inside the house for the keys to his Jeep.

This was not going to be a good night, he told himself as he backed the Jeep out of the drive. A bad night for everyone involved, but especially for the family of Colleen Preston.

3

At first glance, the thing that lay on the front porch of the small white Cape Cod house looked to be anywhere from five and a half to six feet in length. It was sort of oblong, sort of opaque, and in the porch light's yellow glare, it was impossible to identify.

The fact that five or six cops were standing around the object didn't help. From where Beck parked his Jeep, he could see the vague shape and size, and little else. But since he already knew what had been found on Paul and Kitty Preston's front porch a few short hours ago, Beck didn't need to figure it out.

He showed his badge to the first officer he met at the foot of the driveway, the one charged with making certain no civilians came within fifty feet of the house. The last thing Chief Daley wanted was to subject any of the citizens of Ballard to the sad and strange cocoon that held the remains of Colleen Preston.

Beck softly greeted one of the local detectives and continued on toward the porch. Upon hearing Beck's voice, Warren Daley stepped out of the glare and came down the steps as if he carried the weight of the entire Preston family on his back. In a way, he did.

"Jesus, Beck, this is the weirdest shit I've ever

seen." Daley, nearing sixty with a slight paunch and a full head of salt-and-pepper hair, looked pale, even in the light cast by the lamps set up by the CSIs who were hovering over the form on the porch. "You gotta see it to believe it."

He motioned Beck forward, then grabbed his elbow and led him to the porch. Beck shook free and climbed the steps, his eyes on the object that lay just outside the front door. From inside the house came a steady sound of anguished sobs. Beck approached the object which glistened in the light and knelt down.

Inside a cocoon of clear plastic wrap Colleen Preston lay trapped, tightly enclosed from her feet to the top of her head. A closer look revealed that her feet were side by side, her arms behind her, a tiny portion of her tongue showing between her closed lips, her lifeless eyes bulging.

"Holy Mother of God," Beck whispered.

"Yeah. My thoughts exactly," Daley said from behind.

"Her parents found her like this?" asked Beck.

"Her younger brother. Sixteen years old." Daley shook his head. "Imagine coming home and finding this waiting on your front porch."

"Where's the kid now?"

"Inside with his parents and one of the state detectives. I had to call them in. I don't have the crime scene techs to handle something like this, don't have the lab. The usual, we handle okay. Better than okay. But shit like this . . . I'm not too proud to say when something's over my head." Daley shook his head again. "This is serious shit."

"Can't argue that," Beck muttered.

The county medical examiner's van pulled up and a woman in khaki shorts and a dark tank top got out. As she walked toward the house, she pulled on a dark gray smock that covered her to right below her knees. She reached the porch and climbed the steps, her eyes fixed upon the form on the deck.

"Warren. Beck." She greeted them without looking away from the body.

"Viv," the two chiefs responded at the same time.

"Sorry it took me so long," she said, her full attention on the shiny opaque cocoon. "I was at my niece's birthday party in Annapolis. Traffic on the bridge coming back was a bitch."

She knelt down, much as Beck had done.

"What happened to you, sweetheart?" She crooned almost inaudibly. "Who did this to you?"

She opened the bag she carried and took out a pair of plastic gloves, which she pulled on. She drew closer to the form and leaned over it, studying the contorted face of the victim for a few long minutes.

"I don't see any reason to prolong this here, with her family inside." The ME looked up at Warren Daley. "Let's get her over to the morgue and I'll unwrap her there. It's obvious she was killed elsewhere, and the CSIs can continue to look for evidence here. But there's nothing to be gained in unwrapping her on her front porch."

"It's your call, of course," Daley replied.

Dr. Vivian Reilly stood and muttered what sounded to Beck like "one sick bastard," then called to one of the technicians to bring a body bag. She stood between Daley and Beck and watched as the victim was removed from the scene.

"I'll give you a call as soon as I have something," she told Chief Daley before walking toward her van.

"Viv, you ever see anything like this before?" Daley called after her. "You hear about something like this?"

She didn't bother to turn around, she merely shook her head emphatically and kept on walking.

"I suspect if there'd been another like this in the area, we would have heard," Beck commented.

"That's some sick shit." Daley watched the van pull away.

"Warren, have you spoken with Rich Meyer in Cameron?" Beck asked.

"Not for a few weeks, why?" Daley's eyes were still on the van's taillights, just barely visible as they rounded a bend in the road.

"You got that e-mail from him about the girl who disappeared a few weeks before the Preston girl?"

Daley turned to look at Beck.

"You think there's a connection?" He stared at Beck. "You think the same guy . . . ?"

"I don't know what to think." Beck shrugged. "I'm just saying, a girl went missing in Cameron a few weeks before Colleen Preston. I was just wondering if you and Meyer had been in touch about it; if you knew whether or not the Kenneher girl had turned up."

"I'll give him a call first thing in the morning," Chief Daley told him. "No point in getting him out of bed now. Not much he can do at this hour anyway."

"Chief." One of the Ballard officers motioned to Daley, and he excused himself before walking away.

Beck stood to the side of the house and watched the state detectives comb the Preston's front lawn for any evidence that might have been left by whoever dumped the girl's body on the porch for her family to discover. After ten minutes, he waved to Daley, who was discussing something with a few of the state troopers. Daley waved back and called, "Thanks." Beck nodded and walked down the drive to his Jeep, the image of what had once been a beautiful young woman firmly in his mind's eye.

What kind of person did such a thing?

One sick bastard.

Viv had gotten that right.

The following morning local news carried the story. Every channel Beck turned on had a solemn reporter relating the known details, which were few. Twenty-two-year-old Colleen Preston had disappeared more than a week ago and early last night her body had been found on her family's front porch by her sixteen-year-old brother. No cause of death released. No suspects. No comment as yet from the Ballard police department.

With so few hard facts, Beck wondered how so many found so much to say about the tragedy. He turned off the television in his office in disgust.

"Poor thing, that girl." Garland stood in the doorway. "Any idea what that's all about?"

"No clue." Beck sat at his desk.

"I forgot to tell you, Chief Meyer returned your

call while you were on the phone a few minutes ago."
The dispatcher stepped forward and handed him a
slip of paper. "He said to tell you that's his private
line."

"Thanks." Beck turned to dial the number.

"I'm going to grab a cup of coffee," Garland said
as he left the room. "I'll be in the break room if you
need me. Hal's taken over for me for a few."

"Right." Beck nodded absently as he dialed.

"Meyer," a gruff voice answered on the second
ring.

"Rich, it's Gabriel Beck."

"Hey, Beck." Rich Meyer sighed heavily. "Guess
you've got your TV on, too. Some crazy shit, eh? I
heard from Bart Daniels, one of the state detectives,
that girl was wrapped up like some big spider had
snagged her and swathed her in spider silk."

"That's pretty close," Beck agreed. "It's a miracle
that hasn't leaked yet. Daley's trying to sit on the details for as long as he can."

"You saw her? It's true?"

"Yeah. I saw her. It's true." Beck blew out a long
breath. "It wasn't pretty."

"Heard the bastard left her right on her own front
porch, right where someone from her family would
find her."

"The whole family was over here in St. Dennis all
day, stayed late for dinner. Her younger brother was
the first one home, found her when he came home last
night."

"Can you imagine that?"

"No." Beck thought of his own sister. "No, I can't.

Listen, Rich, I was wondering if there'd been any more on that case you e-mailed about a few weeks ago, the missing girl. Mindy Kenneher."

"Nothing, Beck. And you're not the only one who's wondering if she's met the same fate. Jesus, that's all we need. . . ."

"I have to admit I'm wondering. Looking at that body last night, I find it hard to believe this guy hasn't done this sort of thing before. It was all so . . ." Beck searched for the word. "Complete. Not a detail was missed. The body wrapped as neat and tight as you please. There wasn't even an odor. You had the feeling it was all carefully thought out, even how and when the body was left to be discovered. But it looked like, I don't know, like a prop from a movie. I walked away with the feeling that it was all part of something else, that there was nothing random about the how or the why of it."

"All that stuff we learned about in the police academy. About killers."

"Right. It had all the earmarks of someone who was practiced."

"A repeat offender, possibly."

"That's how it looked to me. Of course, I could be wrong." Beck paused. "I hope I'm wrong. But it made me wonder, about this girl of yours who's missing, and I was wondering if she still was."

"Unfortunately, she's still gone and there are no leads. No one saw anything. It's as if she walked out of her office and into the night and just poof, gone."

"I was hoping by now, if she was a runaway, she'd have contacted someone. Her family, a friend . . ."

"There's been nothing. And between you and me, I never saw this girl as a runaway. She's a damned good kid. Good athlete, good grades, never gave her parents a bit of trouble. She seemed to have a great relationship with her mom and dad and her siblings."

"You seem to know a lot about her."

"The Kennehers live across the street from us. I've known Mindy since she was a baby. We've combed this town six ways to Sunday. There's not a trace of her to be found. There's been nothing since she disappeared."

"Must be tough on her family."

"You have no idea."

From where he stood at his office window, Beck could see Vanessa coming up the walk, swinging that furry handbag of hers.

"You're right, Rich. I don't." *And I pray I never do.* "Maybe you want to talk to Warren, maybe put your heads together on this one, see what similarities there might be."

"Jesus, I'm almost afraid to. But you're right. We need to talk."

"Anything I can do, you give me a call. If you want to put together a team to search the woods and the fields . . ."

"Wouldn't be a bad idea. Though if the same guy had Mindy, and I don't want to jump to the conclusion that he does, God forbid, but I'm just saying, wouldn't he do the same thing? Dump her at her house?"

"I don't want to jump to that conclusion, either, but I guess it could happen that way."

"Just between you and me, I'm afraid we're in over our heads here."

"What do you mean?" Beck craned his head to see what his sister was doing. It looked as if she'd stopped to talk to someone.

Shit. Steffie Wyler.

"I mean, this is a small town, Beck. A small police force. We've never investigated an abduction—not saying that's what definitely happened here, but I'd be remiss if I didn't consider it."

"Agreed."

"None of us have any experience with this sort of thing."

"I'm afraid I can't help you there. I'm assuming you've spoken with all of her friends."

"Everyone we could find who'd ever spoke so much as a word with her. Friends, coworkers, hairdresser. The woman who does her nails and the mechanic who fixed her car and pumps her gas for her. We've gone through every aspect of this girl's life. No one knows anything."

"Have you thought about calling on the sheriff's department? Maybe they could give you some pointers."

"You know what that means."

"Yeah, Jake Madison. I can't blame you for not wanting to tangle with him."

"He just makes such a clusterfuck out of everything he touches."

"I can't argue with that. But maybe, like you said, you and Warren . . ."

"Yeah, yeah. I'll give Daley a call as soon as we hang up."

"Have you thought about calling the FBI, see if you could maybe talk to one of their profilers? You know, see if you can get a bead on what type of person would have done this. Seems to me it's a pretty bold statement, wrapping your victim in plastic like that."

He was going to add . . . "and watching them suffocate," . . . but decided against it. He hadn't heard that Viv had issued a cause of death as yet, and it was only his gut reaction that the killer had wrapped the girl up like that so he could watch her struggle to breathe. And from what he'd seen of the vic's face the night before, she'd certainly struggled for air. But until Viv made a statement, he should probably just keep his speculations to himself.

"That stuff's all crap, profiling." Meyer made a dismissive noise. "What's a profiler gonna tell me? This guy has anger issues? He doesn't like women? Bunch of crap."

Beck didn't agree, but he let it ride.

"Well, in the meantime, till something breaks, it wouldn't hurt for all of us to be extra alert. Keep as many cars on the street as we can."

"Right. I'll call around to the other local departments." Chief Meyer paused, then suggested, "Maybe a bunch of us should get together some morning soon, maybe for breakfast. You know, a little informal meeting."

"You just tell me where and when. I'll be there."

"Thanks, Beck. I'll let you know if we turn up any-thing."

"Appreciate it, Rich." Beck hung up and stared out the window, trying to will Vanessa away from the tall blond, but the two women changed direction and headed toward Steffie's ice cream shop across the parking lot from the municipal building. *That's right, Stef. Lure my sister with ice cream, then lay out all the dirty details, get a little sympathy, get her on your side.*

Did women really do stuff like that? he wondered.

Nah. It was just a little paranoia on his part. Steffie hadn't had one good word to say to Beck since he stopped dating her a few weeks back. He'd tried to explain to her that it wasn't her, or anything she'd said, or anything she'd done. It just wasn't working out, as far as he was concerned, and that's just what he'd told her.

Steffie, this just isn't working out.

There hadn't been anything he could put his finger on. He just knew he didn't feel the way he thought a man should feel about a woman he'd dated for sev-eral months. Then again, he doubted he'd ever feel that way about anyone. His track record wasn't very good.

"Whatever," he muttered, shaking it off. Now wasn't the time to worry about what she was telling Vanessa. There were more important things to think about right now.

Like how to make sure what happened in Ballard and Cameron didn't happen here in St. Dennis.

He'd call a meeting first thing in the morning, get

all the officers in, part-timers included, and discuss the need to be a little more vigilant—hell, a *lot* more vigilant—until Colleen Preston's killer was caught. And he'd see what they could do about putting together a team to search the waterfront area for any trace of Mindy Kenneher. Not that he expected to find anything, but still, it wouldn't hurt. With the Harbor Festival behind him, he could spare a few hours to look through some of those old buildings down there near the cove. He certainly didn't want to start a panic, but the towns were too close. What infected one could all too easily infect the others.

On his desk sat the stack of incident reports from the weekend. He thumbed through them, wishing they'd been more attentive to watching the crowd over the weekend. When a town has an open-house atmosphere like the one created by the Harbor Festival, anyone could wander in, blend in.

Even a killer.

4

Beck walked along the cobbled path that led around the cove to the harbor. The midday sun beat down on the back of his neck and he'd already undone the top two buttons on his shirt. He wished he was off duty, wearing a short-sleeved T-shirt and a pair of cutoff jeans. It was that kind of day.

The phones had not stopped ringing since the increasingly lurid reports of Colleen Preston's murder began to leak, and things had just gone downhill from there. By Beck's estimation, over the past twenty-four hours, damn near half the population of St. Dennis had called in to the station asking if a mad killer was on the loose and wondering what Beck was doing to protect them. He didn't blame anyone for being concerned—yesterday he'd called Vanessa and reminded her to be cautious on her date with Mickey Forbes—but the only thing he could tell anyone at that point was to take sensible precautions, not to go anywhere alone, and call the station if anything or anyone seemed suspicious. What else could he say?

He'd been up most of the night and the night before, unable to sleep, unable to escape the image of Colleen Preston's sheathed body lying on the wooden porch. The horror of it was still fresh. The echoes of her heartbroken mother's unceasing sobs still rang in his ears. As surreal as the scene had been, what ate at Beck now was the overwhelming feeling that there was something poised out there, someplace nearby, waiting to strike again. He felt it as surely as he felt the sun beating down on him, and the worst part was that he knew he was helpless to stop it. That sense of apprehension, that feeling that the other shoe would soon drop, made him restless, and the restlessness had driven him to walk.

He'd met with his staff at seven when the shift changed so that he could talk to everyone at the same time. He'd laid out the events of the past few days, describing with as little drama as possible what he'd seen on the porch in Ballard on Sunday night.

"Everyone's saying that girl from Cameron . . ." Gus Franklin, his night-shift sergeant, said.

"I don't want to assume anything, but I don't like coincidences," Beck had replied.

"If it's the same guy, there's likely to be more," Garland had stated quietly. When all eyes turned to him, he explained, "We had something in Boston, not like this, not wrapping the women up like this guy did. But women in their twenties, just vanishing like that. It was like the victims just disappeared from their lives, like they'd been erased. They were just . . . gone. They all turned up in an old warehouse, lined up side by side like dolls across the floor."

The room had gone silent.

"I can put in a few hours down around the cove," Hal said. "Just poke around a little. We're close enough to Cameron that if someone had something they wanted to hide, they might think one of those old buildings down there might make a good hiding place. You got a couple of properties down there, the owners haven't been around in years. Just sitting on them, waiting for the values to go up. At least, that's what Ham Forbes is telling me, and he knows real estate better than anyone else in town."

"You might want to stop at his office later on and see what he knows about the individual properties. Might be worth getting a list of who owns what," Beck said.

"Couldn't hurt," Hal agreed.

"I can stop out around the old boathouse on my way home," Lisa told them.

"While I'm on patrol this morning, I'll check out the old church on Christian Street." Duncan stood in the back of the room. "And there are those abandoned shacks over behind the cemetery. I can make a quick stop."

"All good suggestions." Beck nodded. "Just keep your eyes open. And thanks."

He'd gone from that meeting to one with the mayor and the chair of the town's public safety committee, both of whom wanted assurance that none of the residents of St. Dennis were in danger from whoever had killed Colleen Preston, and possibly Mandy Kenneher as well. That Beck was in no position to give such assurance did not endear him to two of the more politically powerful members of the community. The fact that Christina Pratt, the mayor, had told Beck all he needed to know about the mentality of St. Dennis's elected officials. He'd left her office and headed out the door. If ever he'd needed to walk off a pissy attitude, it was then.

Straight ahead was Singer's Slips, the marina owned and operated by Lisa's husband, Todd, and next to it, his boatyard and showroom. Hot and thirsty, Beck turned off the path and took the concrete steps down to the showroom.

"Hey, Chief, how's it going?" Jay Gannon opened the door for Beck.

"Hot." Beck gratefully stepped into the air-conditioned comfort of the sales area.

"How 'bout a cold one, Chief?" Todd Singer stepped out of his office when he saw his wife's boss. "Water, soda?"

"Water would be great, thanks." Beck followed Todd into the small sitting room off to one side of the showroom.

Todd opened the refrigerator and took out two bottles of spring water. Tossing one to Beck, he asked, "So what can I show you today? We've got a nice special running on some used Whalers. Couple of years old, not too many hours on the motors."

"When I have time for a boat of my own, you're the first person I'm coming to see." Beck sat on the arm of one of the green leather sofas and took a long drink from the bottle. "Unfortunately for both of us, that time hasn't come yet."

"Hey, you have to make time. Nothing more relaxing than being out on the bay early on a summer morning. Or at dusk, when the sun's setting." Todd grinned. "Nothing like it. I guarantee you'd love it."

"I do love it," Beck conceded. "But right now, I'll

have to be content to bum a seat on Hal's cruiser from time to time."

"Ah, now there's a sweet boat." Todd tilted his bottle in Beck's direction. "I caught many a tourist eyeing that little darlin' over the weekend. Lost track of how many people asked about her, if she was for sale."

"You tell Hal? He might cut her loose if the price is right."

"Not a chance." Todd laughed. "I offered to buy that beauty myself, but the price he quoted was three times what she's really worth. Cagey old bastard. He knows there's nothing else like her around here."

"Which is why the *Shady Lady* will be parked in his slip until someone is dumb enough to pay what he's asking." Beck took another drink.

"So if you're not looking for a boat, what brings you down to the marina?"

"Just walking. Thinking." He half-smiled. "Worrying."

"Yeah, Lisa told me the killer who murdered that girl in Ballard might have killed the girl from Cameron as well." Todd shook his head. "She said the medical examiner's report came in, says that girl suffocated inside that wrapping. What kind of a sick bastard wraps a girl up and then lets her die like that? What was that stuff he wrapped her in, anyway?"

"Regular clear plastic wrap."

"Like the stuff you buy in the grocery store?"

"Exactly."

"Must have taken a lot to wrap her up. Maybe the cops over in Ballard should talk to the local stores and find out if anyone's bought up lots of that wrap lately."

"I imagine someone's done that, although frankly, it's the same type you can buy anywhere. One or two packages would have been enough. She was thin. It wouldn't have taken much."

"So you probably couldn't trace it. That's what Lisa said, too." He played with the cap from his water bottle. "You think that girl from Cameron is dead?"

"She could be."

"That's what Lisa thinks, too."

"Well, let's not spread that one around. She may still show up alive." Beck replied, thinking Lisa might be taking a little too much of her job home to share. He'd have to talk to her about that.

"Hey, all these years married to a cop, you don't have to tell me what to keep to myself." He made the gesture of zipping his lips shut. "In our house, the rule is, you don't comment publicly until you've seen it on the news."

"You follow that rule and you'll be right every time."

"Todd, phone," Jay called from across the wide room.

"Chief was there anything . . ." Todd rose from the chair.

"No, no. Actually, I only stopped in to beg a cold drink and a few minutes of your cool air. I need to start back to the station."

"Can I have someone drive you?" Todd offered.

"No, but thanks." Beck rose from the arm of the

chair. "Walking's my therapy. I do most of my best thinking on my feet."

"You oughta wait for a cooler day."

"Should have thought of that myself." Beck finished the water and tossed the empty plastic bottle into the recycling bin. "Thanks for the water."

"Anytime. Want to take one with you for the road?"

"No, but thanks. I'll walk back on the shady side of the path."

"Good seeing you, Beck. Stop in anytime."

"Will do, Todd. Hey, Jay, take care." Beck waved and headed toward the door.

Beck did walk back on the shady side of the path, as far as Charles Street, where he crossed the street to stay in the shade as long as he could. His pager went off just as he'd turned onto Kelly's Point Road. He looked at the number, which was familiar, but since he was only half a block from the station, he waited until he'd returned to his office to return the call.

"This is Chief Beck, St. Dennis PD, returning a call made from this number," he said when a woman answered.

"Chief, I'll get Chief Daley for you," the woman responded. "Can you hold?"

"Yes."

"Beck." Warren Daley was on in a flash. "Something's come up. I'd like you to stop over this afternoon if you could."

"Sure. What's up?"

"I'd rather not go into it on the phone." Daley told him. "Is four o'clock okay?"

"I'll be there."

"Good, good. See you then." Daley hesitated, his voice shaky. "Beck, you're just not gonna believe this . . . this damned case just keeps getting worse and worse. Just when you think you've seen it all. . . ."

It was three fifty-five when a curious Beck parked behind the one-story wooden-frame building that served as the police department for the village of Ballard. Like St. Dennis, but unlike some of the surrounding towns, Ballard had opted for its own force. Several of the smallest towns, without funds to maintain their own police departments, depended on the state police. Ballard, Cameron, St. Dennis, and Hopkins, another few miles down the road, all had their own departments. And all had cruisers parked in the lot on this Tuesday afternoon. Rich Meyer's car sat two spots down from Beck's, and the cruiser from Hopkins apparently had arrived just moments before Beck. He could see Chief Gillespie still seated behind the wheel, talking on his cell phone. Beck delayed getting out of his car until he saw Gillespie's door open.

"Lew!" Beck called to the other man.

"Hey, Beck." Lew Gillespie waited at the foot of the dirt path leading to the back of the building until Beck caught up. "I see you received the summons too."

"Any idea what's up?"

"None. Warren just called earlier and asked me to please be here. He didn't want to discuss it on the phone."

"Yeah, he said that to me, too." Beck frowned.

From the little Chief Daley had said on the phone, Beck had the sinking feeling that something really big was about to play out.

"I see Meyer's here, too." Gillespie looked beyond Beck and added, "And there's Ralston from Sandy Point, just pulling in behind you."

The two men waited for the newcomer to join them.

"What's up, gentleman?" Morris Ralston fixed a smile on his face.

"We were just wondering if you knew, Mo," Gillespie told him.

"No clue." He shrugged.

"Then let's go on inside and find out." Beck gestured toward the building.

"Amen." Ralston slipped his fingers inside the collar of his starched white uniform shirt and gave it a tug. "Too damned hot out here anyway."

The small Ballard police station had four rooms on the first floor, and four more in the basement. The three men were directed down the steps to a small conference room, where Warren Daley and Rich Meyer were seated at a round table awaiting the arrival of the others. Daley rose when they entered, and closed the door behind them.

"It's just us five," he told them, gesturing for the newcomers to take a seat.

"What's going on, Warren?" Ralston asked. "Can we assume this has something to do with that case of yours?"

Daley nodded and reached for a pile of manila folders.

"This is Dr. Reilly's preliminary autopsy report on Colleen Preston. Take a minute and look it over. I want you all to see what's on the loose out there." He passed out the folders.

For the next several minutes, the room was silent, save for the occasional sound of paper rustling. Suddenly the normally stoic Ralston growled, "God damn it, he wrapped up that poor girl alive so she'd suffocate inside that plastic hell. Jesus!"

The others made sounds of disgust and disbelief as they read on. When they'd all finished reading and solemnly closed their files, Daley said, "I've been a cop all my life. Been in this job thirty-five years. I've never had to deal with anything even remotely like this."

He flipped open his own file and read details randomly, "Multiple insect bites cover the entire body."

He turned the page. "Signs of repeated rape. Sodomy."

He turned the page again. "Wrists and ankles bruised and cut showing signs of having been restrained."

Another turn. "End of tongue severed . . ."

"Jesus!" Morris Ralston groaned. "She bit off the end of her tongue!"

One last turn. "Cause of death: suffocation."

Warren Daley closed the file with a pronounced slap and it was clear to everyone in the room that he was close to losing it. His eyes brimmed with tears. "I cannot even begin to imagine what it must have been like for that beautiful little girl for however long it was that animal had her."

He wiped away tears with the back of his hand.

"But let me tell you something about Colleen Preston." He stood. "She did not go easy."

He walked to the end of the table where he'd left his briefcase and brought it back to his seat.

"She never gave up. Never stopped fighting. That may be the only consolation her family has at this point."

Curious eyes watched as he removed a tape recorder from his briefcase and set it on the table.

"Just when you think it can't get any worse, it does," he told them. "Dr. Reilly found this tape inside the wrappings."

He hit play, then sat in his chair, his elbows on the table, his steepled fingers covering part of his face.

"This is your chance, now, Colleen." A distorted male voice filled the room. "If there's anything you want to tell your parents, your brother, your sister, you'll want to do it now."

There was some indistinguishable sound in the background.

"That wasn't nice," the male voice said. "I'm giving you an opportunity to leave something behind that might comfort your family."

"Momma, Daddy, I'm sorry," a raspy voice whispered. "I'm so sorry. I didn't know . . . I never thought he'd . . ." The voice broke into sobs.

"Is that all? This is your last chance, Colleen. No words of wisdom for your sweet little sister?" The voice taunted.

"Fry in hell, you disgusting degenerate psychopathic pig—" she snarled.

The tape went silent.

For a long time, no one could speak.

Finally, when he found his voice, Beck said, "He's not done, and he's no amateur."

"That's what I was thinking." Daley looked around the table, the circles around his haunted eyes deep and dark.

Rich Meyer covered his face with his hands. "If he's got Mindy Kenneher . . . if this is what he's doing to her . . ."

"The girl from Cameron who went missing a few weeks before Colleen Preston?" Gillespie asked.

Meyer nodded.

"If the same man took her, the odds are that he's already killed her," Beck said softly. "She's already lost, Rich."

Meyer sat speechless, contemplating the possibility.

"I asked you all here today because I frankly am at a loss," Daley told them. "We're all small forces, no reserves, no specialists to speak of. I'm thinking if he hit Cameron, and he hit us here in Ballard, where's he going to hit next time? Is there anyone here who thinks he won't strike again?"

"Yeah." Gillespie nodded. "I think to a man, we're all thinking the same thing."

"We have no leads. Nothing. We might have some trace once the county lab reports come back, but that's not going to be for a while. We couldn't get any prints from the wrappings, so we're assuming he was wearing gloves while he wrapped her up. She didn't have so much as a smudge on her, so the ME thinks she was probably washed down real good to remove any trace before he wrapped her up. The CSIs tell me they got very little from her, but they're processing what they did find. Gonna be a while before we know if we have anything that will help. Right now, we're all blind," Daley told them. "Anyone has any suggestions, I'd sure love to hear them now."

"How long had Mindy Kenneher been missing before Colleen disappeared?" Beck asked.

"Mindy disappeared on June first," Rich Meyer told them, then turned to Warren Daley. "The Preston girl?"

"June twenty-six. She disappeared on Tuesday, June twenty-sixth."

"Three and a half weeks between the two." Morris Ralston had taken a small notebook from inside his jacket pocket.

"And today is Tuesday, the tenth of July. Just two weeks since Colleen Preston disappeared." Beck drummed his fingers on the tabletop. "Until we're proven wrong, I think we need to operate on the assumption that we're dealing with a repeat offender here."

"Three weeks between the first and second taking," Gillespie thought aloud. "And he only held the Preston girl for two weeks."

"Which means he's probably looking for another victim," Meyer noted.

"Or maybe he's already found one," Ralston said.

"Anyone reported missing that you know of?" Daley asked. Everyone at the table shook their head.

"Which could mean just about anything." Beck held up one hand and began to count off the possibilities on his fingers. "One, he's taken someone who hasn't been reported missing or who's far enough away that we haven't heard of it as yet. Two, he could be sated for a while. Three, he could have moved on. Four, he could have stopped—"

"What are the chances of that?" Ralston said.

"Not much," Beck agreed.

"Five, he could have been run over by a bus and right now is on a slab in the morgue," Gillespie said, "and six, he could have been picked up on some charge in another state and is now the guest of, oh, Pennsylvania, Virginia, Delaware . . ."

"Or just about anyplace else," Meyer said with disgust.

"Okay, we agree, he could be anywhere right now. Any or none of those possibilities could be the right one." Beck looked around the table at the others, each top man in their respective jurisdictions. At thirty-seven, Beck was the youngest man there. Two were already close to retirement age, another not far behind. "My gut is telling me that he's still around. I think he's going to want to watch, to see what Warren does. He's going to want to watch the press, the papers, and the TV stations. Then I think he's going to do it again."

"I hate to say it, but my gut's telling me the same thing." Chief Daley nodded.

"So where do we go from here?" Gillespie asked. "You thinking about calling in the county sheriff?"

"God, I don't want to do that. I swear I do not." Daley shook his head. "I had three homicide cases I had to work with Jake Madison, and after the last one, I swore I'd never do it again. The man is the biggest pain in the ass I've ever had to deal with. His ego is as big as the Atlantic, and once you confer with him, he totally takes over. Wouldn't be so bad if he knew what he was doing, but he's just a bumblefuck from the word go. I do not want to bring in the county if it means I'll have to deal with him. As important as this case is, turning it over to him will all but guarantee our killer gets away."

"There are some really good men over there, War- ren," Lew Gillespie pointed out. "Some fine detectives, and their lab people are top-notch."

"No argument there, and I'd be the first to say it," Daley agreed. "But unfortunately, they all take orders from Jake."

"So what are you proposing to do?" Gillespie asked.

"Well, I thought I'd start with a press conference tomorrow, tell everyone that we've had this meeting, and that all the local departments are on the same page. We're all going to work together to find this killer." Daley looked from one man to the next. "We all banded together two years ago and we caught that bank robber—"

"Warren, you know you have my total support, and that the St. Dennis force is behind you one hun- dred percent," Beck told him. "But this isn't the same kind of case."

"What would you do, if you were me?" Daley asked Beck.

"I'd do what you're doing, but I'd go one step fur- ther," Beck said. "I'd call the FBI and ask for help. I'd ask for a profiler, first thing, and I'd ask for an agent or two who had experience with serial offenders—"

"Hold up there, Beck," Lew Gillespie protested. "It's too early to start throwing around terms like that."

"I don't think so, Lew. I think this guy's killed before. His whole MO is too sophisticated, too well thought out, too well executed. He's no amateur. I'd bet my life on it."

"I've already told Beck how I feel about this profiler nonsense." Meyer sat back in his chair. "I think it's all a waste of time."

"I think Beck's got a point," Morris Ralston told him. "This killer is accomplished, he knows what he's doing. And even if Mindy Kenneher turned up tomorrow with some story about going to Disney World, even if the Preston woman was the only victim, I don't think it would hurt us to have an idea of what type of person we're looking for. Especially if he's living among us."

"The FBI thing, I'm going to have to sleep on. But the press conference will be called for ten tomorrow morning," Daley told them. "I'm inviting you all to attend, if you have a mind to."

"Might be a good idea." Meyer nodded. "A show of force. Of solidarity."

"Make everyone aware there could be a problem, this guy could be out there. Urge everyone to be particularly careful until we catch this killer," Gillespie added. "Let them know we're all working together to find him."

"And if he's watching, let him know that he's got to

deal with all of us now," Daley noted. "That every police officer in this part of the bay is looking for him. Send him a message."

Beck glanced around the table at the concerned faces, and knew they were all thinking the same thing.

Looking for this guy was one thing. Finding him was going to be something else.

5

The Wednesday morning press conference was winding down. Chief Warren Daley was still at the front of the small room, no podium being available in Ballard. The chiefs of police from the four neighboring departments were seated on folding chairs in the first row, presenting a united show of force against the threat that hung over their small communities.

"Chief Daley." Carl Patterson from the *Bay Chronicle,* standing in the midst of the small group of reporters, raised his hand. "You said the victim suffocated. Can you be more specific? Was she strangled?"

"I'm not going to go into that much detail right now, Carl. The ME still has to issue her final report, so we're just going from the preliminary. And we have to protect the privacy of the family. Until the ME has released her complete findings, I'd rather not put words in her mouth."

"Chief, the rumor that's going around is that the victim was found on her own front porch, all wrapped up in some kind of plastic wrap." Rosalie Ahern from the local morning news show stood against the wall on the left side of the room, which suddenly came alive.

"Hold on, now." Warren Daley's face flushed dark pink and he grabbed on to the microphone. "Hold on—"

"Is that true?" asked Jenna Smith from *Chesapeake Weekly*. "The victim was *wrapped* in *plastic*?"

"Look, I don't know where that story came from—" Daley began but was cut off by the reporter.

"It came from an unnamed source who was at the scene," Ahern said as the camera lights came back on, after having been turned off a few minutes earlier when it appeared the press conference was going to be more of the same old thing.

Daley was clearly flustered, unsure of what to say. He definitely had not planned on disclosing this information, and every reporter in the room, all six of them, sensed it.

Which meant, of course, that it was true.

The room exploded. Daley did his best to calm them all down.

"Chief? Are you going to comment?" Jenna Smith asked.

"I really hadn't wanted to get into this, out of respect for the family. While this is a sensational story for all of you, you need to remember that Colleen Preston was a very real young woman with a grieving family. I want to respect their period of mourning. But that cat being out of the bag now, I can't very well shove it back in, unless I stand up here and lie. And any of you who know me, know that's not my style. So I'll tell you what I know, but I won't speculate beyond that."

Warren Daley took a deep breath. "At ten forty-five on Sunday evening, Colleen Preston's body was found on the front porch of her family home. She'd been totally encased in plastic and suffocation has been ruled the cause of death." He swallowed hard. "As you know, Miss Preston had been missing since the twenty-sixth day of June."

"Did the killer have her all this time?" someone asked.

"We believe that he did." Daley nodded.

"Do you know where she was kept for the past two weeks?" another voice asked.

"No clue." Daley shook his head from side to side.

"Any suspects?"

"We have no suspects, no."

"Chief, there was another woman recently, over in Cameron—"

"Yes, Mindy Kenneher," Daley supplied the name.

"She's been missing for longer than Colleen Preston was. Do the police think she was taken by the same person who killed Colleen Preston?"

Daley turned to Chief Meyer. "You want to take this one, Rich?"

Chief Meyer stood and turned to face the reporters. The camera was still on.

"Right now, we have no information as to the whereabouts of Mindy Kenneher. We have no reason to assume she met the same fate as Miss Preston. That case is still under investigation and we're not going to speculate. When we know something, you'll know something."

He returned to his seat and gestured for Daley to resume control of the conference.

"But isn't this type of thing . . . wrapping up the victim . . . isn't that the type of thing a serial killer does?" Jenna Smith's pretty face crinkled into a frown. "I mean, your normal killer doesn't wrap up his victim, right?"

"Jenna, you watch too much TV," Daley scolded. "Let's not be irresponsible and start tossing around words like that. Right now, we have one victim. Why did the killer wrap her up like that? Maybe he thought it would make it easier—neater—to dispose of the body. Let's not read anything more into this, all right? We have no reason to believe that whoever it was is going to do this again."

"Then why are they"—Jenna pointed to the other chiefs—"here? Why are the heads of five police departments here if you don't think there's a threat?"

"I'll take this one, Warren." Beck stepped forward. "Yes, we all recognize the uniqueness of this killing. But we're here because each of us has pledged to work together with Chief Daley until Colleen Preston's killer has been apprehended."

"Are you thinking the killer is someone local, Chief Beck?"

"That's certainly a possibility. He did know where to take the victim's body." Someone started to ask another question, but Beck held up his hand to hold it off. "Then again, he could have seen her address on her driver's license and gone straight to MapQuest. The point is we don't know anything about the killer except that he's a sadistic SOB. As Chief Daley said, this is an ongoing investigation, and it will continue until the killer is caught. The St. Dennis police department is ready to give whatever assistance Chief Daley wants or needs."

"So what you're saying is, the small towns in this part of the bay have banded together to track down the killer."

"You could say that."

"You think you'll find him before he strikes again?"

"We'll do our best. But since we have no reason to believe he's going to strike again, I think you should be very careful in how you present this story." Beck scanned the scene. The few reporters who'd shown up expecting little from their assignment had been handed a plum. Everyone's eyes seemed to glow with the prospect of covering a sensational murder—maybe more than one. He could feel their excitement and knew they couldn't wait to get the story out there. If they caused an unnecessary panic, well, that would give the story legs. Good for them, hell for everyone else. "Be responsible, okay? Don't be careless with your words."

"Chief Beck, I was at the Harbor Festival in St. Dennis over the weekend," Rosalie Ahearn said as she fished around in her tote bag for something. She pulled out a brochure of some kind and opened it. "It looks as if you have a lot of activities planned to bring tourists in over the summer, lots of special weekend festivals and attractions to keep people coming back."

"The Chamber of Commerce has been very busy." He nodded. "The town's reputation has really started to spread over the past few years. There's a lot there for people to see and do, lots of shopping, good places to eat. I hope you enjoyed yourself."

"I did. But Chief, are you afraid that this killer being out there might scare people away?"

Beck frowned. "First of all, there's no reason to think that Colleen Preston's killer is 'out there.' For all we know, this was a random murder and the killer is long gone. Secondly, you're assuming he's going to kill again, and you're assuming that he's closing in on St. Dennis. None of that follows, Rosalie. I think you're angling for a story where there is none. Let's just keep the facts in mind. So far we've had one victim, in Ballard, which is several miles from St. Dennis. Let's leave it at that, okay?"

"I think she's just saying, with St. Dennis bringing in so many people every week, and it being so close to Ballard—" Carl Patterson began.

"I know what she's saying." Beck turned cold blue eyes on the reporter. "And I'm saying it's a waste of time to speculate in that manner."

"What exactly are you doing to help identify the killer?" Carl persisted.

Beck turned around to Warren Daley and said, "I'll let you take it from here."

"Right now, we're waiting for the lab reports to see if he left us anything to remember him by. At first glance, I'd say he was very careful not to leave any trace, but the lab techs will let us know if he slipped up there. In the meantime, we're looking for other missing persons reports. . . ."

"So you do think there are more victims," Rosalie

noted with some satisfaction. "Are you going to call in the FBI?"

Warren Daley sighed heavily. "No one said anything about there being more victims. But we did feel it would be prudent to check back and see if there were other missing women who hadn't turned up. . . ."

"Over how many years?" Jenna asked. "How many years are you going back?"

"We haven't put a limit on it," Daley told them. "And no, so far, we haven't found any. It was just an idea."

"How about the FBI?" Rosalie repeated. "Are you going to call them in?"

"At this point I see no reason to do that."

"But isn't your department connected to the FBI's VICAP database?"

"Not yet."

"But it's free, isn't it?"

"Last time we looked into it, our computer guy told us we didn't have the right software to support it. And at this time, I've got nothing further to say," Daley told the group. "The investigation is just beginning, so I'll end this with a promise to keep you up to date when we have something to report. Thanks for coming."

Several of the reporters continued to ask questions as Chief Daley made his way from the room. The visiting police chiefs chatted briefly before heading to the parking lots and their cars. Beck had just unlocked his vehicle when he saw Rosalie Ahern walking across the parking lot.

"Chief Beck," she called to him.

He opened the car door and leaned on it, watching her approach.

"I was just about to ask before Chief Daley pulled the plug." She was slightly out of breath as she came toward him. "Have you ever seen a case like this one, where the killer did something like that to his victim?"

"No." He shook his head side to side. "Never saw anything like it."

"Why do you think he did that?" She was squinting, looking into the sun, fumbling in her bag for her sunglasses. "What's your gut tell you about this guy?"

Beck paused. He wasn't about to tell this young reporter, so eager to cover what was most likely her first really big story, what his gut was saying about Colleen Preston's killer.

"My gut's not into speculation."

"Well, do you really think this was a random killing? Or do you think he's going to strike again?"

"Rosalie, I honestly don't know. This guy could be anyone, he could be anywhere. We just don't know." He got into his car and put his seat belt on. "The truth is, we know squat, and until we have something to go on, as Chief Daley said, it's irresponsible to speculate."

"Do you agree with Chief Daley's decision not to contact the FBI to look for similar cases?"

"It's Chief Daley's case," Beck said diplomatically. "It's his call."

"I'm getting the feeling it wouldn't be your call."

"It doesn't matter what I'd do. It's not my case. I'll

help out in any way I can, I'll put on extra patrols until this guy is caught. I'll walk the streets myself if I have to. But I won't second-guess Warren Daley and I won't presume to tell him how to do his job. Maybe you shouldn't, either."

"Is St. Dennis looped into the VICAP system that Carl was talking about?"

"Yes."

"You could probably look for similar crimes on your own, then, even if Chief Daley didn't."

"I don't like the critical tone of your voice. You have no idea what it's like to deal with the budget in a small town."

"But I thought VICAP was a free service—"

"The upgraded computers aren't."

He slammed the car door and rolled down the window.

"Chief, one more thing." Rosalie stepped closer to the car as he turned the key in the ignition. "Where do *you* think Mindy Kenneher is?"

"I don't know."

"Do you think there were others? Before Colleen Preston? Do you think any other bodies will turn up, wrapped up like that?"

"I wish I knew . . ." Beck waved as he pulled out of the parking space and headed for St. Dennis.

". . . so if anyone believes the disappearance of Mindy Kenneher and the disappearance and murder of Colleen Preston are related, they're not saying." Rosalie Ahern was speaking directly into the camera. "When I asked the chief of police in nearby St. Dennis, Gabriel Beck, if he thought there were other victims before Colleen Preston, all he said was that he wished he knew."

"Any plans to bring in the FBI at this point? Isn't that standard when there's an abduction?" The anchor, back in the studio, asked Rosalie, who was reporting from outside the Ballard police department.

Rosalie Ahern was nodding her head. "I asked Chief Daley about the FBI, and he pretty much shot that down. But it was interesting, later in the parking lot, when I spoke with Chief Beck, I asked him if he'd call in the FBI if he were running the investigation, and he gave me the impression that he would. And by the way, they're not calling Mindy Kenneher's disappearance an *abduction* at this point, they're still just calling it a *disappearance*."

"Okay, well, thanks for the report, Rosalie. . . ." The anchor turned to another camera. "In other news . . ."

The theme for *Chesapeake News at Noon* came on a few minutes later as the screen faded to a commercial.

The man watching the broadcast from the privacy of his office smiled as he removed the tape from the old VCR and unlocked the bottom drawer of the filing cabinet closest to his desk. He dropped the tape into what he referred to as his archives and relocked the drawer.

The press conference—What a misnomer that was! A few newspapers and one local TV station showed up!—had tickled him no end. It had really given him a kick to see them all scratching their heads and being so noncommittal. So afraid of saying something that would upset the locals. As if they're not all shaking in their shoes, scared to death the next victim will be in their town, making him *their* problem.

Toying with them all could be almost as much fun as his little girlfriends were.

Which reminded him, he had a little cleanup to do this morning. There was a little problem of disposal he needed to work out.

The solution came to him in a flash, and he laughed out loud.

So Gabriel Beck wishes he knew if there'd been others like sweet Colleen, does he?

He stared out the window, and smiled when he saw the police cruiser pass by.

It was time Beck learned to be careful what he wished for.

6

"I should have said 'no comment,'" Warren Daley said for the third time since Beck picked up the phone. "I never should have let a reporter catch me off guard like that. God damn it, I could just kick myself for getting suckered into that. No way I should have let on about that girl being wrapped up. Just fuels the crazies, far as I'm concerned. Christ, I can't think faster on my feet than that, maybe I should just do what my wife keeps nagging me to do and retire. Maybe it's time."

"You had no way of knowing someone would have passed all the gory details on to the press," Beck replied. "Hey, it happens."

"Yeah, and when I get my hands on the son of a bitch who opened his mouth, I'm going to have his ass nailed to my office wall so I can use it for target practice."

"Who do you think slipped up?"

"I doubt it was a slip. Probably someone hoping to make a little time with Ahern."

"Could be." Beck glanced at his watch. "Sorry I'm going to have to cut this call short. I have a meeting with the mayor and a couple of council members at eight. Second time in two days I've been summoned over to Pratt's office, which is a record. Everyone in town who saw the news is up in arms over this case."

"Tell me about it. Same here in Ballard. At least you don't have a body."

"Thank God for small favors."

"Look, I'm sorry to have called so early in the morning. I figured you'd be up . . . shit, I don't know what I was thinking," Daley said.

"Hey, don't worry about it. Anytime." Beck downed a mouthful of coffee. "Gotta run . . ."

Beck finished off his coffee, his focus on the meeting. He knew the council members were going to grill him about the case in Ballard. What are the chances this guy is going to kill again, and this time in St. Dennis? He'd already heard it from the mayor last night. He heard the panic in her voice, and knew there wasn't going to be a damned thing he could do to calm people down. In retrospect, Warren Daley's press conference, such as it was, hadn't been such a hot idea.

For all his years in law enforcement, Beck's counterpart in Ballard had never had to deal with anything like what had been done to Colleen Preston. The young woman's death, and the manner in which she died, had the entire Eastern Shore shaken up from Chestertown straight on down to Easton.

Rightfully so.

He locked up the house and walked the length of the driveway to where he'd parked his Jeep the day before.

Beck sighed and opened the door. As he slid into

the seat, something in the back caught his eye. He looked in the rearview mirror, and stared for a moment, until it registered.

"Jesus Christ Almighty . . ."

He got out of the vehicle, and shielding his eyes from the early morning glare, peered through the tinted glass before backing away as he pulled the phone from his pants pocket.

He hit speed-dial, his eyes still on the window and what lay beyond.

"Hal. I need you. Now. At the house. Call Lisa. And Duncan. Tell him to make sure to bring the evidence kit. And tell Garland to get the ME over here. Now. I need her now."

He hung up before Hal could ask any questions and opened the back of the Jeep. He got a flashlight and took a pair of clear plastic gloves from a box and pulled them on. As carefully as he could, he opened the left rear door and leaned in.

The body was slightly too long for the bench seat, and so had been left with the legs angled forward. The overhead light automatically came on when the door was opened, and it shed an eerie glow on the plastic encasing the body. There were bubbles of moisture on the outside of the wrappings, and inside the tightly wound plastic was a barely contained mess of fluid. He then went around to the passenger's side to get a better look at the victim. What he saw was the remains of what had been, not so very long ago, a vibrant young woman.

That she'd sucked furiously for air was evident. The plastic was pulled tightly across her face, indented at the nostrils and the mouth. Through the plastic, Beck could see her eyes seem to bulge, and her mouth was open in a grotesque grin, the head tilted back at a slight angle. Fluids had been trapped within the layers of wrappings, blood and urine and feces and whatever else had been released when her abdomen split as her intestines had swollen, then burst with the inevitable buildup of gases.

"Beck." Hal called as he approached rapidly from the end of the drive. "What it is?"

Beck turned and walked away from the Jeep.

"I think it's what's left of Mindy Kenneher. . . ."

It had taken almost an hour for Viv Reilly to arrive, and when she did, she stood next to Beck's Jeep shaking her head.

She glanced at Beck, who stood nearby, and said, "I'll never understand why. I can figure out how, but I cannot understand why."

Beck had personally processed the scene with Lisa and Duncan's assistance, but had found no traces. No fingerprints, no hairs, no fibers.

"It's as if she was transported here in a vacuum," Lisa told Beck. "There's nothing on the outside of the vehicle or the door handle, so we can assume that he used gloves, which would account for the lack of prints. But no fibers? Nothing at all on the plastic?"

"I think I know why." Hal pointed to the grass where the garden hose lay in a careless heap. Water dripped from the spigot attached to the side of the house.

"I haven't used that hose in weeks," Beck said as he

walked toward it. "Duncan, bring a trowel and some paper bags over here. Let's bag up the grass and the top layer of dirt in the areas that are wet. If he hosed down the body, maybe he washed away some evidence."

He waited until the body was removed from the Jeep under Viv's direction, then leaned in to examine the backseat more closely. The fabric was such that he could not tell if it was wet without touching it, so he removed a glove and did just that. In the heat overnight, much of the wetness had evaporated, but the seat was still damp.

"You must sleep like the dead, Chief, for someone to come into your yard, turn on your hose, open up your vehicle, put a body inside, then sneak away." Viv looked over her shoulder as she followed the gurney to her van.

"No dogs in the neighborhood barking last night, Chief?" Lisa asked. "Didn't hear the doors slamming?"

"I sleep on the opposite side of the house and had the air conditioner on in my room last night. I wouldn't have heard anything."

He pointed to the house next door, on the other side of a row of ancient pines.

"You can ask the Dawkins if they heard or saw anything, but it's unlikely. They're both in their late eighties and can't see through the hedge anyway. But maybe someone else on the block heard something during the night, so you and Duncan start going door to door."

After Lisa and Duncan had gone to check in with

the neighbors, and the ME's van had pulled out of the driveway, Hal turned to Beck and asked, "Did you leave the Jeep unlocked?"

"I must have." He rubbed his chin thoughtfully. "We haven't had any break-ins in so long—cars or homes—I just never really worried about it."

He tried to remember what was on his mind when he parked the vehicle the day before. He'd gone to the press conference in Ballard, then drove home. He'd parked in the driveway, then saw a neighbor who'd waved and crossed the street to tell him she'd been a friend of the Preston family for over thirty years and how devastated she was to hear about Colleen. Beck had tried to be sympathetic while at the same time avoiding adding any fuel to the fire of panic that he sensed would soon be spreading throughout St. Dennis if it wasn't checked. He'd received a call from Garland reminding him about his five o'clock appointment, and decided to walk to the station. It had not occurred to him to check to see if he'd locked the Jeep.

"Why do you suppose he did that, left her in your Jeep?" Hal asked.

"His way of giving me the finger, I guess." Beck stood with his hands in his pockets, watching his Jeep being hooked up to a tow truck. As evidence, it had to be taken down to the station where it would be impounded in the small garage behind the municipal building. "Which makes me think he's close enough to have watched the local news last night."

"That's a start." Hal nodded. "More than you knew yesterday."

"And it tells me he's damned clever. Clever enough to not leave a trace of himself, to wash away anything that might have clung to the plastic."

"Wonder what he'd have done if the Jeep had been locked?"

Beck pointed to his house. "There's a porch out front as well as out back. He could have left it at either. If he was determined to leave that package for me, there were plenty of other ways he could have done it."

"So what are you going to do now?" Hal asked.

"First, I'm going to stop in and see Mayor Pratt. Then, I'm going to do exactly what I told Warren Daley to do. I'm calling the FBI."

"You sure you want to do that? I've worked with some pretty damned annoying agents over the years. And you know, once you open that door and invite them in, they take over, and there's no getting rid of them. I got stuck one time for two months with the most obnoxious SOB I'd ever met. Wouldn't go away until the case was closed." Hal shook his head, remembering. "Alphonse Edmonds. He was not only obnoxious, he was mean-spirited. And ugly, now that I think about it."

"All I care about is cleaning up this mess as quickly as possible. This guy has taken me on, and I will use any weapon I can get my hands on to fight him. If the best weapon is the FBI, then fine. Bring it on. I don't care how obnoxious, mean, or ugly their agents are. I just want this bastard and I want him before he finds another victim."

Beck paused, then looked at Hal.

"Unless he already has . . ."

The sun was dipping low in the sky as FBI Special Agent Mia Shields crossed over the Potomac River via the Governor Nice Memorial Bridge, leaving Virginia behind her. Once on the Maryland side, she headed toward Calvert's Ford, one of the small communities on the western shore of the Chesapeake Bay that, sadly, lacked a true beach.

The tobacco fields were just hitting their growth stride on either side of the two-lane road. The tobacco barns were landmarks she'd come to depend on for finding her turn off the main road. She'd been living in Maryland for almost three months, but had been working a job just over the Potomac for the past four weeks, and was still finding her way around. Once she hit the tobacco farm, though, she knew she was on the right road, and knew there were only two more turns before she'd be home.

Not her home, not exactly, she reminded herself. The small house that sat all by itself in the woods belonged to her cousin, Connor, who was once again out of the country somewhere. No one really knew where, except for his boss at the FBI and the director, and word was that sometimes even Connor's boss wasn't sure where or how to find him. Because he'd been gone for so much of the past year, and planned on being back in the States only now and then, Connor had suggested that Mia rent from him instead of renewing the lease on her Arlington apartment.

The complex she'd been living in was crowded and loud. Parties often ran late into the night, even on weekdays, and the parking lot was usually full by the time Mia arrived home from work. While she enjoyed a good party as much as the next person, she also liked a good night's sleep now and then, so when Connor offered the house, she jumped at the chance.

Connor's house in the woods had come as a surprise to Mia. From the outside, it looked like any other bungalow built in the 1920s or '30s. One and a half stories of ugly yellow stone in stucco, it had a wide front porch and a bow window on either side of the front door, windows in the eaves on each side of the second floor. The high ceilings and open spaces inside were atypical, however, and Connor had opened up the interior even more by removing a wall between the dining and living rooms to make one large space. He'd remodeled the kitchen—who knew her cousin was a gourmet cook?—enlarging it to include a built-in banquette in one corner and adding a work island in the center of the room. Off the kitchen was a screened porch. There were two bedrooms and a bath on the first floor, which Connor used, and a large bedroom, bath, and sitting room on the second floor which served as guest quarters. In this case, Mia was the guest.

The biggest surprise awaited outside, where a year ago Connor had an Olympic-sized pool installed. He'd told Mia he'd had it built so that when he was home, he could swim laps to stay in shape any time of the day or night, though she could count on one hand the number of days he'd spent at home since she moved in. Mia suspected she'd gotten more use of the pool than Connor had.

She pulled into the driveway, pleased that there was enough daylight left to enjoy a quick swim and still have time for a leisurely dinner before she had to turn her attention to the file she'd brought home from the office. She'd just completed work on a case and wanted to take one last look at her reports before turning them over to John Mancini, her boss, in the morning.

She parked her car, then emptied the mailbox of that day's offerings—a magazine and two bills amid the junk mail—and followed the flagstone path to the front door. Once inside, she went straight to the kitchen, where she dumped the mail on the counter and poured herself a glass of chilled wine. She leaned on the top of the island and flipped through the magazine idly, barely noting the contents. She turned on the air conditioning to cool off the first floor, then went upstairs to change.

The second floor accommodations were more than adequate for a long-term visit. The closet was large enough to hold Mia's clothes and the sitting room made a great little office. The bedroom windows looked out over the backyard and there were skylights overhead through which she watched the stars. She wondered who might have helped Connor sketch out the renovations for the space when he'd had the house remodeled. She just didn't see her cousin in the décor at all. At least, not the Connor she knew.

She stepped out of the suit she'd worn that day and hung it over the back of a chair with the other garments that had a date with the dry cleaner. She'd been in meetings most of the afternoon and had spent way too much time seated, which resulted in multiple wrinkles in both the jacket and the pants. She pulled on a one-piece swimsuit and slipped into sandals, then went back downstairs. In the kitchen she refilled her wineglass, and grabbed a towel from the back of a chair as she passed through the screened porch. Once outside, she lowered herself into a lounge and sipped her wine. The sun had dropped behind the tree line at the back of the property and spread color through the trees.

Perfect, she thought. This is the perfect way to slough off the day. A little wine, a beautiful sunset, a refreshing swim.

She put the glass on the ground next to the lounge and leaned back, closed her eyes and tried to think pleasant thoughts.

What was it the characters in Peter Pan *used to say? Think good thoughts . . . Christmas. Candy . . .*

Christmas was half a year away, and Mia never did acquire a taste for candy. Except truffles and the occasional chocolate that came in a gold foil box. But pleasant thoughts could not overshadow the other things that ran rampant in her mind. She sat up and reached for her wineglass, drained it, and decided perhaps a swim would help clear her head of the images of the three little boys they'd pulled from a drainage ditch a little more than a week ago.

She set the glass on the table and walked to the edge of the pool and dove in. The warm water washed over her, head to foot, and enveloped her. She swam laps until her arms hurt, then floated on her back watching the stars appear. So much brighter here than they were back in Arlington.

Bless Connor for having offered her his home.

She got out and toweled herself dry, then went back into the house and returned with the bottle of wine and a plate of crackers and cheese.

I'll just have my own little cocktail party. She smiled as she placed the wine and the platter on the table next to the lounge. She refilled her glass and ate some of the cheese standing up. She took a few more sips of her wine before returning to her place on the lounge, where she finished the wine and closed her eyes.

Can't wait until I can close this case. God, I hope I never have to face another family like the Jenners, give them the kind of news I had to give them. Poor babies . . .

She shivered and opened her eyes. For days she'd been trying to wipe out the vision of the three boys, ages two, three, and five, who'd wandered away from their home and ended up in four feet of water in a ditch hundreds of feet from the back of their thirty-acre property. How a two-year-old had managed to walk that far, she'd never know, but the evidence all indicated that they hadn't been abducted and drowned. Rather, it appeared they'd gotten out of their yard while their mother was out front planting marigolds around the mailbox and chatting with a neighbor. Piecing it all together, it looked as if the boys had decided to take advantage of her inattention to explore a bit on their own, and had walked off into the woods at the rear of their property. A quarter of a mile on the other side of the woods, the ground sloped down abruptly, ending in a retention ditch. The sides of the hill were clearly scarred with gouges made by the boy's feet as they slid down to the water below.

Mia rubbed the palms of her hands against her eyelids until all she could see behind them was white light. Better than the faces of dead children, she told herself as she settled on the lounge and lowered the back until she was almost prone, and then wondered if this was how she wanted to spend the rest of her life.

"I'm not a quitter," she said aloud.

She was second generation in the FBI, and she wasn't going to be the first one to quit. Well, her brother Grady had that honor, but he hadn't quit because he couldn't take it. And her brother Brendan . . . well, the less said about him, the better. Once there'd been seven of them . . . *seven*, she reminded herself. Seven Shields, not counting her father and her Uncle Frank, both of whom had retired. The four in Mia's family and Uncle Frank's three sons, Connor, Dylan and Aidan.

Of the seven, there were now only four. Mia and her brother Andrew, Connor and his brother Aidan.

So much for the dynasty her father had once been so proud of.

That she, the only girl in the family, had followed the others into the Bureau had been a point of pride for Mia. She'd worn the badge for nine years now, but recently had begun to question her decision to join. Her career choice was only one of many things she questioned lately.

Until she woke, slightly disoriented with a pounding head, Mia hadn't realized she'd fallen asleep. From somewhere nearby there was a rustling sound. She jumped nearly out of her skin as the small table next to her crashed to the ground, sending the wine bottle and the glass to the grass along with the plate and the remaining cheese.

In the shadow of the porch lights, she made out the silhouettes of several furry creatures who were busy with the cheese and the box of crackers.

Raccoons.

She backed away as slowly and as quietly as she could, doing her best not to draw their attention, fighting an urge to run like hell, until she reached the porch. Once there, she sprinted up the steps and through the door. From the screened porch she watched the young raccoons who, she realized, had no interest in anything other than the tasty treats they'd found.

Lucky for me, Mia thought, *Momma isn't with them, though she's probably close by.*

She stood at the screen and watched the animals chow down on her snack and wrest the cork from the wine bottle, spilling the contents on the grass.

"Thanks, guys, that was a nice chardonnay," she yelled.

After they'd eaten everything, shredded the cracker box, and licked out the wineglass, she said, "You're welcome. Do stop by again."

Eventually the raccoons lost interest in the back-yard, and wandered off into the woods. As amusing as the incident had been, Mia wasn't oblivious to the fact that it could have been a dangerous encounter.

Not to mention the fact that anyone coming into the backyard finding her asleep in her bathing suit in the middle of the night might have had more on their minds than eating her snacks and drinking her wine.

What the hell was I thinking? She chided herself as she locked up the house. Falling asleep in the back-yard is just plain stupid. The fact that the entire back of the property was enclosed by a secure privacy fence made it no less stupid. She shook her head, wondering at her carelessness, and locked up the house.

The clock on the small chest next to her bed read one o'clock.

Jesus. She shook her head again. She'd been in the business long enough to know the kinds of things that could—and did—happen to careless women.

No more cocktails by the pool for me. At least not by myself.

She showered and slipped into a nightshirt and got into bed. As she turned off the light, she noticed the light on her cell phone, which she'd left on the bedside table, was blinking. She picked it up and looked at the number of the last call.

Shit.

She picked up the phone and listened to the message her boss had left for her hours earlier.

"Mia, John. Call me whenever you get this message, doesn't matter what time it is. It's important. There's a new case we need to talk about. . . ."

7

Mia watched the boats out in the harbor from the conference room window in the St. Dennis police department. It was a perfect July day, with the clearest of blue skies, low humidity, and temperatures in the mid-eighties. *What an incredible view,* she thought as a large sailboat entered the harbor, its sails at half-mast. *How does anyone get any work done around here?*

She rested her elbows on the windowsill and tried to keep her impatience in check. The conversation she'd had with John last night had been short and sweet and to the point.

"Female vic found encased in plastic, left in the backseat of the police chief's car, second such victim found in three days. Chief of police has requested assistance. You're the closest agent to the scene. First thing in the morning, you're there. Good luck—it's your baby now."

Or would be, if the chief of police would have the courtesy to show up.

She drained the cup of coffee the dispatcher had brought her when she first arrived over a half hour ago. It was cold and not so bad, as cop coffee went, but her stomach was leaning toward slightly upset and she could have used a Coke.

She'd been told that the chief was in a meeting off-site, but was expected to arrive any minute. She hoped it would be soon. She pushed aside the coffee and stepped into the hall.

"Excuse me," she called to the dispatcher.

He turned to her, the phone in his hand.

"Sorry," she said. "I was just wondering if there was a soda machine . . ."

"What's your pleasure?" He hung up the phone.

"I'd kill for a Coke."

"Can okay?"

"Whatever form it comes in is more than okay."

"Right through that third door you'll find the kitchen. Help yourself to whatever you want."

"Thank you. Sorry to have disturbed you."

"Not at all. I'm sorry you're having to wait so long."

Mia found the kitchen and the promised cold can of soda. She popped the lid and took a long drink. Better than coffee for an upset stomach, she told herself as she returned to one of the uncomfortable chairs in the conference room. Yesterday's local newspaper was there on the table; she scanned the headlines.

ALL WRAPPED UP! shouted the front page of the tabloid paper. *Body wrapped in plastic left for anguished parents! Ballard woman suffocated!*

No wonder everyone's panicking, reading crap like this. What moron gave out all that information to the press?

She folded the paper and tossed it to the opposite end of the table in disgust.

". . . waiting for you in the conference room," Mia heard the dispatcher say.

"Great. Give him some coffee and tell him I'll be in in just a second."

"Ahhh, Chief—"

"Be right there, Garland. Gotta take this call, I'll make it fast . . ."

Why did they always expect a guy? She shook her head. Women had been in the FBI for years, and yet people were still surprised when the agent they were expecting wore a skirt. Or in her case, well-cut black linen pants and a crisp white shirt.

His entrance into the room caught her off guard.

If he was surprised to find that Agent Shields was a woman, he hid it well.

"Agent Shields, I'm Gabriel Beck." He approached her with an open hand and a weary smile. "I apologize for making you wait. I see someone's brought you a drink. Can I get you a refill?"

"No thank you." She took his hand and gave it the firm shake she reserved for those times when she felt she needed to assert herself. She fished her credentials from her bag and handed them over. "I'm sure you'll want to look these over."

He did. When he was finished, he handed them back and took the chair directly opposite hers.

"You've been brought up to date?" He asked.

"Only by the local paper." She pointed to the end of the table.

"That was a pretty bad piece." He shook his head.

"You wonder what people are thinking when they write crap like that."

"They're thinking about how many papers they're going to sell." She folded her arms on the table.

"I'm sure they had a banner day, then." He leaned back in his chair. "I had a long talk with your Agent Mancini yesterday afternoon, I assumed he passed on everything we talked about."

"He told me about the two bodies that were found, how they were found, and where. Both victims were from towns nearby, is that correct?"

He nodded. "Right. The first was found on the front porch of her family home, the second was found here, in the backseat of my car." He added wryly, "My personal car."

"Nice touch on his part. How'd he get the car open?"

"Apparently I'd left it unlocked."

"So he just walked onto your property in the middle of the night and dumped the body in your car and no one heard or saw anything?" she asked.

"Not a thing. It had to have been between the hours of one and five in the morning. I was downstairs reading until a little before one, and I was up again at five. I try to run four mornings each week. I left the house at ten after five and got back around five forty-five."

"And you didn't notice anything at all?"

"The car was parked behind the house, in front of the garage. I left and returned through the front door. It wasn't until I was leaving for a meeting around seven thirty that I found the body."

"The car's been impounded?"

"The lab people are still working on the bare amount of trace our people were able to recover. The killer had apparently hosed down the plastic to remove anything that might have clung to the wrappings before he put her into the car."

"Fingerprints?" she asked.

"Not a one."

"Careful, wasn't he?" She tapped her fingers on the table. "And thorough. Not taking any chances at all. But that's a brassy move, leaving her for you to find. She was from St. Dennis?"

He shook his head. "No. She was from a nearby town, Cameron. At least, we're thinking she was. A young woman named Mindy Kenneher went missing there a few weeks before the woman who'd been found on Sunday night. I'm expecting to hear back from the ME any time now. I was meeting with the chief of police from Cameron when you arrived. He was on his way to the morgue to take a look at the body."

"He hadn't seen her yet?"

"The ME spent hours with the remains yesterday and last night. The condition of the body apparently made it very slow going. As hot as it's been this past week, decomposition accelerated inside the plastic. She—the ME, Dr. Reilly—is very thorough. She's taking her time with this."

"It's my understanding there was a tape found with the first body," she said. "Was there one with the second as well?"

"Yes, but because of the breakdown of bodily fluids inside the plastic, the tape was saturated and has been compromised. Agent Mancini said the FBI labs could work on that, see if they could improve the quality. Unfortunately, right now it's inaudible."

"I'm sure we can help with that. Any chance I can listen to the tape that was found with the first victim?"

"The chief in Ballard has that; I'll have him make a copy. And I've already requested a copy of his file, and the file from Cameron. We'll get you whatever you need."

"Chief, why do you suppose he left the body for you to find?"

"Beck," he told her. "Everyone calls me Beck. And I don't know why he picked me, except for the fact that I attended the press conference Chief Daley held over in Ballard the other day. There were four of us, police chiefs from four communities. Five all together, including Daley."

"Why were you all there?"

"Mostly to let our communities know we were going to work together to solve the case." He made a face. "It seemed like a good idea at the time. In retrospect, not so much."

"Because he—the killer—may have felt threatened? Maybe thought you were ganging up on him? Or then again, judging by his response, maybe he's playing with you. Maybe he saw the whole thing as a challenge? 'You guys think you're so smart, well, I'll show you. You don't know who you're dealing with.'"

"You got that part right." Beck nodded. "We don't know who we're dealing with."

"Why you?" she asked. "There were other local chiefs there. Why did he pick your car and not one of the others?"

"I have no idea. I'm trying not to read too much into it."

He pushed the chair back from the table and stood.

"You feel like taking a walk?"

"Sure."

"Garland, I have my phone if it's important," Beck said as he passed the desk. "We'll be back in a while."

Garland was on the phone, but raised a hand to signal he'd heard.

Mia followed Beck through the lobby and out the front door. She dug in her bag for her sunglasses, then swung the bag over her shoulder.

"Pretty town," she said as they walked toward the water.

"One of the prettiest towns around. I want to keep it that way." He stopped at the end of the macadam drive. "St. Dennis sits right at the convergence of the New River, which you can see straight ahead there, and the Chesapeake Bay, out there to your left, where that big cruiser is headed. During the War of 1812, the town was shelled by the British. Several of the houses in town still have cannonballs embedded in their walls, but none fell. St. Dennis is very proud of that."

"Ahhh, spoken like a proud native," she said. "Born and bred here, I assume?"

"No." He turned and started toward the brown,

shingled building that stood at the end of the parking lot.

"Really? Could have fooled me." She hustled to keep up. "Where are you from?"

"Here and there."

O-kay . . .

"So where are we headed?" she asked.

"I want to give you the lay of the land around here. St. Dennis is split pretty much in two by Charles Street, which is the main road you came in on. Half of the town faces the water, the other half faces the farms on the opposite side of town. Along Charles, we have shops where you can find just about everything. Eateries that run the gamut from pretty damned posh to a storefront with tables on the sidewalk where you can sit barefoot and eat hot dogs. We have an art gallery and an antiques shop and a bookstore where you can find comic books and first editions as well as the latest best sellers. There's a marina where you can dock your boat and a boatyard where you can buy one if you don't already have one." He paused. "We have a population of about fifteen hundred."

She slowed down. She got it.

"That big a commercial district plus a low population equals a tourist town."

"Mostly on the weekends, yeah. And we have several old inns, bed-and-breakfasts, that sort of thing, so we get a lot of people staying around in the summer months. We had our Harbor Festival last weekend. Close as we can figure, our population just about tripled."

"That's a lot of people coming and going, some staying," she said. "So you have to wonder . . ."

"Yeah. Was he one of them?" Beck turned back toward the municipal building. "Let's walk up to town."

He was tempted to add *If you're up to it, in those shoes.*

What was it with women and high heels? He'd seen Vanessa teetering on heels that had to be four inches. And Steffie, too, whenever they'd gone out to dinner. Agent Shields's weren't that bad, and she didn't seem to have a problem keeping up with him, but still. It was one of those things men just didn't get.

"Of course, he could just as easily be a local, living in any one of these small towns. Until we can learn a little more about him, we're all just speculating. One of the reasons I wanted the FBI involved was to have access to your profilers. Maybe help us get a handle on what type of person we're dealing with."

"We can do that. Let's try to get a handle on the whole picture first. We'll start with the victims, see what they have to tell us."

"But they'll send someone, right?" They reached the end of the walk that led to Charles Street and stopped at the corner. "They'll send us someone who can do all that?"

"They did."

He stared at her for a long moment.

"You mean you—"

"I'm trained to do it all." She tried to smile good-naturedly, but a weak grin was the best she could come up with.

"Sorry. I thought you were just here as an investigator."

"That's all part of it. However, if I feel we need someone with more experience, I won't hesitate to call in one of the big guns."

Someone in a passing Buick slowed down to yell a greeting at Beck.

"How's your wife feeling, Tony?" He called back.

"Doin' better, thanks!"

"Tell her I was asking for her."

"Will do!" The driver of the car waved and continued on his way.

"Nice shops." Mia glanced across the street to the row of storefronts.

"Like I said, a little something for everyone." Beck gestured toward the place on the corner. "Let's grab something cold, then I'll give you a short tour."

He held open the door to Sips, a narrow one-room affair that sold only drinks. After a chat with Sam, the owner, about the body in Beck's Jeep while he poured them each a large drink, Beck cut the conversation short.

"Won't take much to feed that fire," Beck said after he and Mia stepped back outside. "It's all anyone wants to talk about."

"How many homicides do you have in the average year?" she asked.

"Average?" He pretended to think it over. "Maybe one. Most I recall was one year when a couple of runaways from Baltimore holed up in one of the abandoned shacks down near the river. One of them flipped out and beat the other one to death with a shovel while he was passed out. We also had a shooting that same year, so that was two. Hal might know of others. You can ask."

"Hal?"

"He was the chief of police before me. He still works part-time when we need extra hands, which we always seem to, this time of the year."

"He was the chief and now he's a part-timer? That sits okay with him?"

"I haven't heard any complaints. Actually, it was his idea."

"Hey, you."

Mia turned to see a pretty young woman step out from the doorway of the shop they just passed.

"You're just going to walk by and not even poke your head in to say good morning?" The woman walked toward them, not bothering to mask the fact that she was appraising Mia from head to toe.

"Good morning," Beck said. "Ness, this is Special Agent Mia Shields, from the FBI. She's here to help out with the investigation. Agent Shields, my sister, Vanessa."

"Oh. Wow. FBI." Vanessa looked impressed.

"Good to meet you." Mia smiled and looked past Vanessa to something that caught her eye in the shop window. The sign over the door read Bling in stylized letters. "You work in this shop?"

"Actually, I own it," Vanessa told her proudly. "My little piece of the world."

Mia stepped closer to the window. "You have some lovely things. That's an interesting bag there . . ."

"It's a fabulous bag. Stop in sometime and take a look while you're here."

"Ness, Agent Shields isn't here to shop," Beck stage-whispered.

"True, but that doesn't mean she can't come by when she has a spare minute." Vanessa smiled broadly at Mia. "Just to look."

"Maybe I'll do that before I leave town," Mia nodded. "Just to look."

"Good." Vanessa turned to Beck. "So where are you off to?"

"Just showing Agent Shields around. I want her to have a feel for the town."

"Don't forget to show her the houses down around the square. And the old church. Oh, and the Breakstone Inn." Vanessa turned to Mia. "It's just gorgeous. We have so many beautiful homes that are totally restored, it's one of the—"

"I don't think Agent Shields is interested in an architectural tour," Beck said.

"Actually, I am," Mia told him. "It helps get a feel for the town and the type of people who live here. I'd like to see—"

She was interrupted by the sound of Beck's ringing phone.

"Excuse me," he said to both women as he took the phone from his pocket and answered. "Beck."

He listened for several minutes, then said, "Thanks. I'll get back to you."

"Problem?" Vanessa asked.

"I'd say so." He turned to Mia. "The body that

was found in my car, the one we believed to be the missing woman from Cameron?"

"Yes?"

"It isn't."

"Isn't . . ." Mia looked confused.

"It isn't Mindy Kenneher."

"So who is it?"

"That's a damned good question." He started to cross the street, motioning for Mia to follow.

"I guess if you had a report of a missing local woman you'd have mentioned it by now." Mia caught up with him on the sidewalk on the opposite side of the street.

"Good guess."

"So it isn't the woman you knew about, the one from the neighboring town." She quickened her pace. "And you haven't gotten word of anyone else missing?"

"None."

"Which means he brought her here from somewhere else just to jab at you a little, or someone's missing who hasn't been reported."

"Judging by the appearance of the corpse, this one's been missing for a while. The flesh was pretty soupy."

"What's your guess, weeks?"

"Tough to tell. Even the ME wasn't sure she'd be able to pinpoint how long the vic's been dead. Given the heat and the temperature that would have built up inside that plastic wrapping, I don't know that we'll ever know for sure how long she's been dead.

Unless, of course, we're able to identify her and figure out how long she's been missing."

"I'll call someone back at the Bureau, see if he can shoot over a list of women who have been reported missing over the past, let's say six months in a fifty mile radius. We'll see if any of them match the vital stats of your vic." They reached the municipal building and headed for the door.

"I'll give the ME a call and see what she's got that we can use. As I said, the body is in pretty bad shape."

Beck held the door and allowed Mia to enter the building first. Garland was flagging him down with a fistfull of phone messages and Beck grabbed them as he walked by, mouthing a thanks to the dispatcher who was busy taking another call.

"There's a phone in the conference room you can use," Beck told Mia. "My office is the next door over. Come on in when you're finished."

"I brought my own." She took her phone from her bag and held it up as she went into the conference room. He had calls to make as did she.

Five minutes later Mia tapped lightly on Beck's open office door then entered without waiting for his invitation.

"Someone in my office is running through the latest NCIC missing-person entries," she told him.

"Great. We'll see if any of them match up with the ME's best guess." Beck leaned against the corner of his desk. "She's thinking the vic is in her mid-twenties, blond hair. Hazel eyes. Five feet six inches tall, weight at the time of her death was probably around one twenty-five. Extensive cosmetic dental work—a lot of porcelain crowns. Expensive stuff. The flesh was in poor condition so she's not sure of any distinguishing marks like birthmarks. There is an old healed fracture of the right forearm, most likely a childhood injury. And that's all we've got to try to match her up with."

"If she's in the system, we'll have her. If not—"

"If not, we go on the six o'clock news and let the world know what we've got. Someone has to be looking for this woman."

"In the meantime—"

"In the meantime, we wait," he snapped.

She stared at him for a long time, then said calmly, "I'll be waiting in the conference room. I'd appreciate it if you'd get me a copy of the files on the two vics—the first one that was found, and the one who's still missing. In particular, I'll need to see all the interviews. Family, friends, coworkers."

He looked at her quizzically.

"Know the victim, know the killer." She turned and went into the conference room, closing the door quietly behind her.

8

Mia rested an elbow on the edge of the table and tried to brush off the twinge of annoyance that flared inside her when Beck had cut her off. Clearly he was used to being in charge. She could deal with that. All her life she'd been surrounded by men who were used to giving orders. What bothered her about Beck was his seeming dismissal of her.

She wasn't used to being dismissed.

Pushing aside her personal feelings, Mia searched her phone's listing of numbers, found the one she wanted, and hit the call button.

Maybe I should remind him that he was the one who called me into this case, she thought as the number rang. *Okay, maybe not me specifically, but he did call the Bureau looking for help.*

"Hey, Will, hi, it's Mia again. Let me give you a different fax number for that information I just requested." Voice mail had picked up and she read off the number of the fax machine in the conference room. "I hope you got this message before you left for the weekend."

She decided to make good use of the few minutes she had to herself. She'd wanted to make a few notes regarding the case, so she took a small notebook and a pen from her bag and began to write a list. At the top went the interviews she'd already requested from Beck, followed by photos of the crime scenes, including the car where the last victim had been left. She'd want to walk Beck's neighborhood at night and she'd want to see the victims, if possible. And she wanted to listen to the tape. Most of all, she wanted to hear the voice of the man who'd devised such a unique method of disposing of his victims.

She paused with the pen in her hand. It was more than merely a means of disposal, she knew. Wrapping his victims in clear plastic was about control and it was about his need to be up close and personal with their death. He wanted to see, to smell, to experience every emotion, every labored breath, every bit of the struggle of his victim as he wound the plastic closer and closer to her face. The sheer terror as the film covered first her mouth, then her nose, the horror in her eyes, all most likely aroused him unbearably, probably to the point of climax.

She wondered if the plastic wrap had been tested for semen.

But of course, the killer had hosed down the victim that had been left in Beck's car. Still, there could be some traces inside the folds of plastic. And what about the one left on the porch of her family's home? She made a note to check that everything that came in contact with both victims had been tested for traces of semen and sweat, including the Prestons' porch steps and decking.

That, too, was telling as far as this killer was concerned. It hadn't been enough to make Colleen Preston suffer. He had to make certain that the people who loved her the most saw firsthand just what she'd gone through.

"Could it be personal?" she murmured aloud.

"What?" Beck stood in the doorway. Mia hadn't heard the door open.

"I was just wondering if the fact that the killer left the first victim—"

"Colleen Preston," he reminded her.

"Yes, thank you. Colleen Preston. We should use her name. I was wondering if maybe the killer left her for her family to find because there's some personal connection. Some reason he'd like to rub their face in it."

"In the fact that she'd been killed?"

"In the manner in which she'd been killed," Mia corrected him. "He wanted them to know he'd had total control over her body and her life and her death. He wanted them to know exactly what he'd done to her. He wanted them to see just how much she'd suffered. How vainly she'd gasped for air. How terrified she'd been. And that he'd orchestrated it all."

She stood and began to pace.

"Why else make the tapes? Why let them hear her last words, if not to taunt them?"

"Because he's a sick son of a bitch."

"Oh, that he is. But this goes deeper than just being sick. This has a personal edge to it."

"You could be right about that. Right now, we need to take a drive."

"Where to?" She slid her bag off the back of her chair and grabbed her notebook and phone from the table, then followed Beck into the hall.

"Sinclair's Cove. It's a bed-and-breakfast about a mile outside of town. I just got a call from the owner. He heard about the woman that was found in my car, and thinks he might know who she is."

"Who does he think she is?"

"One of the grad students who worked for him. She went home for a family wedding in Colorado over the weekend of the first and never came back. Last week he called her parents' house to find out if she'd quit, but they were under the impression that she was here. The Monday after the wedding, she left home to drive back to the inn. They spoke with her once while she was on the road, but they haven't heard from her since."

"And they didn't miss her until her employer called?"

"She's twenty-five years old, she's been living away from home for some time now. I guess she didn't check in all that often."

As they walked past Garland, Beck held up his phone, apparently to show the dispatcher that he had it with him.

"Shit. My car . . ." Beck said when they reached the parking lot and he realized his Jeep was being processed as a crime scene and he'd loaned his cruiser to Hal.

"I'll drive." Mia pointed to the black Lexus SUV parked under one of the few trees with a canopy large enough to provide shade.

"Nice wheels," he said as they walked toward it.

"Thanks." She unlocked it with the remote, then opened the driver's side door and slid behind the wheel.

When Beck got in, she said, "So, I guess this story is the big news around town."

She snapped on her seat belt and turned the key in the ignition, then opened the windows to let out the air that had been cooking inside the closed car despite the fact that the car had been parked in the shade.

"Biggest thing that's happened in St. Dennis since the British shelled it during the War of 1812."

She stopped at the entrance to the parking lot to allow a TV news van to enter.

"Keep going," he told her. "We're not doing the news thing right now."

"Which way?" she asked when they reached Charles Street.

"Take a right."

"I'm going to need to hear the tape he left inside Colleen Preston's wrappings," she said as she made the turn. "And I want copies of the photos from both crime scenes."

"What else?"

"The interviews, I told you that."

"Anything else?"

"I want to walk your neighborhood at night. The Prestons', too. I want to see it the way he did."

"As best we can figure out, he must have been at the Prestons' between eight and eleven. My place, sometime between one and five." He glanced over at her. "You go walking around St. Dennis at that hour, I want to know about it."

"Worried about my safety, Chief?"

"Not funny, Agent Shields." He turned his face to the window. "Not funny at all."

"It wasn't meant to be. For the record, I'm well trained and I'm well armed."

"Good for you. But you're also the right age for this wacko to go after. Don't put yourself in harm's way."

"I never do."

"Make the next right," he told her.

Sinclair's Cove was marked by a white sign bearing the name of the inn and adorned with a painted great blue heron that was life-size and expertly done. The drive was tree-lined and reminiscent of the old South. It wound through a forest of azaleas to a clearing, at the far end of which was a house that took Mia's breath away.

"Wow," she said. "Take a look at that."

"It is something," Beck agreed.

The front of the large white structure was three stories high, with a porch that spanned the entire length, and was adorned with three pillars that went from the porch to the upper roof line. Tall windows graced either side of the front door. The circular drive off to one side of the house left the entire lawn unspoiled, and Adirondack chairs were scattered here and there for the guests to enjoy one of the many views of the bay.

"How old is this place?" she asked.

"Early eighteen hundreds, I think, but you can ask the owner." Beck pointed to the porch where a well-dressed man stood watching. "Daniel Sinclair the . . . I don't know, eighth? Tenth?"

"Come on." She laughed.

"No, seriously. The house has been in the same family since it was built."

"That's crazy."

"Crazy but true. The guy who owns this place is a direct descendant of the one who built it."

She parked in front of one of the outbuildings and turned off the engine.

"That's the river? Or the Chesapeake?" She pointed to the water flowing beyond the rear of the grounds.

"The bay. Most people are surprised when they realize how wide it is."

"I live almost directly on the opposite Shore," she said as she opened the door and got out of the car. "No surprise here."

"Chief Beck." The man who'd stood on the porch now strode across the well-tended lawn. "Thanks for coming out right away."

"That's what we're here for." The two men shook hands, then Beck introduced Mia. "Dan, this is Special Agent Mia Shields from the FBI."

"Called in the big guns, did you?" Daniel Sinclair then offered a smile and a hand to Mia. "Good to meet you, Agent Shields. Glad to know I live in a town where the police aren't afraid to ask for help when they need it. I have to admit I'm surprised that neither Cameron nor Ballard had the sense to call in the feds."

"Well, I'm sure the cases are going to overlap," Mia told him. "We'll certainly share whatever information we feel is relevant to their respective cases."

"Good, good." Sinclair nodded agreeably. "The sooner this bastard is locked up, the better off we'll all be."

"Dan, why don't you tell us about your missing employee?" Beck prompted.

"Holly Sheridan. As I told you on the phone, she asked if she could take a little time off to attend a family wedding in Colorado. At the time, I understood her to mean a long weekend, as in Thursday night through Monday. Of course I said yes. When Wednesday arrived and she did not, I figured I'd misunderstood how much time she'd asked for. When this past Monday came and I hadn't heard from her, I was getting a little pissed off."

"You tried her cell phone?" Mia asked.

"Yes, but it always went straight to voice mail. Finally, I figured, enough already. A family wedding's one thing, but we'd gone beyond the amount of time I felt was reasonable. So I called her parents—we have everyone's next of kin on file here—but they were as surprised as I was that she wasn't here. More, maybe, because they'd seen her off the day she left to drive back here."

"And you said on the phone that was the Monday after the wedding, which would have been July second," Beck reminded him.

"Right."

"So we'd give her a few days to drive back from Colorado . . ." Beck paused, then turned to Mia. "We should check her credit cards, gas cards, ATM withdrawals . . ."

"And find out what route she was following, check with the state police, see if her car's been found." Mia nodded. "Mr. Sinclair, do you know what kind of car she was driving?"

"Holly drove a Ford Explorer. About four years old, I think. White, had some kind of tree-hugger bumper sticker on the back and a thing on the window from the University of Delaware, where she's in grad school. Hotel and restaurant management. That's why she was working here, she wanted the experience. Wanted to own her own bed-and-breakfast someday."

"Was she friendly with anyone here, any of the other workers?"

"Beck, Holly was friendly with everyone, but no one in particular. I can give you a list of everyone who worked her shift, if that would help."

"It would." Beck nodded. "Do you know if anyone was bothering her? Or if she was seeing anyone?"

"Tell you the truth, I don't know anything about her private life. She was living in one of my cottages with one of the other girls, but I never really saw her socialize with anyone in particular outside of work. Holly didn't seem much for partying. She might go out at night once in a while with a group, maybe to the movies, but if there was any partying going on, I didn't know about it."

"What was her job here?" asked Mia.

"Sort of an apprentice chef," Sinclair told her. "She worked all three meals, wanted as much experience as she could get this summer. Up at the crack of dawn for breakfast, worked straight on through the day until dinner was over."

"So she really had no time for much of a social life," Mia said.

"That's what I was saying. If she was seeing someone, I don't know when that could have been. She worked her tail off. Sunup to sundown. Her choice, by the way. Like I said, she wanted as much experience as possible." Daniel Sinclair's voice dropped. "She used to tell me she'd be the first in line to try to buy this place, if I ever wanted to sell it. Which of course, I never would."

"Dan, while we're here, maybe we could take a look at the cottage where Holly was staying," Beck said.

"Absolutely. It's the third one from the end, down near the bay. I think her roommate, Elise Hawthorne, is off this afternoon, so let's walk down and see if she's in." Sinclair motioned for Mia and Beck to follow him down a brick path that led in the general direction of the water.

"Maybe while we're talking with the roommate, you can get to work on that list of employees," Beck suggested.

"Sure. I'll take a run up to the office and have it printed off the computer for you."

"That'd be fine," Beck told him.

"Mr. Sinclair, Chief Beck was telling me the property's been in your family for over a hundred years," Mia said as they walked toward the row of cottages.

"Almost two hundred years," Sinclair corrected. "My ancestor, Harold Sinclair, built the house, pretty much the way you see it today. It's been added to a bit here and there over the years, and we've kept up with modern conveniences, but I feel confident old Harold wouldn't have much trouble recognizing his home." Sinclair smiled. "Actually, there are some who say he's never left."

"Are you saying the place is haunted?" Mia asked.

"Depends on who you ask." He shrugged. "Some claim to have seen a couple in nineteenth-century dress, dancing on the lawn. Could be Harold and his second wife, Felice, could be his son Daniel and his wife Cordelia. She was an English beauty, her portrait hangs in the Blue Room, if you're interested in taking a look."

"I'd love to. Maybe on my next trip out." Mia smiled.

"Ah, all business." Sinclair nodded. "I understand. And here we are."

He pointed to a cottage directly ahead. It was small, clapboard painted white with dark green shutters to match the main house. A brass number three was nailed to the center of the door. Daniel Sinclair knocked several times before it was opened by a sleepy young woman who stifled a yawn.

"Oh. Mr. Sinclair. Sorry." The girl appeared embarrassed. "Am I late?"

"No, no. Nothing like that, Elise." He stepped back and introduced Beck and Mia.

"Chief Beck and Agent Shields would like to ask you a few questions about Holly." He turned to Beck and said, "I'll get that list for you now."

"Thanks, Dan."

"Did something happen to Holly?" Elise clutched both hands in front of her.

"We're not sure," Mia told her. "Have you heard from her over the past week?"

"No." Elise shook her head, her ponytail swinging from side to side. "I haven't, not since she left for Colorado."

"Do you know what route she took?"

"I don't, sorry. We roomed together, but we weren't real close, if you know what I mean. We shared the space, not much else."

"You wouldn't have a picture of her, would you?" Beck asked.

"Actually, I do." Elise looked over her shoulder into the room beyond, as if debating with herself whether or not to let them come inside. Finally, she shrugged and said, "Come on in. Sorry if the place is a little messy, but I've been putting in a lot of hours."

"We understand Holly did, as well," Mia said as she followed the girl into the small front room, which was fitted with a sofa and one armchair.

"Yeah, we all do. It's great experience, you know? Mr. Sinclair is really good about letting us see how the place is run. He teases us about how he's training his competition, but you know there's no place around that can compete with this place."

"Why's that?" Mia asked.

"They have a great chef, they have activities for all ages here, they have boats, the bay. And the guest rooms are gorgeous. All original furniture, fireplaces, balconies overlooking the bay. Gorgeous views, a wildlife preserve right here on the property—I don't know what else you'd look for at an inn."

"I might have to book a room for a night," Mia said.

"You'd have to talk to Mr. S. about that. I think he's pretty much booked solid." Elise headed for the door that opened off to the right. "If you'll give me a minute, I'll get that picture."

She was back in an instant, the photo in hand.

"This is Holly." She held the photo up and pointed to a tall, thin young woman with blond hair. The camera had caught her in a moment of laughter, her head tossed back. Holly Sheridan looked as if she didn't have a care in the world.

"She's very pretty," Mia said softly.

"She really is. And nice, too. She wasn't stuck on herself the way some really pretty girls are."

"Do you know if she was dating anyone? Here or maybe at school?" Mia asked.

"She mentioned a boyfriend, Eric. He's working someplace out west for the summer. She kept pretty busy here. She was in her last year of school and took this opportunity very seriously. There aren't too many places like this that offer paid internships, and she seemed to want to get everything she could out of the experience."

"Do you know what she did on her time off?"

"Not really." Elise shrugged. "She went into town a couple of times a week, but she really spent most of her time here."

"What about her days off?"

"Mostly slept, did her laundry, read. Maybe take out one of the kayaks, swim, relax on the dock," Elise told Mia. "That's pretty much all any of us do. There's no real nightlife in St. Dennis—not that you have a lot of energy left at the end of the day—so you just relax when you can."

"Did she get to know anyone in town, do you know?" Mia asked.

"I wouldn't know, but really, I doubt it. She's only been here since the middle of May, and like I said, she kept herself pretty busy." Elise leaned against the doorjamb. "What happened to her?"

"We're not really sure," Beck told her, looking beyond her to the bedroom. "I guess you share a room, right? The cottage is pretty small, so I'm guessing there's only one bedroom. Would you mind if we took a quick look around?"

Elise's eyes darted from Beck to Mia, then back again.

"What are you looking for?" she asked.

"Anything that might help us to know Holly a little better," Mia replied.

Elise shrugged. "I guess it would be okay. All her stuff is on the left side of the room. The right side is mine."

Elise stepped aside to permit them to enter the bedroom, but stayed in the doorway, slumping against the molding to watch. When Mia took a plastic bag from her purse and slipped a comb into it, Elise straightened up.

"You're taking her hair for DNA, aren't you?" The young woman's eyes widened. "You think she's dead? You think she's the girl in the plastic wrap?"

"We really don't know," Mia said calmly. "But we do need her DNA, yes, hopefully to rule her out."

"I watch TV, I know about these things." Elise's words came in an excited rush.

"Look, Elise, let's not jump the gun, okay? Right now, we're just—"

"You're looking for evidence." It sounded like an accusation.

"We're looking for whatever will help us find out where Holly is and what happened to her." Once again Mia's voice soothed. "If we knew anything for certain, I promise I'd tell you. Right now, all we know for sure is that Holly left Colorado over a week ago and hasn't arrived here yet. Let's just leave it at that for now, all right?"

"But there's that girl they found in the car—"

"She hasn't been identified yet," Mia told her, then turned back to the room. "We'll just be another minute, then you can have your room to yourself."

She went past Beck to the stack of magazines that sat on the floor next to Holly's bed. She knelt down and skimmed through the pile, which consisted mostly of food magazines, with one or two fashion magazines and the local newspaper open to the classified ads. A paperback mystery lay half under the bed.

"Any idea what she was looking for in the want ads?" Mia asked, skimming the ads. The page listed everything from ads for bait—*Night crawlers our specialty!*—to real estate to pets to livestock and boats.

"No." Elise shook her head.

"Mind if we take this photo?" Beck held up the picture Elise had handed him earlier.

"Sure." She shrugged.

"Was I supposed to ask you if you have a warrant?" Elise asked out of the blue. "They do that on TV all the time."

"We had your permission to look around, as well as the permission of the owner," Mia told her as she checked the paperback for a sticker with the name of the store in which it was purchased, but there was none.

She could have added that if a person is deceased, no warrant is necessary, but didn't want to upset the roommate any more than she already was.

"If you're finished, I have to get ready for work now," Elise told them.

"We're done, thanks. We appreciate your cooperation." Beck started out of the room, then paused. "You mind if we take the newspaper?"

Elise shrugged. "Go ahead. It's probably a couple of weeks old by now anyway."

"Thanks, Elise." Mia walked toward the door.

"Okay." Elise nodded as Beck and Mia left the

small sitting room and stepped outside. "I hope you find Holly."

Mia nodded solemnly. She didn't think the time was right to tell Elise that Holly might already have been found.

9

Beck was dialing his phone even before Mia turned the key in the ignition.

"Lisa. Beck." He rested the phone on his shoulder while he strapped into the seat belt. "We have a lead on the vic that was found in my car. We think she's Holly Sheridan, age twenty-five, summer employee out at Sinclair's Cove. I want to give everyone the rundown at the same time, so get Duncan, Hal, and Sue in the conference room now. I should be back in about five minutes and I want to get this investigation moving as quickly as possible. . . ."

Mia followed the lane to the main road, then turned left to drive back into St. Dennis.

"We'll have two meetings when we get back," Beck told her after he hung up from his call. "We'll meet with my staff, as you just heard, then with the mayor."

He waved to a woman passing by on a bicycle.

"I guess it'll be three meetings," he said as almost an afterthought.

"Who's the third?" Mia slowed to make the turn onto Kelly's Point Road.

"The ME."

"Great. I want to get that tape sent out to our lab

as quickly as possible. We have a tech, Jojo Kessler, who is just a genius. If anyone can make sense of the garble, she can. And I can get her to move quickly on it, too."

"How can you be so sure?"

"Jojo has a huge crush on my brother." She smiled.

"Your brother's in the FBI, too?"

"Actually, they all are."

"How many are there?"

"Three." She made a face. "Actually, two now."

"What happened to the other one?"

"He died."

"I'm sorry," Beck told her.

"Don't be." She turned off the engine and opened the door. "No one else is."

She got out of the car, leaving Beck seated in the front seat, momentarily stunned. By the time he followed her from the car, she'd already gone through the front door and into the building.

Beck ignored the three news vans and the reporters gathered at the door.

"No questions at this time." He held up a hand as he passed.

"Then when?" someone asked.

"Has the body that was left in your car been identified? Is it Mindy Kenneher?"

"The only thing I can tell you right now is that it is not Mindy Kenneher."

The reporters began to swarm.

"That's all for now. I have a meeting and I'm already late. But as soon as I know something definite, I'll let you all know."

"You do know something definite, Chief," Jenna Smith said. "You definitely know the woman that you found in the back of your car is dead, and you know she definitely was killed by the same person who killed Colleen Preston."

Beck paused, the door partially open. "You're right, Jenna. I do know those two things. But nothing else has been confirmed." He walked through the door and let it close behind him.

"The phone's been ringing off the hook," Garland told Beck as he approached the desk. "It seems everyone in town has a friend on the EMT squad."

"What are you telling people?" Beck stopped for a moment.

"I'm telling them you've been out of the office all morning and that you'll have a statement later."

"Good. And now that I'm back?"

"You're in a meeting and can't be disturbed."

Beck slapped Garland on the back then walked away. "Those people up in Boston sure did teach you right."

Mia was waiting inside his office when he came in. *Amazing how fast she could move in those shoes . . .*

"I'm going to grab something from the kitchen to drink. Can I get you something?" he asked.

"Anything cold would be fine, thanks," she told him.

"Then we'll head on in to the conference room and I'll introduce you to my officers." His voice trailed behind him. In a moment he was back, a can of Diet Pepsi in each hand. "This okay?" he held one up.

"It's fine. Thank you." Mia took the can he offered her.

"You want a glass?"

"No, this is fine."

"Let's get on with it then." He gestured toward the conference room.

She followed him in and stood while he made introductions all around. She stole a glance at the fax machine that stood on a table near the back of the room, and was disappointed to find the tray empty. She'd have to put in another call for that NCIC report she'd requested.

"FBI Special Agent Mia Shields, meet Sergeant Lisa Singer. Officers Susan Martin and Duncan Alcott." Beck started on the left side of the table. "Hal Garrity, former chief here in St. Dennis, back on the force to help out in the summer. His brother, Phil, works part-time when we need him but he left for Canada on Sunday for a bird-watching trip."

Mia walked from one to the next, shaking their hands and making eye contact, then took a seat near Hal, who leaned over to pull the chair out for her. She smiled her thanks and started to say something, but the door opened and a trim woman in her mid-fifties blew in.

"Beck, what the hell is going on?"

"Mayor Christina Pratt, this is Special Agent Shields," Beck said calmly. "Agent Shields, this is Mayor Pratt."

"Don't get up," the mayor told Mia. "Nice to meet you." She turned back to Beck. "I'd like to know what's going on. What's this about a missing woman—"

"Please, take a seat. I was just about to fill everyone in." Beck closed the conference room door, then leaned on the back of the chair nearest him. "You all know about the body we found in the backseat of my Jeep yesterday. We assumed that the body was that of Mindy Kenneher, the woman who's been missing from Cameron for the past few weeks. Unfortunately, it is not Mindy."

"Do we know who it is?" Mayor Pratt asked.

"We have a damned good idea." Beck took the photograph he'd brought back from Sinclair's Cove from his pocket and held it up. "Holly Sheridan. Age twenty-five, summer employee at Sinclair's Cove."

Beck shared what he'd learned about Holly with the group.

"Duncan, I'm going to assign you to figure out her itinerary between Colorado and Maryland, what route she would have taken, find out what credit cards she had and see if you can trace them. Contact every state between here and there and see if her car's turned up anywhere. I have her family's contact information and I can give you that to get you started."

"When you were in her room, did you find anything that might give you a lead?" Hal asked.

"Nothing."

"Except we do know that she went into town several times each week," Mia interjected. "Her roommate mentioned that. And we found a pile of magazines, a local newspaper, and a paperback book on the floor next to her bed. She could have purchased them locally."

"Did you notice which paper?" Hal asked.

"It was the *Chesapeake Weekly*," Beck answered. "Which could have been picked up anywhere. Neither the magazines nor the book had any stickers that might tell us where she bought them. Now, there are several places in town where they sell magazines, but only two or three where you can buy paperbacks."

"I'll make a copy of that photo and show it around town," Hal told him. "I'll start with Bookends, maybe Barbie will recognize the girl. Only other place I know of in St. Dennis proper that sells books is the Food Mart. I'll see if Bruce or one of the boys remembers seeing her around."

"Make it a clean sweep of all the shops, Hal," Beck said. "We don't know what other interests this woman had, so let's cover the bases right the first time."

"Shouldn't someone talk to the people she worked with?" the mayor asked.

"We've got that covered," Lisa said. "Beck and I already discussed that. I'm on it."

"How long before we know for certain if the body found this morning is Holly Sheridan?" Mayor Pratt looked worried.

Beck looked at Mia. "How long before your lab people get back to you?"

"Well, considering we haven't given them anything yet, I can't really answer that," Mia replied. "If we can send samples out today, maybe in a few days we'll know for certain. Unless there's another means of identification. Maybe get dental records, ask the ME to take a look."

"I'll put a call in to her parents as soon as we're done here, see how quickly we can get those records."

"Why don't you just take the photo out to the ME's office and look at the girl and see if that's her?" Mayor Pratt looked from Mia to Beck.

"I'm afraid she doesn't really look like this anymore, Christine." Beck held up the photo.

"But she hasn't been dead all that long, right? Just a week or so?" The mayor looked confused.

"She was sealed in plastic, Mayor Pratt." Mia turned to explain.

"Yes, so, that should have preserved her, wouldn't it? I mean, no bugs would have gotten to her."

"It's been pretty hot here this past week, as I understand it," Mia said gently.

"Yes. So?"

"So imagine what might happen to a piece of meat if you wrapped it tightly in plastic, then set it out someplace where the temperature was in the high eighties, low nineties every day."

"It would . . ." Christine Pratt blanched.

"Right. It would cook." Mia nodded. "Actually, it would sort of liquefy."

"I see. Well. If we're done here . . ." The mayor stood and looked at Beck. "Beck, if I could see you in the hall . . ."

She left the room without looking back, leaving a silent group behind. Beck stepped out behind her.

"She was in a hurry all of a sudden," Hal noted dryly. "Left her handbag on the back of the chair."

"I'll run it out to her." Lisa took the bag and left the room.

"I didn't mean to upset her." Mia told Beck when he returned.

"Hey, she asked." He shrugged, then looked around the room. "Anyone have anything to say? No? No questions? You all know your assignments, let's get moving."

Everyone stood and started toward the door.

"Oh, one more thing. No one talks to the press or to anyone else. No one."

He made eye contact with each member of his staff.

"If anyone in this room does not understand what that means, speak up now, because if there's a leak, if I hear something coming back that I didn't personally put out there, someone's head will roll. Any questions?"

There were none.

"All right then." He pushed in the chair he'd leaned on. "Agent Shields, if you're ready, we'll take a run out to see Dr. Reilly. Maybe she'll have something to tell us."

The lab was located in the basement of one the county-owned and -operated assisted-living facilities.

"This is a little weird," Mia noted as she parked her car near the entrance. "You have all these elderly folks out here for their afternoon strolls, and downstairs you have the morgue? Am I the only one who thinks this is strange?"

"Hey, the county had the space here." Beck shrugged. "At least you didn't make any lame jokes about the residents not having far to go when they pass from one life to the next."

"Don't think I wasn't tempted," she said as she got out of the car. "Which way?"

"Door around the side of the building." Beck joined her on the sidewalk.

"Well, that's certainly better than using the elevator in the main lobby."

He laughed and led the way to the door leading to Dr. Reilly's quarters, one flight down behind a black door. Beck knocked, then tried the knob.

"Hey, Beck," Vivian Reilly greeted him as he opened the door into her office.

"Viv." He held the door for Mia, then allowed it to swing closed behind her. "Viv, this is Agent Shields from the FBI."

"Good to meet you." Vivian put down the files she held and extended her hand.

"Thanks. Nice to meet you, too." Mia took the hand that was offered. "I hear you've been busy."

"And not in a good way." The medical examiner shook her head, then turned to Beck. "This latest one, the one from your car? What a mess. I hate to turn her over to her family like this."

"They're having a hard enough time as it is." He nodded. "I called them while we were driving out here. Had to ask them to get their family dentist to have Holly's dental records overnighted. The dentist is the girl's aunt, so there's no problem getting the records. I can tell you the Sheridans are reeling from this, especially not knowing for sure if this is their daughter."

"As any parent would be." The doctor put her files

down on the desk. "I'm assuming you came to see her, not me. Let's go."

Beck and Mia followed her down a short hall and through a heavy metal door into the county morgue, which was dimly lit and cold.

"Let me just get a little more light in here," Dr. Reilly said as she flicked on the wall switch. She walked to one of the drawers built into the wall and partially slid it out.

"We've had to keep her somewhat contained," she explained, "since so much of her was falling apart."

"Tough to make the call on cause of death," he said.

"Yes and no. Because of the decomposition, it's harder to find any of the usual telltale signs. But there's enough to convince me that she, like Colleen Preston, was alive when she was wrapped up." She turned to face the victim. "The lungs and the brain show sign of bleeding, the eyeballs are bulged. All signs that her body was trying to force her to breathe. Wrapped up the way she was, the lungs couldn't expand, they couldn't get oxygen, that caused the petechial hemorrhages in the eyeballs, the lungs, the mouth. What hadn't fallen away held the evidence."

"So you're saying suffocation?"

"Yeah," the ME told him. "Just like Preston."

"She have any distinguishing marks, Viv?" Beck asked.

"Birthmarks, tattoos?"

"A tattoo, yes. On the upper part of her right arm there was something. Not sure what it was originally, but I can tell you it was green."

"Green," he repeated.

"Yeah. The ink they used was green." She pulled the drawer all the way out. "Here, take a look."

He bent closer, seemingly oblivious to the odor and the grotesqueness of the corpse.

"I see some loops there. Not enough flesh, though, to see the entire shape."

"Unfortunately, some of the meat just fell off the bones," she said, then glanced up at Mia to see if there was a reaction. Finding none, she continued. "As you know, the victim was in a state of partial decomposition when she was found."

"The woman we think this might be . . . she'd only been missing for a week. Could that be possible, that she'd deteriorate so much in so short a time?" Beck asked.

"Wrapped up the way she was, in this heat . . . and if she'd been left in a place that was closed up so that the temperature went over one hundred for days on end, yeah, she could have turned soupy pretty quickly." She looked at Mia again and said, "Sorry."

Mia shrugged.

"How long have you been with the FBI, Agent Shields?" the ME asked.

"Almost nine years."

"Then I guess you've seen pretty much everything," Vivian said.

"I have now," Mia replied.

"I feel the same way," Viv assured her. "Bastard who did this—"

"Enjoyed every minute of it," Mia murmured.

"Yes. He probably did." Vivian drew a hand

through her hair. "How do you find him? How do you stop him?"

"We get to know him through his work," Mia stated matter-of-factly. "We let him lead us to him. If we pay close attention to what he's already told us about himself, sooner or later, he'll lead us right to his door."

"Do you really believe that?" the doctor asked.

"Absolutely," Mia assured her.

"What has he told you about himself so far?"

"Well, there's the control thing." Mia looked at Beck. "We've already talked about that. How he likes to be in control of the entire situation, probably from the first moment he picks out his victim. If her flesh hadn't decomposed, I'd expect to see signs of restraints, bruises or marks on her wrists, her ankles. He would have had her every move under control."

"The first victim, the Preston woman, she did have those marks," Beck recalled.

Mia nodded. "For however long he'd had her, she would have been restrained except for those times he either wanted sex or wanted to reward her."

"If you're a good girl, I'll untie you for a while," Beck said.

"Exactly. And he's a neat freak, efficient. He kills his victims in a way that lets him maintain maximum control and watch every last excruciating breath she takes, while it also eliminates any messy cleanup on his part." Mia crossed her arms over her chest. "No fuss, no muss, no nasty smell, as long as she's all wrapped up. He could keep them for months, for years, even, and they'd remain nice and tidy. A bit mushy inside the plastic, but nothing he'd have to deal with."

"Don't you wonder how a soul gets that twisted?" the doctor asked.

"All the time," Mia said simply.

"I mean, what makes someone want to do something like this?"

"The mayor's pretty adamant that we ask the FBI for a profiler," Beck spoke up. "That's what she wanted to talk to me about when she called me out of the meeting this morning. Are you going to be insulted if we do that?"

"No. As I told you earlier, I've had a lot of training, but standing here, looking at what he did to this woman, I'm thinking you're going to need to explore the why in order to find the who. And we'll need someone with more experience than I have to help figure out why. I have pretty good instincts, but I'm not a psychologist. And frankly, I think that's what you need here."

"Do you want to make the call, or should I?" Beck asked.

"I'll do it. I'll call my boss. We have several really good people, but there's someone I'd like to request."

"The sooner, the better," Beck told her.

"While I do that," Mia said, "if you could get the audiotape you found with the body to Beck, and give us a sample of hair we can get DNA from, we'll be pretty much finished here. Unless Beck has something else in mind?"

"No, just the tape and the samples."

"I'll get both right now," The ME told him.

Mia called her office and spoke for several minutes. When she was finished, she told Beck, "My boss has agreed to check into the availability of the person I've requested. At the very least, we'll have someone by tomorrow."

"Great." He held up the evidence bag with the tape in it. "Too bad we won't have this ready by then, but the other tape will be available."

Dr. Reilly approached with another small bag, which she handed to Mia.

"Hair. You'll let me know if it matches?"

"Absolutely."

"Good." She turned back to the gurney that held the body. "We want to be able to send her home as soon as we can. I hate to see them stay here for too long. It just doesn't seem right."

"We'll do our best," Beck promised. "And I'll let you know as soon as we have a positive ID."

"Thanks." She smiled wanly and turned her back, and prepared to return her charge to the cold drawer where she'd been kept.

10

"Here's the copy of the file I promised you." Beck handed the fat brown envelope to Mia. "There's a copy of the tape that was found with Colleen Preston, copies of the photos of both victims, and copies of the statements. Everything you asked for."

"Thanks. I'll read it over tonight, bring myself up to speed."

"Good." He nodded.

"So." She stood and hoisted the heavy file. "I'll see you in the morning."

"Right." Beck nodded again.

"Any particular time?"

"We start early, so whenever you get here, someone will be here."

"Okay, then. See you tomorrow." She started toward the door, then stopped and dug into her pocket. "Here," she said, "here's one of my cards. In case something comes up and you need to get in touch with me."

"Good idea." He took a card from the supply on his desk and held it out to her. "Here's mine. In case you have a flash of inspiration while you're reading the file."

Mia slipped it into her wallet. "Thanks."

"I'll see you in the morning then."

She gave a small wave and left his office. Her heels clicked on the tiled hall and he heard her say something to Garland in passing. The heavy front door slammed shut and the sound echoed across the lobby. The municipal offices closed at five. It was now almost seven, and everyone had gone home. Everyone except the police.

Beck stretched to get the kinks out, and decided to take a walk into town to get some dinner. The rumbles from the direction of his stomach reminded him that he hadn't eaten all day. He could grab a quick bite at Lola's up there on Charles Street and be back at his office by eight for the meeting with the town council. Everyone was stirred up—not that he blamed them—but making wild assumptions like some of the ones he'd heard that day would only serve to make the residents panic. No need for that. The situation was serious, he wasn't going to downplay that. But they'd approach it in a professional manner and they'd catch this bastard, sooner or later.

It was the later that had Beck and everyone else in town nervous.

When he reached the corner of Charles and Kelly's Point, he glanced across the street and saw movement in Vanessa's shop. He crossed when the traffic moved on and pushed open the door to Bling, where he saw his sister waiting on a pair of customers. Vanessa looked up and smiled broadly when she saw him.

"I'll be with you in a minute," she told him.

"No hurry."

He wandered around the shop, poking at this item

and that, all the time wondering why women bothered with such things as beaded handbags with rows and rows of fringe hanging down in uneven strands, or necklaces made out of small pieces of colored stones that wound around and around the wearer's neck.

"Make a good weapon," he muttered under his breath.

"What was that?" Vanessa called to him from the cash register. "Are you talking to me?"

"No. Sorry. Just thinking out loud."

When he heard the bell over the door jingle, he walked to the front counter.

"Boy, you'd think with all the buzz about St. Dennis on the news people would be staying away in flocks," she told him as he approached. "But it looks as if this is going to be another busy weekend."

"Well, it could be one of several things. Either they haven't heard about the killer—"

"They have. No one's talking about anything else."

"Then maybe they figure if he's going to strike again, it's not going to happen to them, or else they're a little excited about being here, tempting fate."

He turned and looked out the window. "Maybe they're thinking, it might even be someone right here in town. Maybe someone I passed on the street today. The guy who gave me change at the drugstore, or the guy who waited on me at lunch. Or maybe the guy who—"

"Stop it, Beck. That's creepy."

"This guy's a creep, Ness. He could be anyone. If

he's here in St. Dennis, chances are he's someone we know."

"Don't say things like that." Vanessa visibly shivered. "I don't know anyone who could do such terrible things."

"Ah, but that's the point," Beck told her. "This guy doesn't have the mark of the devil on his forehead. Shit, if he did, we'd have a lot easier time finding him. He looks just like anyone else. He fits in, and maybe has for a long time."

"If he's been here for a long time, why hasn't he killed people around here sooner?"

"We don't know that he hasn't. We don't know that every girl who comes to the Eastern Shore in the summer has made it home. We don't know that he hasn't been traveling around and killing somewhere else. The truth is, we don't know jack-shit about this guy."

He paused, thinking about what Mia'd said earlier.

"Except that maybe he has a thing about being in control of women."

"Sounds like my ex-husband," Vanessa said. "Come to think of it, it sounds like just about every guy I've met since I was fourteen."

"Don't joke about it."

"Who's joking?"

The bell on the door rang and a middle-aged woman poked her head inside the shop.

"Are you closed?" she asked.

"I'm open till nine," Vanessa said brightly. "Come on in."

Beck slapped a hand lightly on the glass counter.

"I'll be running over to Lola's for dinner, then back up to the department for a meeting at eight. If I'm out by nine, I'll stop by and see you home."

"Not necessary," she told him. "I'm grabbing a bite to eat with Rocky after I close up."

"Rocky Simon who owns the art gallery two doors down?"

"Uh huh. He just got some really nice stained glass in and he said I could stop over and be the first to take a look."

"Is that sort of like 'Come on over and I'll show you my etchings'?"

Vanessa rolled her eyes and lowered her voice to a whisper. "Rocky is gay, Beck, and even if he weren't, he's like, my best friend."

Beck frowned. "Rocky Simon is gay?"

Vanessa rolled her eyes again and walked to the back of her shop to tend to her customers.

The man sitting at the table next to the front window of Lola's Café watched as the chief of police went into Bling and closed the door behind him. From where he sat, he could see the counter where the cash register stood—he knew precisely where, because he'd been inside on several occasions—and he watched Vanessa moving behind it as she completed a sale for the two women who had just left the shop and now stood on the sidewalk. Debating where to go next, he figured. A little more shopping, or maybe a little dinner. Maybe just ice cream; maybe a stroll down to the docks and a plate heaped with crabs and a cold beer.

They turned and walked several storefronts down to Bookends and went inside.

Excellent choice, he told them silently. The new mysteries were put out today. He'd been in there himself around five, and chatted with Barbara, the owner, about the latest blockbuster thriller. He'd ended up buying the book—"A really scary serial-killer book," Barbara told him as she'd handed a copy to him right out of the box—and they'd discussed the likelihood of there being a real serial killer right here in St. Dennis.

Barbara was adamant in denying that such evil could invade their town. "He has to be from someplace else," she'd told him. "No one in St. Dennis is that depraved, that cruel . . ."

He'd agreed solemnly that surely the killer was from out of town. Perhaps Cameron, he'd suggested with concern, or maybe Baltimore. Maybe one of the summer people.

"That's what we were thinking," she told him. "Nita Perry and I had lunch today down at the Captain's, and Rexana was saying that she's watching everyone who comes and goes through their place. She and Walt get real busy on the weekends—let's face it, it's the crabs that bring so many people down here to the Chesapeake in the first place—but she's keeping an eye on things. Watching for someone suspicious looking, you know?"

He'd nodded, but couldn't help adding, "I don't think you can really tell by looking at someone if they're a killer or not, though, Barb."

"That's pretty much what Nita said. She said one

time—this was years ago, when she had her first antique shop, back in Virginia—she had a guy come in and buy a couple of Oriental rugs. Before she could have them delivered, she found out he'd shot his next-door neighbor right through the head because the guy's dog kept peeing on his wife's roses and she'd been bitching about it day and night."

"I wonder why he didn't just shoot his wife."

Barbara had looked momentarily shocked, then slapped his arm playfully and said, "Oh, you!"

He watched Beck exit the shop and walk directly across the street. He waved and greeted the chief when he came through the door into Lola's and made some idle chitchat before the waiter interrupted by bringing him his check. He was still chatting with Beck as he took several bills from his wallet and placed them on the table, then stood to leave. They exchanged a few more friendly words, then he left, waving good-bye to the owner and leaving the chief of police to his dinner.

He walked outside and stretched, glancing over at Bling. *Now there was a fancy piece.* He smiled to himself. The thought of playing house with the chief's sister was unbearably tempting.

Might be prudent to wait to see how Beck handles things these next few days, see how good he is. Him and that pretty little FBI agent. *Talk about a fancy piece.* He shook his head, remembering how her hips had swayed as she'd walked in those high heels across Charles Street earlier in the day. Oh, yeah, that back porch had a real pretty swing, as his grandfather used to say.

Right now, though, there was the matter of that little cutie from over in Cameron to deal with.

She'd been a real firecracker, hadn't she? he thought fondly as he poked at one of his eye teeth with a wooden toothpick he'd grabbed on the way out of Lola's.

Well, all good things must come to an end.

He waved to a pedestrian across the street as he walked around the corner to his car, where several rolls of plastic wrap and an eight-pack of audiotapes were tucked into the trunk of his car.

He took his time, enjoying the peace of a perfect summer night.

11

Salsa or cheese?

Mia stood in front of the open refrigerator and debated the meager dinner choices. She hadn't eaten since she'd picked up a muffin and a cup of coffee on her way into St. Dennis that morning. It was a little after eight and she was too tired to cook and too lazy to go for takeout, so she was stuck with what she had on hand.

She decided to go with the salsa, having snacked on cheese last night. Besides, it would go nicely with the bottle of red wine she'd opened and taken out onto the screened porch, where she'd set up a sort of temporary camp. The file she'd brought home lay open on the wicker table and the lamps had been turned on and repositioned where they'd shed the most light for reading. She poured some of the salsa into a bowl, grabbed the box of crackers from the counter, and with her foot pushed open the door that led from the kitchen to the small porch. She moved the table closer to the loveseat and sat, placing what would serve as dinner to the right of the file and surrounding herself with the extra cushions.

She filled the wineglass, then raised it in a mock toast and said, "Here's to you, all wildlife lurking outside the fence. The pool is all yours. I've work to do. Tonight, however, snacks are not included."

The setting sun left streaks of color in the low clouds that hugged the horizon, so she sipped her wine and watched until the last bits of lavender faded into the darkness.

"Time to work."

She opened the file and began to read, then looked around for her phone before remembering she'd left it in her bag on the counter.

Mia retrieved the bag, found the phone, and set it next to her. She wiggled a bit to find a comfortable spot, then tucked a few more pillows behind her. Leave it to Connor to find a sofa with seat cushions that felt like concrete.

Well, she reminded herself, *he does spend most of his time in places where—let's face it—even this uncomfortable thing would seem like a luxury.*

She smiled, remembering how shocked everyone in the family had been when her cousin actually bought a house for himself.

"So, does it have indoor plumbing?" Connor's brother, Aidan, had asked with a perfectly straight face.

"Are you going to buy a real bed," Mia's brother Andrew had chimed in, "or are you going to use that grass mat you used to take camping?"

"Indoor plumbing, real furniture, a kitchen with a real stove and refrigerator." Connor had laughed good-naturedly. "Granted, it's tucked away by itself on a dirt road, but since I spend so much time alone,

I figured a little bit of isolation will make it really seem like home."

Well, he got that part right. It's isolated.

Mia shifted again on the sofa, lifted her glass to take another sip, and frowned when she found it empty. She hadn't remembered draining it, but not a drop remained. She refilled it and went back to her reading.

An hour later, she'd gone through all the interviews connected to the Colleen Preston murder. From what Mia read, it seemed that Colleen had been a really special young woman, liked and respected by everyone who knew her. That a stranger had taken her from those who loved her . . .

Ah, she told herself, there's the thing. It wasn't a stranger. She knew it in her gut.

Her rumbling stomach reminded her to eat, so she dipped into the salsa with the crackers and ate for a minute or two, focusing on what she'd just read. She drank a little more wine, then went back over the interviews to track the victim's movements on the day she disappeared.

8:45 - left home for work at women's clothing store in shopping center near Chestertown

9:30 - arrived at work

1:00 - left store for lunch with friend at restaurant in shopping center (coworker interviewed—nothing out of the ordinary discussed, no mention of anyone or anything bothering her. Looking forward to upcoming weekend in Ocean City, MD, with three friends)

3:15 - took break in store
5:45 - rang up last sale
5:58 - left store through back door

Mia put down her pen and refilled her glass. She went back through the notes made by the officers who first investigated the case, but found no description of the area behind the store. Was it a private parking lot? Who had access to it? Was someone waiting there when Colleen left work?

She blew out a long breath. In her mind's eye, she saw the young woman leave, saw the door close behind her. Saw her starting for her car . . .

She squeezed her eyes shut, not wanting to imagine what came next. Bastard. Had he taken her there, or had he followed her, taken her someplace else? Was he an acquaintance, or someone she knew well enough to trust?

She rubbed her temples. Sometimes the job just plain hurt.

Over the course of the two hours since she'd started reading, her muscles had cramped. She stood to stretch, reaching her arms over her head and bending from side to side, almost losing her balance as she leaned to the left. She caught herself on the arm of the loveseat and righted herself. *Must have been sitting longer than I thought,* she told herself.

She sat on the edge of the cushion and picked her bag off the floor, opened it and began to search through the contents. When she found the small tape player, she removed it and set it on the table, then slipped in the copy of the tape Beck had given her.

She poured another glass of wine, then punched play.

"This is your chance, now, Colleen. If there's anything you want to tell your parents, your brother, your sister, you'll want to do it now."

There was a sound she couldn't make out in the background, then, "That wasn't nice. I'm giving you an opportunity to leave something behind that might comfort your family."

"Momma, Daddy, I'm sorry. I'm so sorry. I didn't realize . . . I never thought he'd . . ." Then sobs.

"Is that all? This is your last chance, Colleen. No words of wisdom for your sweet little sister?"

"Fry in hell, you disgusting degenerate psychopathic pig . . ."

Mia's hands were shaking. She stopped the tape and sat in silence, tears welling.

Colleen Preston's sobbing plea spoke directly to Mia's own conscience. It spoke of that moment of recognition that there would be no second chance to make this right, no way to turn back the clock to that moment she'd somehow ended up in this nightmare. Mia knew that Colleen had wept not for herself, but for her parents, and the unspeakable pain her death would cause them. She'd wept because she knew that the loss of her life, her suffering, would bring infinite grief and sadness to those who loved her.

"It's all about expectations," Mia said softly. "Your parents expect certain things of you. In your case, your parents expected you to outlive them."

Colleen must have felt that she had placed herself in harms way. *I didn't realize . . . I never thought he . . .*

Realize what? That this person you maybe knew—this *he* you perhaps trusted, was a raging maniac? That by befriending this person or maybe by merely speaking to him, making eye contact with him, stopping to answer a question for him—somehow you left yourself open for him to abduct you? Torture you? Take your life?

If something bad happens because we don't realize the consequences, are we just as culpable?

Momma, Daddy, I'm sorry . . .

Mia could relate. How many times over the past two years had she whispered those same words?

"You're going to have to be the little mother now," an uncle had told the seven-year-old Mia on the day her mother was buried. "You're the only girl in the family, you're going to have to keep your brothers in line, just like your mother did."

Yeah, well, we all know how that turned out, don't we? If I'd been anything like Mom, I'd have known something was wrong. I'd have seen it coming. . . .

But I wasn't like her, and I never saw what surely she would have seen. Dylan, Missy, even Brendan—they'd all still be alive if I had. None of that crazy shit would have happened.

I just wasn't big enough to fill her shoes.

Mia tossed back what was left of the wine in the glass.

The phone rang, a lightning bolt of sound that jolted Mia out of her trance. She cleared her throat, hoping to clear her head at the same time, and picked up the phone after checking the caller ID.

"Annie, hi."

"Hey, Mia. Sorry to call so late, I should have looked at the clock before I dialed. I was speaking with John about a case and he asked me to give you a call when we finished. He said you called him earlier, about a case you wanted to discuss with me?" Anne Marie McCall, one of the Bureau's most respected profilers, was Mia's first choice to work on this case.

"Right, I did. I have this case over on the Eastern Shore, maybe you heard about it? The killer is grabbing these girls off the street . . . maybe not off the street, we don't know where he's getting them or how, but he keeps them someplace and rapes them. At least we know the first one was raped repeatedly; the second one, she was just pretty much mush—"

"Whoa, Mia, slow down. You're not making any sense," Annie said. "You're rambling."

"Sorry, sorry." Mia's voice cracked. "It's just so sad, Annie, and I thought maybe I could do the profiler thing, but not this case. Not this time. It's too complicated. The killer's too smart and if we screw up, another young girl is going to die. Maybe another one already has because we don't have a clue—"

Annie interrupted, asking quietly, "Mia, are you all right?"

"Well, yeah, I'm fine, but these two vics we have . . . Annie, if you saw what he did to them . . ."

"Mia, what's going on?" Annie hesitated for a moment. "It isn't like you to fall apart like this."

"I've never seen a case like this."

"You've seen plenty of hard-core stuff over the years. I've worked with you on other cases."

"Not like this," Mia protested. "I've never seen anything this evil."

"Mia, I have to ask . . . Have you been drinking?"

"I just had a little wine, while I was reading through the file."

"How much?"

"Just a little, really." Mia picked up the bottle and was surprised to find it was almost empty. No wonder her head was spinning and her focus was off. She took a deep breath. "I guess I didn't eat as much as I should have today. I missed lunch, I missed dinner, then tried to snack on salsa and crackers, and I opened a bottle of wine to have while I was munching. I guess I lost track."

"You do this often?"

"Of course not." Mia forced herself not to snap. "I just got home late, and I was working my way through this file and just not paying attention. It's all so sad, Annie. This guy is a demon. He's a monster. This is one of the worst things I've ever seen."

"Okay, tell me what you know."

Mia stumbled through the case, unaware of how she was ambling this way and that. Finally, she said, "And he leaves these tapes inside the plastic wrap, all wrapped up inside with their bodies. You hear him talking to her, you hear his voice. And you hear her,

Annie, she's crying and telling her mother and father how sorry she is . . ."

"I see," Annie said softly.

"Here, I'll play it for you—"

"No, no, Mia, don't put the tape on. Leave it for now. Close up the file and go to bed; you sound tired. We'll listen to the tape when I get there."

"I hate to ask you, it's the weekend."

"It's okay. Evan's working both days anyway. I'll be there by afternoon so we can sit down and go over the case together."

"Okay." In spite of herself, Mia felt tears begin to well up again. "Maybe by two? I'll need to tell Beck."

"Who's Beck?"

"He's the chief of police in St. Dennis. I think he might be a very interesting man. Cute, in a hard-cop, all-business sort of way. Not that I'm interested in that type."

"Of course not. Nothing appealing about cute, interesting, hard-edged cops who do their job."

"Ha. You should know."

"I do know. Now, do us both a favor. Don't play that tape again. Just put everything in your briefcase and go to bed, all right? You need some sleep. And put the wine away for tonight, hear?"

I put it away, all right.

"Sure. Thanks, Annie."

"I'll see you tomorrow. Now go to bed."

"See you tomorrow."

Mia hung up the phone and slipped it into her bag. She closed the file and put it into her briefcase and snapped the lid. Took everything back into the kitchen.

Set the plate with the remaining crackers on the counter and the empty wine bottle on the floor next to the trash can. Locked the back door and turned off the lights. She wouldn't listen to the tape again, as she promised Annie.

She wouldn't need to play it again to hear that tormented voice. It was there, in her head, amid the jumble of her own pleas for forgiveness.

Momma and Daddy, I'm sorry. I'm so sorry . . .

12

Mia waited patiently outside the manager's office in the rear of the apparel store where Colleen Preston had worked. The national chain clearly catered to young women—there were racks of colorful summer merchandise and accessories. The store sold everything from straw hats and flip-flops to summer formal wear. At the glass counter to the right of the door, several of the employees gathered, speaking in hushed voices. Judging by their furtive glances in her direction, Mia assumed the topic of conversation was the reason for the FBI's presence.

Clarise Holden, the store manager, appeared in the doorway, offering an apology. "I'm sorry to keep you waiting, Agent Shields. I was on the phone with the national office. We're all so upset about Colleen . . ."

"Understandable. I'm sorry you weren't notified directly. Hearing about it through the news has to have made it even harder for you and your employees."

The store manager, a thin woman in her thirties, responded flatly. "It's been a terrible shock to us all. Colleen was such a cheerful person, so nice to the customers, even the crankiest ones. She never complained about her hours or anything else."

"Ms. Holden, are you aware of anyone who might have been bothering Colleen?"

The woman held up a hand laden with silver rings. "I already answered all these questions for Chief Daley. Have you spoken with him? I'm assuming you're working with him?"

"I did read the statement you gave to the Ballard police," Mia said circumventing the question. She had not contacted the local police, and had not spoken with Daley. "You told him you really didn't know much about the private life of any of the employees."

"That's correct. And I still don't. I'm sorry, but Colleen just came in here and did her job. She didn't hang around before or after her shift, and we never had a conversation about anything that didn't pertain to her employment here."

"Was she friendly with any of the other girls who work here?"

"Danielle Snyder. They worked the same shifts and sometimes took breaks together."

"I'd like to speak with her. Is she in this morning?"

"She is. I'll get her, if you'll excuse me."

Mia moved her handbag from the floor to her lap to permit the older woman to open the door. Clarisse Holden stood in the doorway and waved to someone, then stepped back inside the office. A moment later, a young woman in her early twenties stepped into the room. She had red hair and blue eyes and freckles, and under other circumstances might have appeared perky.

"You wanted to see me?" she asked warily.

"Danielle, this is Agent Shields from the FBI. She wanted to ask you a few questions about Colleen."

"I already spoke with the police," Danielle told Mia.

"I know you did." Mia turned in her chair to make eye contact with the young woman who appeared flustered. "But I wanted to talk to you for a minute about Colleen."

"Okay." Danielle nodded.

"We're trying very hard to find the person who killed her, Danielle. I know you've been asked this before, but if you can think of anyone who might have been bothering her, someone she might have mentioned, even one time . . ."

Danielle shook her head. "She never said anything about that."

"How about someone from one of the other stores in the shopping center? Was there someone who came in to see her? Did she ever mention that anyone in particular got on her nerves?"

"No, nothing like that."

"Ms. Holden said you and Danielle often worked the same shifts. Were you working the day she disappeared?"

"Yes."

"Do you remember the last conversation you had with Colleen?"

Danielle's eyes misted, and she nodded. "Yes. She was talking about going away that Friday with one of her girlfriends from high school. They were going to Ocean City for a long weekend. They'd rented a condo or something."

"Do you know who the other girl was?"

"I only met her once. Jessica Flynn. She and Colleen had lunch together the day before . . . before Colleen disappeared."

"Do you know how I can reach Jessica?"

"I think she lives in Ballard. She just moved back home, I remember that. She had been living in College Park, but she came back because she got a teaching job with the local school district. She got her master's in May, I think she said. She stopped in here a few times since she'd moved back. She and Colleen were pretty tight."

"Thank you, Danielle," Mia said. "You've been very helpful."

"Can I go back to work now?" she asked.

"Yes," Mia told her.

"And thank you, Ms. Holden." Mia pushed back her chair and stood. "I appreciate your time."

"Of course." Clarise Holden stood as well.

"By the way, the parking lot behind the store . . . is that accessible to the general public?" Mia asked.

"Yes. Each of the stores has so many parking spots allotted for their employees, but occasionally a customer will park back there. It's not a private lot, if that's what you're asking."

Mia thanked her again for her help, and left the store. Danielle was huddled with a coworker near a display of beach bags, discussing, no doubt, her interrogation by the FBI.

Mia got into her car and drove to the back of the shopping center. Behind the stores, parking was a narrow strip, two rows deep, with an entrance and exit a mere one-car width. Each store had a solid metal door opening out to the parking lot, but none had a window. Unless someone else was leaving their store at the same time Colleen had left, no one would have seen if she'd met up with someone when she left work that day. According to the statements taken by the Ballard police, no one saw anything.

She thought it might be worth a shot, so she drove back around to the front of the center and went store to store, but learned nothing new. No one had seen Colleen leave that day.

On her way into St. Dennis, she called information and got a number for Jessica Flynn's parents' home. Jessica was at home, and agreed to meet with Mia immediately.

"Anything that can help," she told Mia.

Following the directions Jessica gave her, Mia arrived at the Flynn home in less than fifteen minutes. Jessica was waiting for her on the small front patio. When Mia pulled into the driveway of the split-level home, Jessica walked to meet her. She was tall and pretty, a confident looking young woman with a mane of light brown hair and a tan she must have been working on for several weeks.

"Hello, Jessica," Mia said after she'd gotten out of the car. "I'm Agent Shields. Thanks for agreeing to see me right away."

"I don't really know what I could tell you that might help, but you can ask me anything."

"I just have a very few questions, Jessica."

"Call me Jessie, please." The girl pointed toward the house. "We can sit up there, if you want."

"That would be fine, thank you." Mia followed her to the patio and sat on one of the cushioned chairs. "Jessie, I heard you had lunch with Colleen shortly before she disappeared."

Jessie nodded. "I drove over to the store on Monday, the day before . . . before." She swallowed hard. "I had to give her money for the place we were renting on this trip we were taking. We were leaving on Friday for Ocean City for the weekend, and Colleen was going to see the guy who owned the property to pay him."

"Was she meeting him that day?" Mia bit her bottom lip. This wasn't reflected in the police file she'd read.

"No, I thought she was going to see him Wednesday."

"Do you have a name? Do you know where she was supposed to meet him?"

Jessie shook her head, "No. It was someone Colleen knew who had a place to rent. She was handling everything. I just gave her my share of the rent at lunch. She was going to meet the owner and give him the money and get the key to the place."

"Do you know the address of the place you were renting?"

"It was someplace on the beach." Jessie toyed with a strand of hair. "She said it was right on the beach, and the owner was giving us a real good deal on the rent."

"Condo? Single home?"

"Condo," Jessie said. "It's in one of those high-rises right on the beach, that's all I know."

"And she never mentioned the name of the person she was dealing with?"

"No."

"Do you know how she found out about the place?"

Jessie hesitated and made a face, as if trying to recall. "I think she said he told her about it."

"So it was someone she knew?"

"Maybe. Or maybe someone she called. I know for a while there, she was checking some places online."

"Any particular website?"

Again, Jessie shook her head. "No. She called and told me she'd found a great place that was still available for the following weekend and did I want in, and I said sure."

"Do you remember when that was?"

"A few days before I met her for lunch. The end of the week before, I think."

"So you met her and gave her your share of the rent." Mia looked up from the notes she'd been taking. "Was she planning on paying the owner in cash, did she say?"

"She said she'd put it in her account and write a check to the owner."

"Do you know if she did that? If she wrote the check?"

"I have no idea. I never saw her again." Jessie's bottom lip trembled. "Do you think it's him, the condo guy? Do you think he killed her?"

"I think we need to speak with him," Mia said, "just as we need to speak with anyone who might have seen Colleen or had dealings with her that day."

"I wish now that I'd asked more questions," Jessie told her. "I wish I'd made her tell me who he was."

"What do you mean?"

"When I asked her, she just said it was someone she'd met, and he was giving us a special deal, so he didn't want his name passed around, because he usually charged more and he didn't want anyone to know he'd given it to us for so much less. Do you think that was why it was such a deal?" She started to cry. "Because he wanted to kill her?"

Beck had just walked into the kitchen at the station when he looked out the window and saw Mia pull into the lot. She parked in the same spot she'd parked in the day before. He watched as she got out of the car and slammed the door, locked it with the remote, and dropped the keys into her bag. It was hard for him to look away, same as it had been the day before. Mia was one of those women that you couldn't help but notice.

And Beck had noticed pretty much everything.

He'd noticed the thin gold band she wore on the middle finger of her right hand, her gold hoop earrings, and the small diamond set in a gold circle that she wore around her neck. Hair so dark it was almost black, worn straight down around her shoulders, neat but not fussy. Eyes as green as emeralds. She dressed conservatively in tailored linen, but then there were those mile-high heels. She was slender and not too tall, and feminine in the same way his sister Vanessa was feminine. *Girly,* he thought, but knew she wasn't as much of a cream puff as she appeared.

A cream puff wasn't likely to make it through the rigorous FBI training.

And there'd been that odd comment about the one brother who was dead . . .

Overall—that odd comment aside—the package was pretty nice.

Still, he had a bone to pick with her.

He realized his mind was wandering. He snapped back to the task at hand—getting a cold drink for the FBI profiler who sat in his office. He grabbed a bottle of water from the refrigerator and a paper cup and went back into his office.

Mia arrived seconds after he'd handed the water and cup to the profiler.

"Hi, Beck," Mia said as she entered the room with a perfunctory knock on the door. "Hi, Annie. You made it."

"Your directions were great, thanks." Anne Marie McCall smiled as Mia dragged a chair closer and hung her bag on the back.

"I had a very interesting morning," Mia told them.

"So I heard." He replied dryly from behind his desk.

"From . . . ?"

"From Chief Daley over in Ballard. He got a call from the parents of Jessica Flynn asking about the FBI agent who'd interrogated their daughter less than an hour ago."

"Yes, that was me. So?"

"So he wasn't happy, thought I'd done an end run around him by sending you over there."

"I'm trying to find a common link between the vic-

tims, so I followed up on some witnesses his department interviewed. And, by the way, picked up a bit of
information his people missed. So what's the big
deal?"

"The big deal is he's pissed that he wasn't informed
first." Beck sat in his chair and returned her stare.
"Look, most of the communities around here are covered by the state police, but there are a few that have
retained their own departments. St. Dennis is one, Ballard is another, Cameron . . . there are a few more. The
point is, we try to stick together, work together—"

"And he's pissed because he thinks you sent me
into his town to second-guess his officers."

"That pretty much sums it up."

"I'm sorry, I had no idea. Last night, I was reading
through the file, and it was in my head that the guy
we're looking for is local. Maybe not from St. Dennis,
but close enough to know the town. I mean, obviously, since he knew where you lived. I thought if we
could figure out what the victims had in common,
we'd be closer to figuring out who he is. I called this
morning when I was on my way to Ballard but you
weren't in."

"You could have left a message."

"I did. I left the message for you to call me."

He leafed through the messages in his in box, then
held one up.

"My apologies," he said, silently cursing the fact
that he'd somehow missed the message.

"Look, I'll call the chief over there and tell him you
didn't know I was going to do interviews this morning."

"I told him that."

"And he believes you?"

"Of course. We're friends."

"Which makes this even more difficult. I see." She nodded slowly. "I'll make certain that I reach you next time."

"Fine. Now, are you going to tell me what you found that Daley's people missed?"

"Yes, but I think we need to bring Annie—Dr. McCall—up to date on the case."

"Chief Beck has already done that," Annie told her. "He was just filling me in on some of the observations you made about the unsub."

"How'd I do?" Mia asked.

"From what I've heard about the case so far, I think your comments regarding his need for control are right on the money. And I agree, this man has very serious issues with women. He has a need to abuse them, degrade them, totally dominate them. I think when you find him, you'll find that he has what appears to be a seemingly normal life, even a normal love life. He could be married, or has been. He's very good at keeping this other side of himself hidden."

"You think we'll find him?" Beck asked.

"Absolutely. He'll lead you right to him, if you give him enough time. The downside of that is, the longer it takes to find him, the more women will die."

"As far as we know, this is his third victim," Beck told her.

The profiler shook her head.

"He's way too accomplished to be a novice. He's

got his act down pat. I'm sorry to say he's had lots of practice. No one starts out at this level of expertise."

Beck turned to Mia. "You were going to have someone at the FBI look into similar crimes . . ."

"And we'll have his report as soon as he finishes it, yes. But there's a strong possibility that there won't be any matches."

"Because maybe his victims haven't been found?"

"Exactly." Mia nodded. "These murders are unique. I think if there were others with similar characteristics in the system, we'd have heard by now. They'd pop right out."

"Maybe what we need is a run of missing women from this area over the past ten years," Beck said thoughtfully.

"Let's start with five," Mia suggested. "I think if he'd been at this for more than that, some of his victims would have surfaced by now. Let's see how many cases of missing young women on the Eastern Shore remain unsolved."

"Do we want to limit the area?" Beck asked.

"No. Let's go farther. So far, none of the victims have been tourists, they've all been living within a ten-mile radius, but who knows if he's roamed, or how far. Let's do the Eastern Shore to the ocean," Annie suggested.

"That's easy enough to get." Beck stood. "I'll have Garland start on that right away."

He excused himself from the room.

"So how are you feeling?" Annie asked.

"I'm fine. Why?"

"You sounded a bit tired last night," Annie said

gently. "I was worried that maybe you've been working too hard for too long without a break."

"I'm okay. I don't need a break."

"Mia, we all need a break once in a while."

"I'm okay, really. But thanks."

"I'm going to have to stick around to read over the files Beck has had copied for me. It's going to take me hours to get through it all. Any chance I could bunk in with you at Connor's tonight?"

"Sure. I'd love to have you stay."

"Thanks. I'll call Evan and let him know where I'll be."

"Do you think he'll mind? After all, you've only been married for what, six months now?"

"Six months and eighteen days, but who's counting?" Annie smiled.

Beck came back and closed the door behind him.

"Garland is on it. He'll let us know as soon as he has some results," he told them.

"So what else do you need, Dr. McCall?" Beck asked. "You have copies of the files, the photos, the reports . . ."

"That should keep me busy for a while," Annie said. "Perhaps we could meet in the morning and go over the case?"

"Whenever you're ready," Beck replied.

"Let's say eleven tomorrow assuming you work on Sunday. That should give me enough time to get through all this. If I feel I need more time, I'll give you a call."

"Sunday's are like any other day around here."

Beck nodded. "Thanks for making room in your schedule for this, Dr. McCall. I'm sure you're busy."

"It's an intriguing case. I'm looking forward to examining the files."

Beck turned to Mia. "Before you leave . . ."

"Right, Jessica Flynn. She's the girl who was going to rent a condo in Ocean City for a long weekend with Colleen Preston."

"We know that."

"Yes, but what you don't know is that according to Jessie, Colleen was supposed to be meeting with the owner of the condo on Wednesday—the day after she disappeared—to pay for the rental and get the keys. But what if she met up with him a day early?"

"Would it be too much to ask that Jessie knows the name of the owner?"

"It would be," Mia told him. "It seems that Colleen was the only one who had any dealings with the owner. She made all the arrangements. Jessie didn't even know where this place was located, except that it's a high-rise right on the beach."

"Of which there are dozens in Ocean City."

"Anyone around here own one of them?" Mia asked.

"Only about a third of the population of St. Dennis," Beck said.

"Why would you buy a place on the ocean if you live on the bay?" She wondered.

"There's been a building boom in Ocean City over the past ten, twelve years. Like I said, there are dozens of those high-rise condos on the beach. Lots of people have bought them as investments and rent them out. Then there are people who like the ocean, and a condo is an affordable way of having that weekend place. At least it used to be affordable, I don't know what those places are going for now. If it's rented during the summer, it can pretty much pay for itself." He sighed. "So, yeah, many people around here own condos in Ocean City."

"Don't people who rent mostly go through rental offices? Would you deal directly with the owner?" Mia asked.

"You might if you knew the owner personally," Beck replied. "Then again, there's always the possibility that there was no condo, that it was just a ruse to get her to meet him someplace. And maybe Jessie just assumed that the person who had the key was the owner instead of a rental agent."

"Jessie told me that she'd given the money to Colleen and that Colleen was going to give this guy a check."

"Then we'll check with her bank and get a look at her recent transactions," Beck said. "We'll need a warrant, but that won't be a problem."

"Do you think there'll be a check?" she asked.

"Nah. I think the whole condo thing was a means of getting to Colleen. But it's a thread to pull on. So let's see if anyone knows if Holly or Mindy had any dealings with anyone in real estate before they disappeared."

Beck glanced at his watch, then stood. "Now, if you'll excuse me, I have a meeting with the mayor. Dr. McCall, unless I hear from you, I'll see you at eleven. Agent Shields, you'll be there?"

"I will."

"Good." He started toward the door, then stopped. "You're not planning on that walk around my neighborhood in the middle of the night tonight, are you?"

"No." Mia walked into the hall ahead of Annie. "Tonight I'll be reviewing the file on Mindy Kenneher. And I promise, if I have any thoughts about interviewing anyone connected with the case, I'll give you a heads-up."

"I'd appreciate it." Beck turned off the light at the wall switch. "The chief of police over in Cameron was pretty adamant about not bringing the FBI into his investigation."

"We'll bring him around," Mia said over her shoulder as she and Annie headed for the lobby.

"No doubt you could," Beck said under his breath as he watched her walk down the hall. "No doubt at all . . ."

13

"So, what's it like, living out here all by yourself?" Annie sat at the kitchen table and watched Mia fill a pot with water and put it on the stove to boil.

"Quiet. If I didn't work so much, I don't know if I could stay," Mia admitted. "You're actually the first visitor I've had since I moved out here."

She opened a box of pasta and tossed it into the pot, then added, "Unless of course, you count the wildlife. Deer. Fox. Raccoons."

"You could always move back to Arlington," Annie reminded her.

Mia made a face. "Too far. John's been assigning me to a lot of the action on the Eastern Shore. Over the past few months, I've had several cases in Delaware. I think once Connor comes home and wants his house back, I may consider moving to Wilmington. It would be more convenient, I think, and there are some nice areas around the waterfront."

"You mean Wilmington, Delaware, not North Carolina."

"Right." Mia searched the cupboard for a jar of spaghetti sauce. She found it behind a box of cereal she'd brought with her when she moved in, but had never opened. She opened the jar, poured it into a pan, and set it on a burner.

She opened another cabinet and took down two wineglasses. She handed them to Annie and said, "Would you mind opening the bottle I picked up on the way home tonight? It's still in the bag next to my purse there on the counter. The opener is in the drawer to your right."

"Sure." Annie did as requested. After she poured wine into both glasses, she handed one to Mia and said, "Speaking of Connor, any idea when he'll be back?"

"Not a clue. I never know. About a month ago, he breezed in around 3:00 A.M., scared the shit out of me, stayed two days, then disappeared again." Mia laughed. "He's like a shadow, you know? He goes off and does whatever it is that he does, comes back, reports to whomever it was that sent him there in the first place, gets another assignment and poof! Gone again."

"I've noticed he's been doing much more of that over the past year or so." Annie tossed it out there and waited for a reaction. When there was none, she added, "It's almost as if he can't stay in one place for too long."

"Connor loves to travel." Mia shrugged. "He always has. And he's always been into that covert thing. Sometimes I almost think it's a game to him."

"That's one game I wouldn't want to play. The stakes are very high."

Mia turned to Annie. "How do you know?"

"We talk sometimes," she said simply.

"You mean between assignments?"

"Sometimes."

"Does he tell you where he goes? What he does?"

"Not with a great deal of specifics, but sometimes he just needs to unload. And I guess me being a psychologist, he feels safe unloading to me."

"The fact that you were going to marry his brother probably has nothing to do with it."

"I'm sure it has a lot to do with it." Annie studied Mia's face.

"Does he ever talk about Dylan?"

"Of course. We both do."

"Even though you're married to Evan now?" Mia asked.

"The fact that I was lucky enough to find someone else to love, who loves me, doesn't mean that I've had my memory erased. I did love Dylan; Evan knows that. He also knows that I would have been married to Dylan by now if he hadn't died."

"You mean if my brother hadn't killed him." Mia's jaw was squarely set. "If my brother hadn't murdered him—"

"We both know how Dylan died, Mia," Annie said softly.

Mia picked up her glass and took several sips of wine.

"Sometimes I don't understand how you can still be friends with all of us."

"You're kidding, right?"

Mia shook her head.

"I've worked with members of your family for as long as I've been with the Bureau, Mia. At one time or another, I've worked with every one of you. I have great respect for you and Connor and Grady and Andrew as professionals, and I care about all of you very much. And Aidan—hell, my sister is married to him, he's soon to be the father of my first nephew. And yes, we'd have been family if Brendan hadn't killed Dylan." Annie took a deep breath. "I like to think you're still family, and not just because your cousin married my sister."

"Are you really that forgiving?"

"Mia, there's nothing for me to forgive. No one was responsible for Brendan's actions except Brendan. No one is to blame, except Brendan. Please tell me you don't think that any one of you could have stopped him from doing what he did."

Mia shrugged. "Andy and I have talked about this a million times, why we didn't see what he was doing, why we didn't know how evil he was. . . ."

"Why would you have?" Annie's eyes narrowed.

"He was our brother, we knew him better than anyone." Mia laughed harshly. "We should have known."

"You know of a person only that which they choose to show you. Brendan obviously had a great stake in not letting anyone see what he'd become. He was very careful to never slip out of character." When Mia started to protest, Annie held up a hand. "I'm the specialist in behavior. If anyone should have noticed that something was off with him, it was me. But I never did, not for an instant." She tried to smile. "Even when he set out to kill me, I never saw it. I was just lucky that his plan was interrupted."

"By his partner. A child smuggler."

"We take our saviors where we find them." Annie leaned her elbows on the table. "And Luther Blue will spend the rest of his life in a federal prison for his crimes, not the least of which was shooting Brendan in cold blood. At least the operation was shut down."

Mia drained her glass and reached for the bottle to refill it.

"Until someone else picks up where they left off."

"That's always a possibility, of course," Annie said, "but I know that entire area is being watched pretty closely. I doubt you'll see truckloads of children being smuggled out of Santa Estella again. Let's be grateful for that much, okay?"

Mia opened a cabinet and took out a colander and set it in the sink.

"Look, there are a lot of bad things going on in this world, I don't have to tell you that. You deal with it every day, just as I do. We do the best we can to be part of the solution, not part of the problem."

From where she sat, Annie could see that Mia had tears on her face.

"It's Brendan's sin, Mia, not yours," she said gently.

As if she hadn't heard, Mia grabbed the pot from the stove and drained it in the sink. She put the spaghetti on plates and topped it with sauce, then placed one before Annie.

"You might want to move your file. Spaghetti sauce finds a million ways to splatter when you're trying to read."

"Right." Annie sighed and moved the file aside.

She watched Mia refill both wineglasses and move her own files out of the way so she could sit across the table from Annie.

"So," Mia said. "How is Mara feeling? It must be so exciting for her and Aidan, with the birth of their first child so close. . . ."

And just that quickly, Mia had changed the topic and hadn't brought up Brendan's name again for the rest of the evening, Annie recalled later. Once dinner was over—a dinner during which Mia had just about polished off the rest of the wine—Mia excused herself to go up to her room with her file, presumably to work.

Annie had settled into Connor's room and studied the case files Beck had given her earlier that day, but her thoughts kept returning to the woman pacing the floor above. It didn't take a doctorate in psychology to see that Mia was very troubled.

Finally, when the sound of footsteps overhead ceased, Annie got out her phone and dialed a number that very few people knew. She listened as the phone rang until voice mail picked up.

"Connor, Annie here. Hope you're safe and well, wherever you are." She paused. "Please give me a call when you're able. There's something I need to talk to you about."

14

"Everyone seated? Got your coffee, your tea, whatever? Once we start, I don't want any interruptions, so whatever it is you need, get it now. Anyone?"

Beck stood at the head of the table in the conference room where once again he'd gathered his staff behind closed doors for what he referred to as a "situational update" on the Holly Sheridan case. Everyone who'd had an assignment was expected to report their findings, and everyone present was expected to be tuned in to whatever information was being shared.

Noting that everyone appeared to be set, he continued.

"First, I want to thank all of you for giving up Sunday morning with your families. If circumstances were different, we'd have waited until tomorrow. Agent Shields is with us again today, along with her colleague, Dr. Anne Marie McCall, who will offer her insights once everyone else has reported on their piece of the pie. Any questions?" Beck surveyed the room. There were none.

"Then let's get started. Duncan, you're first up." Beck pointed to the officer who sat halfway down the table to his right.

As Duncan cleared his throat, about to begin, the door opened and Christina Pratt hurried into the room.

"Am I late?" she asked.

"We're just about to start," Beck told her.

"Great." The woman settled into a seat to the left of Mia and took a small notebook and pen from her handbag.

Mia caught Beck's eye to see if he'd noticed, but he hadn't appeared to. She made a mental note to call it to his attention. Letting civilians have confidential information made her nervous, whether that civilian was the mayor or the guy who sold you coffee in the morning. When that information was written down, it made her doubly so.

"Do I need to remind you all that what is said here, stays here? Anyone not understand what that means?" His eyes surveyed the room. "Anyone?"

No one spoke up. Mia hoped the mayor understood that that meant her as well.

"We'll be having a community meeting once I've sorted through everything we discuss here today, but I will be the one who decides what information is made public and what we keep close to the vest." He leaned over the chair, his arms resting on its back. "Duncan, let's do it."

Duncan Alcott's fingers tapped so lightly on the table that only those seated to either side could hear the sound. He was tall and thin and wore military-style glasses and a crew cut. He'd joined the force under Hal as a patrolman, and had never distinguished himself as either a great cop or an especially poor one. He was pretty much average in every way. There'd been a few flare-ups over the years—like the times he'd been bypassed for a promotion he'd wanted, and about a decade ago there'd been an incident in a bar down in Cambridge—but for the most part, he'd been reliable and trustworthy. Because he had no family in the area, he could be depended on to work holidays and weekends, which made him popular with his fellow officers. He had nearly twenty years in uniform and preferred traffic and night patrols, and Beck was content to let him remain in his comfort zone. Efforts over the years to fit him into any other mold hadn't been successful anyway. Hal had once described Duncan as "a good soldier," and Beck found it still fit.

"Um, well, Chief asked me to figure out Holly Sheridan's itinerary between Colorado and Maryland. What roads she took and that sort of thing." Duncan cleared his throat again. "The victim left her parents home in Denver on Monday, July second. She filled up her Explorer right outside of Denver, headed onto to Route 70, took it all the way to St. Louis, then dropped down onto 64 into Kentucky, then picked up 79 into West Virginia. Around Morgantown, she got onto 68, took it as far as 70, took it straight on over to Baltimore." He looked up at Beck and asked, "Do you want every stop she made? She had an overnight in Columbus, Missouri, and made a number of gas and food stops."

"Are any of them particularly relevant?"

"Just the last one."

"Which was?"

"She stopped in Wye Mills." He glanced at the two FBI agents and added for their clarification, "That's in Maryland, not far after you come off the Bay Bridge. You probably drove through it on Route 50."

Mia nodded. She remembered.

"Anyway, the victim stopped for gas at a mini-mart off Route 50, 1:00 A.M. on Thursday, July fifth. Filled up her tank, went inside, got a soda and a snack. Got her on tape," Duncan said. "Can't see outside near the pumps, though, so I checked in with the manager, which is how I got a copy of the tape."

He held it up.

"The manager called in the guy who was working that night, showed him the tape." Duncan continued his flat recitation. "He did recall the victim, but he—"

"Holly Sheridan," Beck reminded him. "Let's use her name once in a while. She was someone's daughter, someone's sister. Let's give her a little dignity."

"Right." Duncan reddened. "Anyway, the witness recalled Holly Sheridan coming in that night. She bought a diet Pepsi and a packaged sandwich. She opened the soda and drank it standing there, said she'd been on a long drive and how good it felt to stand and stretch her legs and how happy she was to be back."

"Did you ask if there was anyone else pumping gas at the time?"

"Yes, but he said there was no one there when she arrived." Duncan held up the tape. "I noted to him that maybe a minute before she left the store, you could see a flash of headlights reflected in the window, and he said he thought someone did pull in. The manager pulled the receipts for the night and found a cash sale was made about five minutes after the vic— after Holly's credit-card sale."

"So the other customer would be on the tape when he came in to pay," Hal Garrity spoke up. "Let's see it."

"Sorry, no. After seeing the tape, the attendant remembered he had walked Holly outside and was standing by the door. The second customer had a ten dollar sale, handed the guy a ten, and didn't want a receipt."

"Any description, of the customer or the car?" Beck asked hopefully.

"Said the guy was maybe mid-thirties, medium height and build, had a baseball cap on, didn't see his hair, didn't really look at his face. Doesn't really remember much about him except that he was driving a dark SUV. Didn't catch the make."

"Guy works in a gas station and doesn't notice what someone was driving?" Hal shook his head skeptically.

"He said he too busy watching Holly walk across the parking lot to her car. He said she was wearing some pretty hot shorts."

"Swell," Beck muttered. "Well, at least we know she made it to Maryland, and if she ran into someone, or someone followed her, it was close to home."

He turned to Duncan. "Nice work."

"Thank you." Duncan went red again.

"Guess her car still hasn't turned up," Beck said.

"No, sir. But this morning I did check again with

the state police, just to make sure they know we're still looking."

"Great. You keep on that." Beck turned to Hal. "You were going to show Holly's face around town."

The older man nodded. "I did. I made fifty copies of that photo you got from her roommate, and I passed it around. Turns out she's been just about everywhere. Barbie down at the bookstore said she was in once a week, picked up a mystery or a romance and whatever new food magazine had come in since her last visit. Rocky at the gallery said she'd stopped in the weekend of the art show; there were several works she admired but she didn't buy any."

"Either Barbie or Rocky mention if she was with anyone?"

"She was alone the three or four times she stopped in at Barbie's, and Rocky thinks she came into the gallery alone and left alone." Hal shook his balding head. "Steffie says she was in for ice cream a couple of times, but doesn't think she was with anyone. Said she chatted with her a few times, that Holly was pretty outgoing. Said she talked to whoever was in the shop whenever she was there."

Hal glanced down the table at Beck and added, "And no, she doesn't remember anyone in particular, just the usual assortment of locals you get at any given time on any hot day."

Hal passed a photo of Holly around the table. When it reached Christina Pratt, she said, "I've seen this girl around. I think it might have been at Steffie's. Founders Day weekend, after the concert, I think it was."

"Do you remember who else was around?" Beck asked.

"Only half the town. Including you and your sister." The mayor took a final look at the photo before passing it across the table to Lisa Singer. "I remember seeing you there, because my son had his kids that weekend and my five-year-old granddaughter was fascinated by Vanessa's shoes, and—" She stopped and laughed self-consciously. "Well, suffice it to say, half the town was in line for ice cream at Steffie's after the concert." She turned to Lisa Singer. "You were there too, weren't you? You and Todd and your boys?"

Lisa nodded. "We were, though Todd got a call from someone who'd been in the week before looking at a boat and had to leave."

"So there you go." The mayor looked around the table. "It would be easier to make a list of the people who weren't there. Which means Holly Sheridan was in good company."

"Maybe not all good," Beck reminded her. "If that's where he first saw her, not so good at all."

"You think he's from St. Dennis?" Christina Pratt frowned.

"I do," Beck nodded. "I can't think of another reason for him to have left the body of a girl who was living here in the back of my car. But maybe our profiler will have some thoughts on that, and we'll get into that later, once we've finished this discussion."

"If he's from St. Dennis, then chances are we all know him." The mayor looked around the room.

"You have his voice on tape. Why didn't someone recognize it?"

"He used a device that distorted the sound." Beck turned to Lisa. "You're on."

"Chief asked me to talk to Holly's coworkers, see if I could find out more about her social life." She thumbed through some notes. "Seems she didn't really have one, at least not this summer. This girl was all work, almost all the time. Took some time to rest up between shifts, but that's about it. According to Dan Sinclair, she was determined to learn as much about running a B and B as she could."

"Any of the guys working at Sinclair's seem interested?" Beck asked.

"Not really." She shook her head. "Everyone seemed to like her, but no one seemed to be overly interested. Keep in mind that Dan Sinclair only hires interns who are really into the whole B and B thing. He only hires seniors or grad students, and interviews them all pretty carefully. The University of Delaware faculty recommends students who are serious about learning the business, and most return every year until their graduate work is completed."

"Talk about training the competition," someone commented.

"Apparently, Sinclair's been doing it for years," Lisa replied.

"Is there a boyfriend?" Beck asked.

Lisa nodded. "Eric Johnson. He was at the wedding, flew out of Denver on Sunday night to Montana, where he's doing some sort of internship with the forest service."

She glanced up at Beck and added, "I checked. He arrived on time Monday morning. He was there all week."

Lisa turned a page in the folder and continued. "Holly's parents are having her dental records sent out here ASAP—the mother's sister is the family dentist, so there's no problem getting those. They're going to express them, so I expect to see them by ten-thirty tomorrow morning. I'll take them right over to Dr. Reilly when they arrive. The sooner we can make a positive ID, the better."

"Did anyone mention if Holly had a tattoo?" Mia asked.

"Actually, yes. One of her coworkers did. She had a Claddagh on the upper part of her right arm." Lisa nodded.

"In green ink?"

"Traditional color for the Irish symbol, yes." Lisa stared at Mia. "Why do you ask?"

"The victim found in Chief Beck's car had a tattoo in that very place," Mia told her. "The design wasn't clear due to the decomposition of the body, but the ink was clearly green."

"So there's not much of a question . . ." Hal stated the obvious.

"None in my mind," Beck replied.

"Holly hasn't been identified as a victim to the media as yet, right?" Mia asked.

"Right. Even though I've been ninety-nine percent certain all along that it's her, I hate to release information that hasn't been positively confirmed. We sent some of Holly's hair from her brush to the FBI lab along with hair from the victim to make sure the DNA profiles match, but I'm sure it's her."

"When are you going to make that public, Beck?" Mayor Pratt asked.

"As soon as the dental records are received and the match is confirmed," he told her. He turned to Lisa. "Have warrants been requested for the computers and cell phone records of the three known victims?"

"Yes, but we couldn't get to Judge McIlvain to sign them until Friday night. We called the cell companies yesterday, and faxed over his warrants, but we probably won't have the records in our hands until tomorrow morning. Holly Sheridan's laptop was in her car, which we have yet to find, but I've asked the Ballard and Cameron PDs to pick up the computers from the Preston and Kenneher homes. The parents didn't demand warrants; they're eager to do whatever they can to help. If I don't have a response by noon, I'll follow up again."

"Do we know if anyone else is missing?" Mayor Pratt asked. "I mean, if this guy is from St. Dennis—and I'm still not buying that he is—would he just have started doing this out of the blue? Wouldn't there have been other women missing before these three?"

"I think those are good questions for our profiler." Beck turned to Annie. "Want to take it from here?"

"As your chief has noted, my name is Anne Marie McCall. I'm a psychologist, I'm a supervisory special agent, and I work primarily with agents assigned to a specific unit within the Bureau." Annie stood. "For starters, I don't believe these are your offender's first kills. The manner is way too sophisticated for an amateur. He's definitely not new at this game. He's played before. We just need to find out where, and when, and I believe Agent Shields has something on that. Mia?"

"Yes. There's nothing for the past year, but back in 2001, a young woman on vacation in Dewey Beach went missing. Kim Bradley, twenty-one years old, from Penns Grove, New Jersey, a new graduate of Salisbury University, rented a beach house with a few of her sorority sisters. A group of them went to a club in Rehoboth"—Mia paused to refer to her notes—"a place called the Elephant Room. When it was time to leave, she was nowhere to be found. She stumbled into the house around six the next morning, bruised and hysterical. Said she'd met a guy in the bar, they went outside for some fresh air, he forced her into his car at knifepoint and raped her."

Beck turned to Lisa. "Find out who the officer in charge of that investigation was and talk to him, get everything he's got. And find out where the rental property was and who they rented from."

His attention returned to Mia. "What else do you have?"

"Two rape-abductions in that same area, June and September of the previous year, both college girls. Pretty much the same story. Met a guy in a club, stepped outside, then bam! I've requested copies of the files, and will have someone from our field offices follow up and interview the victims. One is in Columbus, Ohio, the other is in Boston. Those were the only local missing persons we found, but there's always the possibility that he lived elsewhere at some point, and may have been active there. There are thousands of missing persons reported every year. There's no way we could narrow the field."

"I'm assuming you also ran a check nationally for cases with similar MOs?" he asked.

Mia nodded. "There have been many rape-abduction-murder cases where the victim was held for a period of time, but none where the vics have been suffocated as these women have been. While I think there's a really good chance that what we're seeing is an escalation over his previous activity where he abducted and raped but did not kill—as Dr. McCall said, this guy's no beginner—it's impossible to sort out all of the rape-abduction cases over the past five to ten years just by looking at the data reports. The victims I mentioned earlier were all college girls, all from out of state, and all the abductions occurred in beach areas. None were held beyond the actual rape, none mentioned being restrained. I understand that the area from Dewey Beach in Delaware down through Ocean City, Maryland, is very popular with young people." She paused, then added, "There's no way of telling how many others there might have been over the years. Rape victims don't always report the crime, and girls of this age under these circumstances are often reluctant to call the police."

"Because sometimes it's a matter of the girls picking up a guy in one of the clubs and getting more than they bargained for," Lisa said. "They're embarrassed to admit they made such an error in judgment."

"Exactly. They think maybe they set themselves up

for it, going off with someone they didn't know, so they're reluctant to complain to the police." Mia nodded. "I will request that as many of these women as possible be tracked down and interviewed to see if we have a pattern in the MO and to see if we have physical descriptions of the subject that match up, but that's going to take some time."

Beck ran a hand wearily over his face and nodded to Annie to go on with her presentation.

"I've had an opportunity to study the files on the three women and while I can't pretend to have all the answers, I can share some insights based on my twelve years experience doing this sort of thing." She leaned against the far wall, her hands in the pockets of her skirt. The petite blond woman, always immaculately dressed and professional, began to weave her words into a compelling narrative. Everyone in the room hung on her every word.

"For starters, the man you're looking for has massive control issues as far as women are concerned."

The mayor snorted.

Annie appeared amused. "You had something you wished to say, Mayor Pratt?"

"The guy ties women up and keeps them tied up, then rapes them, and when he's done with them, he wraps them in plastic and suffocates them. It doesn't take an FBI profiler to figure out that he likes to be in control. And I'll bet you're going to say those issues stem from his relationship with his mother."

Still smiling, Annie nodded. "Oh, there's a good chance they do. This is a man who reflects pretty much what we see in most of our serial killers. His approach may differ, his MO may be different, but scratch the surface and you'll find he and Ted Bundy are brothers under the skin. He really doesn't like women very much."

"So he's probably single, right?" Sue asked.

"Not necessarily, no. He may be married, in a long-term relationship, or divorced. The women he's been involved in are probably very complacent, nonaggressive, which permits him to have his way, to feel superior."

"And if she protests?" someone asked. "Or becomes more assertive?"

"Then he'll react to that. Sever the relationship, have an affair, something that restores the balance to his world, where he is king and women are there to please him."

"Not in my house." The mayor's comment elicited light laughter.

Annie smiled, then continued. "Now, let's take a closer look at our man. He's very organized. He has his victim picked out in advance, he's probably stalked her and studied her so he knows where, when, and how to get to her. He takes with him what he needs to get the job done, which in his case is some rope—we know he keeps his victims restrained when he's not with them. . . ."

She glanced around the room. Every eye was on her.

"How do we know? Even without the medical examiner's description of the marks on the wrists and ankles of the two victims she's examined, it would stand to reason. In Colleen Preston's case, for example, she'd been missing for several weeks, but the body, when found, hadn't started to decompose, so we know she hadn't been dead long enough for the tissue to begin to break down. I believe your ME determined she'd been dead for less than twenty-four hours. The marks on her wrists were both old and fresh, meaning she'd been in those restraints for long enough for the earliest ones to heal over. So if he's had her for weeks, he's had to leave her alone for hours at a time, and he's not going to let her roam freely. He would have known ahead of time exactly what he was going to do. Everything would have been planned very carefully, as dictated by his fantasy. And you all know that most of these killings have their genesis in fantasy, right?"

All of the law-enforcement officers nodded their heads.

"So you know, then, that the primary source of pleasure for the killer is his ability to control his victim."

"Doesn't he enjoy the sex?" the mayor asked.

"Yes, he does, because the sexual attack is his best way to control," Annie said, "because a large part of the control is in degrading his victim. Making her feel totally powerless, totally under his control, totally humiliated. That's what he gets off on. He has to make his victims feel utterly helpless. That is his primary motivation."

"Why?" Susan asked.

"Because at some point in his early development, someone important to him made him feel powerless, and that feeling of powerlessness, of helplessness, made him angry and frustrated. So for kids who never learned to channel those feelings into something constructive—sports, for example, or academics— they very often try to comfort themselves by making others hurt, too."

"So we're back to Mom again," the mayor said.

"I'm afraid so," Annie acknowledged.

"I never really understood that," Lisa admitted. "I mean, I've read it all, I even took courses in college, but I don't understand how hurting someone else can make you feel better."

"That's because you are emotionally healthy," Annie told her. "Believe me, I've given a talk like this to a group of convicted multiple murderers and to a man, they all sat there nodding their heads, agreeing with every word I said. They immediately understood how being able to dominate another human being— having the power of life and death over someone else—can make a man feel superior. How that power overcomes their real feelings of inadequacy. Suddenly, they are invincible."

"And it's the mother's fault, these feelings of inade- quacy." Christina Pratt crossed her arms over her chest defensively.

"Who has the most control over the developing child? Not always, but most frequently, the mother," Annie replied.

"So if Mom controls the child, locks them in the closet and abuses them or something like that—"

"Yes, Mayor, those things happen. Unfortunately, they do. I've heard heartbreaking stories of abuse from these men. No mercy had been shown to them, therefore no mercy will be shown to their victims.

"But it doesn't have to be anything as overt or dramatic as extreme physical or mental abuse. Very often the abuse is much more subtle. Divorce of the parents at a young age, parents who are unable to show affection or who are demanding, perfectionists, or parents who separate themselves from the child—I've seen all of these conditions in the backgrounds of offenders I've studied. Alienation from one or both parents has been seen to be a factor in some cases."

"But it isn't always the parents. . . ." Hal said.

"Of course not. There can be other adults—uncles, cousins, grandparents, even older siblings, or neighbors, friends of the family. Sometimes the abuse is at the hands of other children. Bullying is abusive. Maybe the child is overweight or has a physical disability, something that makes him different. If the abuse is harsh enough, the child may escape through revenge fantasies. He might learn very early just how powerful fantasies can be."

"Then how come every kid who gets teased or bullied in the school yard doesn't end up a serial killer?" Lisa asked. "I was an overweight kid and was teased mercilessly, but I've never wanted to kill anyone because of it."

"Really? Are you sure?" Annie turned to face Lisa from across the room. "Think back. You never wanted to hurt any of the kids who teased you?"

Lisa looked thoughtful for a long moment, then smiled. "Well, maybe a little . . . but I never thought about killing anyone."

"Everyone gets pissed off at someone or other at some time in their life. You think of a thousand ways to retaliate. We all do it. The difference between those of us who grew up to be serial killers and those who did not is that most of us learned other ways to deal with our anger and frustrations. Most of us had a safety net in place, or learned how to construct one for ourselves, and we managed our feelings and moved on. But some kids never get past it; they never learn to move on. And some of those kids fantasize about what they would do to get even, and get fixated on revenge. For those kids, acting out those fantasies becomes their way of alleviating pain. They do unto others what has been done unto them."

The room was very quite for a moment, then Hal said, "So the abuse can be mental as well as physical."

"Absolutely. One of the major forms of rejection cited by serial killers who have been interviewed wasn't sexual abuse, it was an unstable home."

"Back to Mama again," the mayor said dryly.

"Many times parents have no idea that their actions are having a negative effect on their children. I've seen cases where the mother was very dominant and the father was outwardly very complacent, but inwardly, he was very resentful of the control the wife exercised over him. In cases like that, Dad may play the buddy role with the son. 'Hey, it's you and me, son.' And the son grows up to resent his mother's control the same way his dad did, resents the disdain with which his mother treats his father, because the son identifies more with the father. Mom rejects Dad,

Mom is rejecting the son. Do the parents view this situation as abusive? Of course not. But often in situations like this, the boy will fantasize about showing his mother that he's every bit as powerful as she is."

"There are a lot of powerful women in the workplace," the mayor reminded her. "Just look around the table . . . Lisa, Sue . . . hell, even me. Are we running the risk of turning our sons into serial killers?"

"Look, it's always a matter of choice, and it always comes back to fantasy." Annie told her. "It's one thing to have those fantasies—many children do. But it's something else entirely to act them out. The serial offenders we've studied all came from backgrounds where they felt powerless to control their situation—whatever that situation might have been—and never developed the coping skills necessary to overcome it. So it follows that there's a really good chance that our current offender came from a similar background. He's abducting these girls so that he can control them, and by doing so, he's become powerful, superior. That's the bottom line on this guy."

"So we're looking for someone local who came from a background where he was neglected or rejected by his parents or teased by his friends," Sue Martin said.

"That could be anyone." Christina Pratt frowned. "Christ almighty, my own son went through a period where he was pissed off all the time at everyone because he had a minor speech defect and sometimes at school the kids made fun of him. Does that mean he could be the killer?"

"What it means is that when you identify the killer,

you will find there was some sort of difficulty in his background."

"I thought a profiler was supposed to be able to tell us who to look for." The mayor closed her notebook with obvious annoyance. "So far, you've just talked about generalities. Oh, he could be this, he could be that. I haven't heard anything yet that could help us figure out who he is."

"Profiling isn't an exact science, it's merely a tool, Mayor Pratt. I can study the victim and the crime scene—and in these cases, we don't even have crime scenes, we don't know where these women were abducted and we don't know where they were kept or killed. I can tell you what type of personality is most likely to commit this type of murder. But I cannot conjure a name out of the air." Annie did her best to hide her growing impatience with the mayor. If she'd understood Mia correctly, Christina Pratt had been the one who'd wanted a profiler assigned to the case. Why was she being so argumentative now that she had what she'd wanted? "That's like asking me to pull a rabbit out of my hat.

"Other things you might want to consider," Annie continued, "is that this man has been able to fly under the radar for a long time. He's very practiced at keeping that anger and need to control in check. I think he's probably married, or has been. He may be a father, and if so, outwardly he might dote on his children, though inwardly he might be indifferent to them as individuals. He sees them as his creations, and therefore, in his eyes they are perfect. He's socially capable, sexually active, and may well live with a partner from whom he's successfully hidden his inner self. He's also good at controlling his own emotions—if you listen to the tape he made while he was preparing to kill Colleen Preston, you'll hear no evidence of excitement in his voice. He's in total command, and he's very cool about it. There's a hint of superiority in his tone. He's also going to be very interested in how the media covers his story, which is why so often you hear about the killer showing up at a funeral or a press conference or a community meeting." She paused and looked across the room at Beck. "I'm assuming that's one of the reasons behind the meeting you're calling?"

"That's one reason, of course." Beck nodded. "But both the mayor and council and I think the residents have the right to know what's going on. They need to know how to protect themselves."

"One way of doing that is by finding the common thread amongst the victims," Annie told him. "What did they have in common?"

"Well, we know they were all in their early twenties and lived within about six miles of each other," Lisa said. "They were all reportedly fun-loving, pretty, girls—"

"There are probably hundreds of pretty girls who like to have a good time in the area. What was it about these girls that attracted the killer?" Annie leaned on the end of the table.

"They all liked the beach."

"Why do you say that, Lisa?" Beck asked.

"I was going to get into it when we talked about Mindy Kenneher. Whose background, incidently, is very similar to Colleen Preston's in terms of her family life, education, job, that sort of thing."

"Get back to the beach." Beck gestured with his right hand for her to get on with it.

"Well, you know how Colleen was planning on a weekend at the beach with a friend?"

"Are you telling me Mindy was going in on a condo in Ocean City?"

"Rehoboth Beach," Lisa told him. "She and two of her friends."

"Tell me you have the name of the person who owned the beach house." Beck stared at her.

"No. Mindy was handling the arrangements. The other girls don't even know what street the house is on."

"And you were going to tell me this when?"

"Actually, I was trying to right before the meeting but you were on the phone. I only just talked to the girlfriends this morning. Unfortunately, no one seems to know who the property owner is." Lisa paused, then added, "Including her parents. I already asked. And I called the Prestons. They don't know who Colleen was renting from."

"We need those cell phone records," Beck told her. "If you don't have them in your hand by ten tomorrow morning, call the companies again. There's a good chance the victims may have been in contact with the so-called property owners by phone."

"So we need to find out who owned the place in Dewey and the place in Rehoboth from those two older cases Agent Shields mentioned earlier."

"I'll do the follow-up." Lisa nodded. "And I'll contact Ballard and Cameron PDs and see if anything showed up on the victims' computers."

"When shall we have this town-hall meeting?" the mayor asked.

"The sooner the better," Beck told her. "I'd like to do it tomorrow night, if we can get the word out."

"I'll call the local radio stations as soon as I get back to my office." Christina Pratt stood to her full five feet ten inches. "I'll also have a flyer made up immediately and ask the local shops and restaurants to hand it out to their customers. You think maybe seven, seven thirty, Beck?"

"Seven thirty is good," he agreed.

"Fine." She stepped away from the table and pushed in her chair. "I trust I'll see you all then."

"That should do it," Beck told the others as the mayor left the room, "unless someone has a question."

"I have a question." Sue directed her question to the two FBI agents at the opposite end of the table. "If you're right and the killer is from St. Dennis and he's at the meeting, how will we know who he is? I mean, we know everyone in town. How are we supposed to know who we're supposed to be watching, or what we're watching for?"

"Well, that's a good question," Beck replied. "I guess the best we can do is keep our eyes open and hope that he somehow does or says something that makes him stand out."

"What are the chances of that?" Hal asked.

Beck shrugged.

"Pretty much what I thought." Hal nodded. "Slim to none. . . ."

Mia shrunk back from the bright sunlight as she stepped outside the municipal building.

"Should have brought my shades." She raised her hand to shield her eyes.

"You don't have to walk me to the car," Annie told her. "Go on back inside."

"It's okay." Mia joined Annie on the sidewalk. "I want to. It's the least I can do, after you pulled yourself off another case to look at this one, especially on a weekend. I owe you big time, and I'm sure Beck appreciated it."

"And you'll pay up, one of these days. But what's with Pratt?" Annie frowned. "I sensed hostility there."

"I don't know. I'm guessing she's a mama who resents her kids' problems being foisted back onto her." Mia shrugged. "And she probably watches too much TV. Thinks the profiler should be able to show up and pull a list of names out of her butt."

"Don't I wish I could," Annie said. "Damn, but that would make all our jobs easier, wouldn't it?"

"Yeah, no more long, drawn-out, boring investigations. Just, 'Hey, it's either Tom, Dick, or Harry. Let's get DNA and see which of them did it.' Sorry she seemed to be picking at you."

"Not the first time, won't be the last." The two women reached Annie's car. She unlocked it and dropped her briefcase onto the backseat and her handbag onto the front passenger seat. "Thanks for the hospitality last night. It's been a long time since we've been able to visit with one another. It was good to have some time to chat."

"It was. Let's not wait so long between visits." Mia gave Annie a hug.

Annie got into her car and slammed the door, then rolled down the window. "Mia, if there's something bothering you—"

"There isn't."

". . . or if you just want to talk about anything, you know I'm always here for you, right?"

"Thank you. I appreciate that." Mia pushed back the lump that was beginning to form in her throat.

"Just don't ever hesitate, okay?"

"Okay. Thanks, Annie, but I'm fine. Just a little tired."

"Then take some time off. When was your last vacation, anyway?"

Mia shrugged.

"That's how agents burn out, Mia. I've seen it happen too many times. Don't let it happen to you. You love your job too much, honey."

"I know. I'm fine, really." Mia backed up so that Annie could turn the car around.

Mia waved good-bye, then stood in the parking lot and watched Annie leave. When the car had disappeared, she stuck her hands in the pockets of her light jacket and walked back into the building, her head down. She could talk to Annie if she had to, she knew that. But what could she say? Forgive me for not knowing that my brother was going to kill your fiancé? The fact that Dylan hadn't been the intended target really didn't matter. Brendan had set out to murder his own flesh and blood. How do you get past that?

And why, she asked herself for the thousandth time, why hadn't she seen it coming?

15

Mia spent Monday morning in the conference room making calls. So far, she'd requested that her boss send agents from Columbus and Boston to interview the victims of the rape-abductions from 2000 and 2001, faxed copies of the reports she had to the office, and discussed the cases with the agents who'd been assigned. The first time she glanced at her watch, it was almost one in the afternoon and Beck was standing in the doorway, "Want to run up to Charles Street and grab some lunch?"

"Sure. Just give me a minute."

"I'll be next door."

Mia packed her notes into her oversized leather shoulder bag and looked inside for her phone. She listened to several messages, one from her brother Andrew, and one from a friend from the office wanting to know when they could get together for dinner. She saved both to return later.

"Do you mind if we walk?" Beck asked when Mia came into his office.

"Not at all."

He glanced at her feet as he came around the desk, and Mia smiled.

"It's the shoes, isn't it?" She was clearly amused. "You're wondering how I can walk in them."

"It crossed my mind."

"Nothing to it." She walked ahead of him into the hall. "You just put one foot in front of the other."

Beck laughed and tapped Garland on the shoulder as he passed by and held up his cell, to let him know he was leaving the building but had his phone. Garland nodded, never missing a beat in his conversation.

"Damn, but it's hot," Beck said when they'd walked outside.

"At least we'll be in the shade most of the way."

They walked in silence for a moment, then both started to talk at the same time.

"So what did you think—"

"How do you suppose—"

"Go on," Beck said.

"I was just wondering what you thought of Annie's assessment of your killer."

"She said pretty much what you did. That the guy is a control freak, that the whole restraint and rape thing is acting out a fantasy. I didn't hear anything that surprised me, but I think when we catch this guy, we'll find him to be pretty much the way she described him."

"Your mayor didn't appear to think so."

"Christina can be a hard-ass sometimes. I think she was looking for more of a portrait than a profile. Plus Dr. McCall may have struck a nerve. I hear her son was a handful when he was younger."

"Has he straightened out any?"

"He better have. I think he's got his eye on my sister."

Beck paused when they reached the corner. "What are you in the mood for?"

"I eat just about everything," she told him. "Where do you usually go?"

"Lola's. She has a nice variety, so chances are you'll find something that suits you."

"Great. Lola's it is. Which way?"

"This way." Beck started to the left, and Mia followed.

Café Lola was a half block away in a centuries-old brick house that had two dining rooms facing Charles Street and a second, smaller room overlooking a narrow courtyard where several tables had been set up.

"Inside where it's cool, or outside in the shade?" the cheery hostess asked after greeting Beck.

"Cool. Definitely." Beck turned to Mia. "Unless you'd rather sit out in the courtyard?"

"Inside. Please. If God wanted us to sit out back and sweat our butts off, He wouldn't have invented air conditioning."

"A table inside would be fine, Hannah," Beck told the hostess.

"What's good here?" Mia asked once they were seated and she'd scanned the menu.

"Any seafood is good. The specials are usually great. Lola buys right off the boats when they come in early in the morning."

"There really is a Lola?" Mia folded her menu and placed it on the table.

"Right over there in the doorway." Beck nodded his head slightly to the left, and Mia turned in her seat.

"The woman in the chef's apron? Tall, thin, white hair?"

"Yes."

"Not to be obnoxious, but she appears to be, oh, roughly, one hundred years old."

"Close. She's ninety-one."

"Ninety-one! And she's still running a restaurant?"

"Says she's not retiring for another four years. And then," Beck said, grinning, "she's going on a world cruise."

"I'm betting she makes it," Mia said, a touch of awe in her voice.

"Oh, she'll make it, all right. She still walks down to the docks every day, waits for the boats to come in, looks over the catch, picks out what she wants. The old guys give her first pick. If she's late, they wait for her. The other restaurants don't like it, but there's not much they can do about it."

The door opened and Mia looked up.

"Isn't that your sister?" she asked.

Beck turned around.

"Yeah. And speak of the devil . . ." he muttered.

"The devil?" Mia frowned.

"Hi, Beck." Vanessa waved and headed in their direction, a dark-haired man following in her wake.

"Hey, Ness. Who's minding the store?" Beck

greeted her, then turned to his sister's companion and nodded. "Mickey."

"Cindy came in early today. Hello, Agent . . . Shields, was it?" Vanessa smiled at Mia.

"Yes. It's Mia. Nice to see you again." Mia returned the smile.

"This is Mickey Forbes." Vanessa introduced Mia to the dark-haired man.

"Good to meet you." He showed a lot of very white teeth. "I heard the FBI was called in. Working with the chief here on that psycho killer we've got running around, right?"

"Ahhh . . . yeah."

"So what's the latest on that?" Mickey leaned toward Beck. "I heard you had a profiler looking over the case. Was that cool or what?"

"Cool. Yes, indeed, it was cool." Beck nodded slowly.

"So what did she say? You get a bead on this guy?"

"More or less," Beck told him.

"You have the coolest job, I always tell Ness, boy, if I could only be your brother—"

"There's always the police academy, Mick," Beck said.

"Yeah, I think about it, you know? But there's child support and that sort of thing." Mick shook his head side to side. "The timing isn't good."

"Doesn't appear to be," Beck replied. He turned to Vanessa. "I think Hannah has your table ready."

Vanessa looked over her shoulder. "Oh. Right." She turned back to Mia and said, "Don't forget to stop in sometime. I'll give you a great price on that bag I saw you eyeing in the window."

"I might do that. Thanks."

"See you later, Beck. Mia." Mickey followed Vanessa to their table on the opposite side of the room.

"You don't care for him much, do you?" Mia asked when they'd gotten out of hearing range.

"No. Didn't like him before he started going out with my sister, don't like him any more now that he is."

"Any particular reason?"

"I think he's a hothead and a lady's man. He's been separated from his wife for less than a year, and he acts as if he was never married. Vanessa needs a guy like him like she needs a hole in her head." Beck crossed his arm over his chest. "And believe me, that's the last thing she needs."

"She seems pretty steady to me, not at all like an airhead."

"Airhead might be too strong," he conceded. "Let's just say she doesn't have very sound judgment when it comes to men. Her track record isn't too good."

"Well, we've all made mistakes in that area at one time or another."

"Two disastrous marriages by the time she was twenty-two is one mistake too many in my book."

"Two? Ouch."

"Yeah. Big ouch."

"Guess you didn't think much of either of them."

"I'm sure I wouldn't have, had I met them."

"You never met your sister's husbands?"

"I didn't even know I had a sister until about two years ago."

"How could you not know?" Mia frowned as an elderly waiter stopped by their table to take their orders.

"What's the catch of the day, Jim?" Beck asked.

"Best blue-claws this side of the bay. Lola says she's ready to steam up a bunch of 'em just for you, Chief."

"That's a tough offer to resist, but I have a meeting in about an hour, and every time I eat crabs, I end up making a mess."

"Well, I guess we can't take you anywhere, can we?" The waiter chuckled.

"I'm afraid you're right. Lola can save me some of those steamers for later, though." Beck smiled.

"We can do that, and right now we can send out a big plate of crabs and spaghetti for you and your friend."

"That sounds wonderful. I'm in," Mia told him.

"Chief?"

"Sounds good to me."

"You want a cold glass of beer with that?" Jim asked.

"Now, James, you know I'm working. What would people say if they saw the chief of police sitting here drinking in the middle of the day?"

"You have that big plate of spaghetti in front of you, they'll say, Jimmy, bring me some of what he's got."

Beck laughed and handed over the menus.

"I'll bring over some iced teas then, if that's all right."

"That's fine for me." Beck looked at Mia, and she nodded.

"Now, is he a contemporary of Miss Lola's?" Mia asked after Jimmy disappeared into the kitchen.

"Nah. He's just a young pup. Barely eighty."

"Sounds as if someone in St. Dennis has discovered the secret to longevity."

"Unfortunately, some life spans have been shorter than others," he reminded her.

"How do you suppose Mickey found out about Annie being here this morning? I know some towns have a great grapevine, but that's pretty fast even for a small town like this one."

"I'm guessing his mother told him," Beck said dryly.

"His . . ." Mia's eyes widened. "You mean Mayor Pratt?"

"Right."

"Different last name," she said. "Divorce, remarriage?"

"You're pretty quick for a fed." He leaned back while their drinks were served. "Sorry. No offense intended."

"None taken." Mia looked across the room to where Vanessa was engaged in an animated conversation with Mickey Forbes. "Did you notice she was taking notes this morning?"

"Was she?"

"How discreet is she? I mean, is she the type who'd leave her notebook on the kitchen table for anyone to pick up?"

"I hope not. I'll remind her, though."

"Why is she so involved in this investigation?" Mia frowned. "I don't remember the last time I saw an elected official sit in on a case conference."

"Under our town charter, the mayor is in charge of public safety, which means the police department. Technically, we answer to her. Fortunately, she stays out of my way for the most part, but she does feel her position gives her the right to know what's going on with any case at any time. I have no grounds to argue with her, so generally, I don't. I think she's more involved with this case because it's caused such a firestorm and she's gotten a lot of calls from residents. I guess they feel if the killer can get that close to the chief of police, no one is safe. And they'd be right."

"What does he do for a living?" She watched Mickey Forbes from across the room. "And please don't tell me he's in real estate."

"No, he's not—he sells luxury cars and owns a sporting goods store—but his father is in real estate."

Mia raised an eyebrow.

"Commercial real estate. He owns a lot of rentals here in town and built a few of those strip malls you passed on the way into town."

"Do you think Mickey fits the profile?"

"Good Lord, don't even put that idea in my head. The last thing I want to think about is my little sister dating a serial killer." Beck rested both forearms on the table and stared at Mickey Forbes from across the room for a long time. Finally, he said, "Jesus, I guess just about anyone in this room fits it in some way."

He exhaled and took a long drink of water.

"The guy in the yellow shirt over there at the bar? Carl Jackson? He's the town Realtor. Last I heard, he was renting properties over in the beach communities. The guy next to him? He lost custody of his kids to his ex-wife after he was brought in on domestic abuse charges." Beck seemed to know everyone in the place. "The guy in the plaid pants? He still lives with his mother over on St. Mary's Place. Never married. Momma never liked any of the girls he brought home. He turned fifty-one last week and Momma is still buying his clothes."

He looked across the table at Mia. "If that isn't control, I don't know what is."

"You checking them out?"

"Sure. Jackson, however, as you may notice, weighs about three hundred pounds and he's pushing fifty. He's on crutches a lot because his knees are taking a pounding. You think he's capable of carrying anyone anywhere?"

"Well, there is the real-estate connection, maybe someone in his office . . ."

"Only person he employs is his wife. And frankly, we both know the condo, the beach house, were most likely bait. Those places might not even exist."

"True. If you're planning on killing someone, lying about owning a condo at the beach probably isn't a real issue."

"The truth is, you start breaking down a group, you're going to find a number of men who can fit the profile. So you tell me, how do you start to eliminate some and focus on the others?" he asked. "How do you cull from that herd?"

"Actually, the herd will start to cull itself," she told him. "Like Annie says, sooner or later, he'll lead you to him."

"How many more women are going to die between now and then, Agent Shields?" His face hardened.

"I can't answer that," she told him, "and it's Mia, please."

"All right, Mia. How do we get him to identify himself?"

"You've scheduled your meeting for tonight, right?"

He nodded.

"Let's see who shows up. Let's see who shows the most interest. Open the meeting to Q and A, see who asks the most questions, who makes suggestions. Maybe we can start to make a list of people to take a closer look at."

"You really think that's going to work?"

"You have a better idea?"

"In the absence of any physical evidence, I guess not."

"By the way, we have agents assigned to track down and interview the victims of those beach assaults from two, three years ago. I'll let you know as soon as we have something on them."

"Terrific. Would love to get a description out of them."

"Be honest. You're hoping the descriptions of the

rapists in all three cases match up, and you're hoping to get a name out of it."

"Yeah, but I'm also hoping to win the lottery next week. That probably won't happen, either."

Beck's phone rang, and he answered it immediately. He said little, then finally, "Thanks. Thanks for staying on it."

He placed the phone on the table and told Mia, "That was Lisa. She received the dental records on Holly Sheridan and drove them out to Dr. Reilly. She waited to see what Viv would have to say, and she didn't have to wait long, as it turned out. Holly Sheridan apparently had extensive reconstructive work done after a riding accident when she was fourteen. All of her teeth on the left side, top and bottom, had crowns. All Viv had to do was open the girl's mouth and look."

"Crowns?"

"Capped north and south."

"Well, at least we know for certain."

"Yeah, and so should Holly's family." Beck stared at the mountain of pasta in front of him. "Look, if you wouldn't mind, I think I need to get back up to the office."

"I don't mind," she told him.

"Sorry to bail on you . . ."

"Don't apologize. I understand completely. Go on. I'll finish up and meet you back there."

He started to signal for the check, but Mia stopped him.

"Don't worry about it. I've got it. Just go. Do what you have to do."

"Thanks." Beck stood and pocketed his phone. "I'll see you back at the station."

Mia nodded and watched him leave the restaurant, his face darkening with every step he took.

He's thinking about what he's going to tell the Sheridans, she thought. What could be worse than calling a mother and father to let them know their child has been positively identified as a murder victim? Mia shivered. It was a call she'd had to make several times herself, and she knew just how hard the next half hour or so was going to be for Beck.

She picked at the food on the plate in front of her, her appetite gone, but not wanting to leave the restaurant to head back to the municipal building. She was pushing a chunk of crabmeat around with her fork when a shadow crossed her table.

She looked up to see Daniel Sinclair approaching.

"Agent Shields, isn't it?"

"Yes, Mr. Sinclair. Nice to see you again."

"Ah, I see Jimmy talked you into the crabs and spaghetti."

"He did. And they definitely live up to their reputation."

"I've been trying forever to talk Jimmy into leaving Lola and coming to work for me, but he'll have none of it." Dan Sinclair paused and added, "Actually, I've tried to talk Lola into coming and cooking for me when she retires, but she keeps putting off giving me an answer."

"Word is that Lola's planning on a long cruise when she retires," Mia repeated what Beck had told her.

"Oh, I meant after the cruise." Sinclair smiled.

"Well, good luck with that."

"There's talk of a meeting at the community center tonight," he said. "Do you know anything about that?"

"Yes, I think Beck mentioned seven thirty, but you might want to check with the station. And I think they're going to give the information to the local news stations so that as many people as possible hear about it. I suspect there will be some information on the early local news."

"Is there a suspect?"

"No. The chief just wants to make sure all the information that's circulating is correct."

"Oh, right. Squelch any rumors, that sort of thing."

"Right."

"Well, I guess I'll see you then." He started to leave.

"Mr. Sinclair, any chance I could get a room at your inn tonight? It just occurred to me that the meeting might run late, and I have a distance to drive."

"I'm sure we can accommodate you. Just come on over after the meeting and go to the front desk inside the lobby of the main house. We'll have something reserved for you."

"Great. Thanks. I appreciate it."

"My pleasure." He touched a finger to the brim of an invisible cap and started toward the door. A middle-aged woman holding the hand of a small child was coming in just as he reached it, and he paused to hold the door for them before turning and giving Mia a wave.

Well, she thought, at least I won't have to make that long drive back to Connor's. Maybe she'd duck into Bling at some point between now and the meeting and pick up something to wear tomorrow, maybe take a look at that cute bag. She always had an emergency bag in her trunk with toiletries and a nightshirt, but she didn't usually travel with an extra set of work clothes. She'd been wanting to look around in Bling anyway, and this would give her a good excuse. It was as close to downtime as she was going to get this week.

She looked out the window and watched Dan Sinclair walk to his car on the opposite side of the street. He stopped in front of the art gallery and chatted with a young woman with long blond hair and a very short skirt.

A man in his early thirties came out of the gallery and spoke with the pair on the sidewalk. Shortly another man, also in his thirties, walked out of the bookstore with a bag under his arm.

Right there, right before her eyes, could be three viable suspects. Any one of them could be the killer.

Her head began to hurt. There seemed to be no end to the potential suspects in St. Dennis. She watched the men across the street for a few more minutes, then turned her attention back to the room. It seemed half the town was in Lola's.

Without any physical evidence, there was no way to start eliminating suspects from the pool. Unless, of course, someone did something to distinguish themselves at the meeting tonight. Or unless the lab found something in the folds of plastic.

She'd call the lab for an update on her way back to the police department. As far as culling a credible suspect from the herd, she'd just have to figure out a way to do that between now and seven thirty.

16

Mia watched the crowd trickle into the community room of the St. Dennis municipal building. It was a little after seven and already the room had begun to fill up through the wide double doors. By the time the meeting started, it would be standing room only.

"Some crowd, eh?" Hal Garrity had appeared at her elbow.

"It's great, don't you think?" Mia nodded enthusiastically. "Shows that the residents are taking the situation seriously."

"That, and not wanting to miss out on the chance to be on TV." He pointed discreetly to the cameras that were being set up to the left of the podium. "And let's not forget that there isn't a whole lot going on around here on a weeknight."

"You have to think the merchants are worried about losing business if this case isn't solved soon."

"Thing about St. Dennis"—he leaned closer and lowered his voice—"is that most of the shop owners aren't worried at all. These past few years have been boom times around here. No one ever really expected the town to take off the way it did. Oh, some gambled on it, like Ham Forbes. Of course, some could say he had the inside track on buying up all the real estate he could down there on Charles Street."

"That would be the mayor's ex-husband?" Mia recalled that the mayor's son's last name was Forbes.

"Right. Say what you want about Christina Pratt, but she's been right on target, far as the tourist thing. She pushed for money for renovating the harbor, pushed for grants to restore old buildings, pushed for everything she could get to spiff up the town." Hal nodded in the direction of the mayor, who'd just entered the room. "Yeah, I'd call her a real visionary. She looked north at Chestertown and south to St. Michael's and saw no reason why St. Dennis couldn't offer as much in the way of atmosphere. And of course, shopping."

"She was the catalyst?"

"Worked relentlessly to get what she wanted, got everyone who was anyone on the bandwagon with her. Paid off, I'd say."

"Which one is Mr. Pratt?" Mia studied the three men who had accompanied the mayor into the room.

"None of them," Hal told her. "He's been gone about five years now, went back to Connecticut, where he came from."

"Divorced?"

"Yes. Complained to anyone who'd listen that she put all her energy into the town, none into the marriage, and he split."

The mayor and her companions made their way through the crowd. As they approached the spot where Mia and Hal stood, she touched the man closest to her on the arm and said, "Hamilton, have you met Agent Shields?"

"I haven't had the pleasure." The very handsome silver-haired man dazzled Mia with a smile. "Ham Forbes, Agent Shields. So, you're here to help Beck catch the bad guy."

"With any luck."

"I'd have thought luck wouldn't be an issue," he said smoothly. "I would expect the FBI to come in here with a game plan and take care of business."

"We're doing our best," she assured him.

"Yes, well." He straightened his tie. "Let's hope that's enough."

He nodded to Mia and Hal, then resumed following his former wife through the crowd to the front of the room.

Mia watched him with an amused expression on her face.

"Am I supposed to guess why she divorced him?" she asked.

"You'd be wrong." Hal chuckled. "He divorced her."

"Really?" She thought that over for a moment. "A little too much ego under one roof?"

"Yes, and most of it hers." Hal waved to a neighbor. "Don't let him fool you. He's developed a little spine over the past few years—remarried and divorced since they split up—but he was never in charge in that relationship. Christina calls the shots in everything she does."

"Must make those town council meetings fun."

"They are, actually," Hal said with a wicked grin.

"The thing is, she's the best mayor this town ever had. She had the vision, and she had the guts to see it all through. St. Dennis would be just another sleepy bay town without her. The other side of the coin is that she can be the very devil if you don't see things her way."

"I think Beck mentioned that she spearheaded the revival of the town."

"And happily sunk that spear into the back of anyone who stood in her way," he said. "But she's made more friends than enemies, because she was dead-on about what St. Dennis could become. A lot of people made a lot of money because they listened to her and invested in the right places at the right time."

"Including Hamilton Forbes."

"Especially Ham Forbes. He owns more of St. Dennis than anyone else in town."

"Does he own beach property? In Dewey or Rehoboth, maybe?"

"Not as far as I know. He's kept his holdings right here in town. Likes being a big fish in a small pond." Hal seemed to study her face. "I know what you're thinking, but no, Ham's kept it all right here. If he'd bought property over in Rehoboth or Ocean City, we'd have heard about it. He likes to talk about what he has. Compensation, I'm thinking, for what he lacks."

"Actually, I was thinking about his son."

"As far as I know, Mickey doesn't own anything except the two businesses. He did have some interest in a property out along the highway, but he sold that when the new shopping center went in. Going to end up paying for his divorce, from what I hear."

"The center right outside of town? The one with the movie theater and the fancy coffee shop and the gym?" Mia had passed it several times. "That must have been some divorce settlement."

"Yeah, I heard Callie—the soon to be ex—is making out pretty good. Mickey was lucky to keep the sporting goods store. I'm not sure he minded though. He wants out of the marriage, but he wants his kids taken care of, too. So he'll give Callie pretty much everything she wants."

"I'd think sporting goods would do well around here."

"Very well. He carries a lot of fishing and hunting gear, along with the sports paraphernalia. Runs some soccer clubs, lacrosse, softball." Hal laughed. "Time was, if you were into sports, all you needed was a pair of sneakers and a ball, maybe a glove and a bat, but that was as complicated as it got."

"You play a sport back then, Hal?"

"Played some minor league baseball, yes, ma'am." He nodded. "Some thought I'd make it to the pros, but my number came up in the draft. One day I was on the mound throwing my fastball, the next I was dropping out of a helicopter into a jungle in Vietnam. Spent the next twelve months dodging bullets."

"One of my uncles was in Vietnam," she told him. "My dad said he wasn't the same person when he came back."

"None of us were," Hal nodded solemnly. "For any number of reasons . . ."

Beck walked up behind him and put a hand on Hal's shoulder.

"We're just about to start," Beck said. "Either of you have any last-minute thoughts?"

"Just that you might want to ask the TV cameramen if they'd scan the crowd from time to time." Mia suggested. "We can borrow the tape later and see if anyone stands out in any way."

"I thought I'd ask both of you to keep an eye on the crowd. I think you both know what to look for."

"I'll take the right side of the room, Agent Shields can take the left," Hal offered.

"Fine with me," Mia agreed.

"Let's get this moving, then." Beck made his way back to the podium, stopping to talk to each of the cameramen he passed on the way.

By the time he reached the front of the room, Mia had wandered to the front left side where she had a good view of the crowd, as well as the door leading to the hall.

"Good evening, thanks for coming," Beck was saying. "You all know why we're here, but for those of you who may not have heard the whole story, or who may have only heard rumors, let me start at the beginning. Last Sunday night, the body of Colleen Preston was found on her parents' front porch . . ."

Beck began to recite the saga, from the time Colleen's body was found. Mia turned her attention to the crowd. She felt certain the killer would be here tonight—no way would he miss out on this—and she knew, too, there was only a fair chance his behavior might call the attention of even a trained eye. She knew the basics—he'd be a white male in his early to mid-thirties. She guessed he'd be well-dressed—he had the means to have a vehicle to transport his victim in, and access to some place secluded enough to keep her for a period of time, where he knew she wouldn't be discovered. He's going to be very interested in the proceedings tonight, and he's going to be hanging on Beck's every word. But at the same time, he's going to be feeling very smug. After all, he knows what no one else in the room knew. He knew who he was, what he'd done, and how. She hoped his smugness might manifest itself in some discernible way, but knew better than to bet on that.

Mia's eyes scanned row to row, front of the room to the back. There were more than enough white males in their mid-thirties, none of whom appeared to be reacting in an untoward manner. She strolled along the side of the room slowly, hoping to get a better look at the small group standing along the wall. She thought there was a good chance that the man they were looking for would select such a vantage point rather than a seat. Standing along the side would offer him the opportunity to watch the faces of the people in the audience. He'd get to see the looks of horror and fear on their faces as Beck laid out everything that had happened over the past week, and their fear would give him power over the entire room.

She smiled at the members of the St. Dennis police department who ringed the room. On her side of the room, Duncan Alcott leaned against the wall, halfway between the first row of chairs and the last, his arms folded. He stole an occasional glance at the crowd, but for the most part paid more attention to Beck than to his surroundings. Mia watched him pull a stick of gum from his pocket, unwrap it, and fold it slowly into his mouth, never taking his eyes off Beck. Behind him stood a group of seven or eight girls who appeared to be of high school age. Behind them, Lisa Singer stood next to a tall, good-looking, dark-haired man—her husband, Todd? Further back, Mia saw Vanessa Keaton standing with Mickey Forbes.

Mickey's eyes were shining with excitement, and a chill went up Mia's spine. She realized he wasn't the only man in the crowd who was tantalized by the whole bondage and rape scenario Beck had laid out, but he was the only man in the crowd who was spending a lot of time with the police chief's sister. She knew the killer would want to keep his finger on the pulse of the investigation. What better way to do that than to wine and dine Beck's sister? Then again, he could probably learn all he wanted to know from his mother.

She wondered if Mickey owned any property that neither Hal nor Beck knew about. Did his father own abandoned buildings that his son had access to?

And there was Lisa Singer's husband. How much closer to the investigation could you get without actually being a part of it?

Then again, as she'd said before, there were a lot of potential suspects here in St. Dennis.

There's the balding man there in the back of the room, by the door. And that guy standing there at the end of the last row, watching the crowd instead of Beck, his face void of expression.

And who knows how many possible suspects Hal was mentally lining up on the opposite side of the room?

". . . and take some questions, if anyone has any," Mia heard Beck say, as she tuned back in.

There were the usual questions. Did the police have any suspects? Did they think he was going to strike again? What could the people of St. Dennis do to protect themselves? How was this going to affect the tourist business?

"You don't really think this killer is someone from St. Dennis, do you?" a man in one of the middle rows asked.

"Actually, we do." Beck nodded. "Everything points to him being local. He knows the area, he—"

"A lot of people know the area." The man stood, his arms crossed defiantly over his chest. "You're telling us this killer—this fiend—is one of *us*? I want to know how you can make a statement like that. Some of us are more than a little upset that you think one of us could be a deranged killer."

The room went very still.

"Jack, the facts are what they are," Beck told him.

"So we have to look at everyone with suspicion? Our neighbors, our friends, our sons, our brothers?" He was growing increasingly agitated.

"Until we bring him in, yes." Beck nodded. "Within reason, of course. Jack, no offense, but the killer is probably about twenty years younger than you, and probably in a little better shape. We're pretty sure he's in his early to mid-thirties, and he's strong enough to overpower these women and carry them as dead weight to the places he chooses to dispose of them. Which he's done with apparent ease, by the way. He didn't seem to have much trouble carrying a victim through the yards on my street to my driveway."

"How do you know he carried her through the backyards?" someone asked.

"Because one of my neighbors is an insomniac who was sitting on his front porch all night and never saw or heard a thing. So we know nothing passed by the front of the house," Beck explained. "Then again, there's a good chance he could have come in by boat, tied up at the dock at the end of the street, and walked along in the shadow of the back fence until it ended. From there, he would have been walking behind the garages, so he could be fairly certain he wasn't going to be seen at that hour of the night."

"Well, mid-thirties and strong could apply to a hell of a lot of men around here," another man in the crowd said. "How can you tell who's a likely suspect and who's not?"

Beck reiterated Annie's profile to the crowd.

The group had grown very quiet once again. Beck looked across the room to her and said, "Agent Shields from the FBI is here with us. Agent Shields, is there anything you want to add?"

"There is." She stepped forward, gathering her thoughts as she walked to the front of the room. Maybe there was a way to get the killer's attention.

"I agree with Chief Beck that the man we're looking for is from St. Dennis, as does one of the FBI's best profilers." Mia took the microphone from the stand and walked slowly around the room. "But I'd go one step further and say that I believe he's in this room."

A loud angry buzz seemed to flow from the front of the room to the back. Mia held up one hand.

"You all watch TV. You know that a serial killer is likely to be drawn to the media coverage of his crimes, right? He wants the attention. He wants to know what's being said about him." She strolled down the center aisle, her eyes scanning the crowd on both sides. "He wants to sit here—or stand—and feel superior to everyone in this room, especially the chief and his department. To me. To you. Right now, he's hanging on my every word. He wants me to tell you how very smart, how very clever he is."

She stopped in the aisle and looked around. The room had gone silent again.

"Well, he is very smart. Very clever. The profiler and I were saying just this morning that he's not like anyone we've seen before. The way he kills is unique. He really has his act together. He's highly organized and he very carefully plans every aspect of his crime from the abduction to the torture to the disposal of the bodies. I suspect he's as organized in every aspect of his life."

"Chief Beck didn't say anything about the victims being tortured." A woman several rows to Mia's left said loudly.

"What would you call being held captive for an indefinite period of time, shackled, repeatedly raped, then when he's finally done with you, when he's taken everything you have, including your dignity and your will to live, he wraps you in cellophane starting at your feet, until your entire face is covered so that you fight for even your last dying breath?" Mia said more sharply than she'd intended. "If that isn't torture, I don't know what is.

"Something else—he's very sophisticated; the fantasy he's living out is highly evolved. He's a very confident man. Maybe owns his own business. And he's bold. It takes a very bold man to do what this man does. There's a high degree of risk here, taking the entire operation into consideration."

As Mia made her way back to the front of the room, she made it a point to meet and hold the gaze of every man there. She was looking for a challenge.

"If he's so smart and he's so sophisticated, why did he leave that girl's body on her front porch?" someone asked. "And it doesn't seem so smart to me to leave a dead body in the police chief's Jeep."

"After a while, I suspect he needed to brag a bit." Mia smiled. "Genius needs to be recognized."

"So he's showing off?" a young woman in the front row asked.

"Exactly." Mia nodded. "For all his intelligence, all his sophistication, he is, at heart, a show-off."

She'd reached the podium and returned the microphone to its stand.

"There's one other thing about him that we know for certain," Mia told the silent crowd. "The man we're looking for is a sadistic coward. He has to tie his victims down to control them. He gets the greatest sexual satisfaction from torturing his victims. That's what he gets off on. He fantasizes about how he can dominate his victims, how he can degrade them through various sexual acts, and then he lives out his fantasies. He makes sure their death is a long, drawn-out affair. It's slow and deliberate and he savors every second of it. By then, he's humiliated them, he's stripped them of everything, and he's kept them restrained so that he has total control over them. But without those restraints—without the duct tape and the chains, and the hours he forces them to spend alone—without those weapons, he is nothing but a weak little man. He's a coward. He can only be satisfied by tying a woman up and raping her." She looked around the room and added coolly, "Can you think of anything more pathetic?"

She stepped back from the microphone and nodded to Beck before walking down the center aisle and out the door.

17

Mia sat in the Adirondack chair, her legs stretched out straight in front of her, her head resting against the hard wooden back. She closed her eyes and listened to the waves lapping at the shore, and felt almost as if she were being rocked to sleep. Not that she wanted to fall asleep out here, on the wide lawn behind Sinclair's Cove, but it was a restful moment.

She'd made one stop on her way out of town before driving to the inn from the meeting in St. Dennis.

"I'd like a room," she'd told the pleasant young man behind the desk when she arrived.

"I'm sorry. I'm afraid we're booked to the rafters."

"Mr. Sinclair said there'd be a room for me."

She frowned. She hated the thought of having to drive back to Connor's house now. She was tired and feeling worn out.

"Oh." The desk clerk reached under the counter and pulled out a small slip of paper. "Agent Shields?"

"Yes."

"Mr. Sinclair called earlier and asked that we refresh one of the cabins for you. He said to apologize that we could not accomodate you in the main house." He handed her a key on a long leather circle.

"Last cabin on the left as you go around the back of the building. May I take your bags?"

"No apologies necessary. And I only have a few bags." *Just the ones under my eyes, one from Bling, and, oh yes, the one holding the bottle of Pinot Grigio on the passenger seat of my car.*

"Please let me know if you need anything," he told her. "We have breakfast starting at seven, though we can make arrangements for coffee and muffins earlier, if you like." He smiled. "A lot of people come for the fishing and they like to get an early start."

"No fishing for me," she promised, "and hopefully no early start."

She turned toward the door and noticed the portrait hanging over the fireplace. Following her gaze, the clerk told her, "That's the late Mrs. Sinclair. Pretty lady, wasn't she?"

"Mr. Sinclair's wife?"

"Yes."

"What happened to her?"

"She drowned four years ago."

"What a tragedy," Mia said.

"It really was. She was really nice." He lowered his voice. "A little on the bossy side, but we all liked her anyway."

"How did she drown?" Mia would have expected someone who lived on the water to be a strong swimmer.

"Boat overturned. She took one of the small outboards to do a little crabbing and stayed out too long. Who knows how that happened. Storm came up real fast and she couldn't get back in. Mr. Sinclair took it real hard. He's been raising the kids—Danny and Delia—on his own. Doing a good job, too. They're nice kids."

The desk phone rang and he excused himself to answer it. Mia thanked him for the key and went through the lobby to the front porch. After parking her car in the lot, she walked around the back of the inn and followed a cobbled path to the last cabin.

There were lights on, both inside and over the front door. For a moment, she wasn't sure she was at the right place. But it was definitely the last cabin. She slipped the metal key into the door and pushed it open.

Her cabin was almost identical to the one in which Holly Sheridan had stayed at the opposite end of the row of similar structures. The small front room contained a white wicker sofa, a matching chair, and an end table that held a tall ceramic lamp, the base of which was a seagull with its wings half opened. A basket of fruit, cheese, and crackers was on a tiled tray had been placed upon the coffee table. A fairly new television sat on a stand in the corner and a neat pile of current magazines was stacked on the end table.

Next to the tray something lay folded inside white tissue paper. She slipped a finger through the tape and pushed aside the paper to find a navy blue T-shirt with a silk-screened image of the inn. A note on the tray from Daniel Sinclair welcomed her to the inn and apologized that the only shirt they had was an extra large. "We give them out to all our guests," the note informed her, "but last week we had a sorority reunion and went through all the smalls and mediums."

Mia held up the shirt in front of her. It was indeed large, but it was a nice gesture. She refolded the shirt and took it into the bedroom and left it on the foot of the double bed, which had been turned down. She peeked into the bathroom and found fresh towels and two water glasses, along with the obligatory soaps, toothbrush, toothpaste, and mouthwash.

She went back into the sitting room and sat on the edge of one of the sofa cushions and picked through the basket of fruit. She immediately bit into a green apple. She'd missed dinner and was starving. A few pieces of cheese and several crackers later, and Mia felt herself begin to revive. She stuck the key in her pocket, took one of the glasses from the bathroom, grabbed the bag holding the wine and her handbag, and went outside into the dark.

When she arrived at her cabin, she'd noticed the chairs set to overlook the bay, and chose the one closest to the water. She took the corkscrew from her shoulder bag and opened the bottle, and poured herself a glass. Stretching herself out in the chair, she sipped her wine and watched small dark birds darting across the water.

She was on her second glass of wine when she realized the small birds were bats.

"Oh, swell," she muttered, pulling herself into a ball and hunkering down in the chair. "Maybe they won't see me."

The moonlight was bright on the bay; except for the presence of the bats, it was a near-perfect night. It was quiet, except for the beating of the occasional wing overhead and the croaking of the bullfrogs from the marsh on the far side of the inn. She tried closing her eyes and willed herself to ignore the bats.

They're eating insects, she reminded herself. *That's good, right? The more they eat, the fewer mosquitoes to bite me. They have no interest in me.*

That's what her big brother always told her.

The thought of her big brother brought a pain to her heart.

"Go away, Brendan," she whispered to the night. "Crawl back into that little corner of hell where you're going to spend your unhappily ever-after, and don't come back. . . ."

A sound behind her drew her attention and she looked over her shoulder. The shadow of a man stretched out across the lawn, growing larger as it drew closer.

When the figure was about twenty feet away, it demanded, "Want to tell me what that was all about?"

Beck. And he didn't sound happy.

"What was *what* all about?"

"That little show you put on back there. What the hell were you thinking, taunting him like that? Were you trying to get him to come after you?"

She pulled her gun from her bag. "Better me than someone else."

"Yeah, sure. If he comes at the place and time you want him to."

Beck stood five feet away, looking down at her. From the chair, he appeared to be about twelve feet tall and most foreboding.

"The problem, as I see it, is that he's going to be doing the choosing, Mia."

"Maybe so." She put the gun back, then sat up and grabbed the bottle by its neck. "Would you like some wine? There's another glass in my cabin. I could—"

"I don't drink."

"I didn't used to." She set the bottle back on the ground and took a sip from her glass.

"What happened?"

"Shit." She told him matter-of-factly. "Shit happened."

He picked up the bottle and appeared to be looking at the label.

"How'd you get here?" she asked.

"Borrowed the car from Hal." He tilted the bottle in her direction. "How long have you been doing this?"

"Oh, roughly a half hour."

"I meant—"

"I know what you meant." She waved a hand dismissively. "That was my weak attempt at humor."

He replaced the bottle on the ground near the chair.

"None of my business, I know, but I'm curious. You don't have to answer."

"Since I got back from Indiana." She leaned her head back and looked skyward to avoid his eyes.

"What happened in Indiana?"

"We had this case . . . twenty-two-year-old guy killed his whole family. Mother. Father. His sisters. Their husbands and children." Her voice dropped with each word until Beck was almost leaning into the chair to hear her. "Eleven people in all. He killed every one."

"I guess there's no point in asking why."

"Oh, there was a why. His father wouldn't cosign a loan for him to get a new car, so he shot him and his mother. Went to the first sister's, asked the brother-in-law, who also declined, since the guy with the gun was unemployed. Shot him, too. Then I guess he figured, aw, fuck it, and he went house to house and just blew them all away."

She cleared her throat.

"And after that, there were these three little boys in Virginia. . . ."

They sat in silence until Beck broke it by saying, "You mentioned once that your brother—"

"Yeah, yeah. Doesn't take a genius to draw a line between the guy with the gun in Indiana and the guy with the gun in my family." She waved her glass in his direction.

"Want to tell me about it? What happened with him?"

"I'm sure you read all about it. It was a really big story about two years ago. FBI agent behind a child-smuggling ring, runs into his cousin while preparing to take a shipment of kids out of some small Central American country, later attempts to assassinate the cousin, kills the cousin's brother by mistake. The networks, the newsmagazines, the papers, they just couldn't get enough of it."

"That was your brother? The killer?"

"Good old Brendan." She took a gulp from the glass and stared into space. "This case in Indiana, when they spoke with the neighbors and with friends, they all said how close the family was. An ideal, all-

American family, they all said. Well, they used to say that about us, too."

"People on the outside, they never really know what's going on."

"Well, in our case, apparently no one on the *inside* knew, either. He never showed a thing, never gave any one of us a hint that something was evil and twisted inside him. And the thing is, none of us ever saw it." She leaned forward in the chair again and whispered, "Why didn't we know?"

"Because he obviously didn't want to share that part of his life with you."

"But you're family, you should *know*." Her eyes welled but no tears fell. "And here's the thing that's killing me. Connor—who my brother had intended to murder—still treats me like the princess."

"The princess?"

"I was the only girl in the entire family." She nodded. "That's why I was the princess." She leaned forward and added, "That's why I should have been the one to know."

"The one to know about Brendan?"

She nodded.

"I'm not following that."

"I was supposed to be the momma. I was supposed to take care of the boys the way Mom would have. And I did not do that."

"I thought your brothers were all older than you."

"They are."

"And the cousins, the other three guys? They were all older, too?"

She nodded.

"Then why were you supposed to be responsible for them?"

"Uncle George said so," she told him solemnly.

"Uncle George?"

"My mother's uncle."

"When did he tell you that?"

"When everyone came back to the house after my mother's funeral."

"Uncle George told you that you were supposed to be the little mother because your mother was dead?"

"Uh-huh."

"Mia, with all due respect, Uncle George has his head up his ass. That's the dumbest thing I ever heard."

"I agree. It was stupid and cruel and it was sexist, and my mother must have turned right over in her grave, but I was seven years old and I had just watched my mother be put in the ground." She sniffed and wiped her face with the back of her right hand. "I still wasn't clear on whether or not she was going to come back. I mean, even if she could get out of that box, how was she going to dig through all the dirt?"

Mia took a deep breath. "You know, no matter what you tell a child about death, they really don't understand a damned thing you're saying, because it's all beyond their experience.

"I clung to the adults around me for a long time because I had to. They all became much more important to me than they had been before she died. So when one of them told me something so profound, I believed it. I believed it for a long time."

"You still believe it."

"I try really hard not to. But it's still in there."

"You need to find a way to get it out, once and for all." He paused for a moment. "Have you thought about maybe seeing someone . . . ?"

"Yeah, I have." She tried to smile. "But basically, I'm lazy. I'll try to deal as best I can with something before I'll break my routine and try another way of dealing. It's the way I'm wired."

Beck picked up the bottle again. "This is not a good way to deal."

"Maybe not," she conceded, "but at least I can sleep at night. For a while, I could not."

"You didn't have problems sleeping before you left for Indiana?"

"Not really. When I first moved, it did take me a few days to get accustomed to the sounds in the new house, but for the most part, I was okay." She thought that over for a moment. "But I'd been traveling a lot for several months. That's why Connor suggested I move into his house."

"Your cousin Connor?"

"Yes. *Super* Special Agent Connor Shields," she stage-whispered. "We tease him about being the real international man of mystery because no one knows where he goes or what he does when he gets there."

"You share a house with him?"

"Not really. He's never there. That's why he offered me the house. I was traveling a lot and rarely at my apartment, which was expensive, and he had bought this house but he wasn't there either, so he suggested I give up my apartment and move into his house. Then I could save money and buy a house of my own." She laughed softly and said, "No one knows how Connor found this place—it's butt ugly, by the way, a sort of mustard yellow, stone-set-in-stucco bungalow on a forgotten road in the middle of the woods. And no one can figure out why he wanted to buy it, since he's never around. But he bought it and he moved into it, remodeled, then promptly left the country."

She paused, then looked at Beck and said, "You really think I'm going off the deep end, don't you? I'm not, and I'm sorry if I've given you that impression. I just have trouble sleeping, that's all."

"I think you have a lot on your plate," he said softly. "And I also think you might want to talk to someone professional, because if you keep doing that"—he pointed to the glass in her hand—"you're going to have a bigger problem than not being able to sleep."

"I know you're right," she said, but did not put the glass down. "And for the record, I tried sleeping pills, but they made me too groggy in the morning. I've tried meditation, hypnosis, acupuncture, and exercising until I can barely walk. Nothing seems to relax me except a few glasses of wine at night. I know it isn't smart, but . . ." She shrugged.

"Don't you have a headache when you get up?"

"Sometimes, but I don't really drink that much. I mean, I don't pass out or anything. I just drink until the voices stop and I can sleep." She rolled her eyes. "Oh, now I've really done it, haven't I? Now you think I hear voices."

She set the glass down on the grass at her feet. "The voices I hear are those of my brother Grady, my cousin Dylan. Grady's dead wife Melissa. And when I say I hear them, it's because I talk to them sometimes. I ask Brendan why, though he doesn't really have an answer. I tell Dylan how much I miss him, and I tell him about Annie and he tells me it's okay where he is. I tell Melissa how sorry I am that she and Grady didn't get to live their life, and she tells me to take care of him and not to let him waste his life mourning for her. Does that sound crazy?"

"Actually, no, it doesn't."

"Did you ever talk to someone who was gone?"

He nodded. "Yeah, I have."

"Family?"

Another nod.

"See? No one can mess you up like your family."

"You have no idea . . ."

She waited to see if he'd elaborate, but he did not, and she let it pass. She started to reach for the glass again, then changed her mind and drew her hand back.

"Mia, why did you challenge him like that?"

She knew exactly which *he* Beck was referring to. Personal time was over. It was back to business.

"I looked around that room, at all those people, and I knew he was there. I could feel him. I could almost smell that superior attitude of his, sense the challenge he was sending out, and I had to toss it back at him.

"I knew he was in that room, and he knew I knew it," she continued. "And he also knew I had no idea who he was and he was enjoying that a little too much. It pissed me off. The longer it takes us to figure out who he is, the more likely it is that another young woman will die. I can more than take care of myself if he comes after me. You think most of the young women in this town can say the same?"

"So you put a big target on your back?"

"We have nothing, Beck. We don't know why he picked the women he picked, or where he met them or how he convinced them to come with him or where he keeps them. There are three crime scenes for each of these killings, and the only one we can explore is the last one, the place where he disposes of the bodies. And those scenes have yielded us exactly one big fat zero's worth of trace. This guy is so good. He doesn't leave a crumb."

"So we know he wears a condom when he's assaulting the girls and wears gloves while he's wrapping them up."

"Which leads us nowhere." She sighed deeply. "He's going to take another victim again, very soon. He's due for another fix, that high he gets from living out his fantasy."

"Aren't you afraid of being part of that fantasy?" Beck lowered himself to the grass and sat down.

"No. I'm more afraid for someone else. That pretty girl who works at the ice cream place, or that cute little waitress in the sandwich shop or even Vanessa, maybe." She pulled one leg up onto the seat and leaned forward on it. "You think your sister would hold up under that type of torture for very long?"

"No." He shook his head. "No, she wouldn't hold up at all. Vanessa just doesn't get that anyone would want to hurt her."

"After two bad marriages?" Mia raised an eyebrow. "She is trusting."

She hesitated, then added, "Would she be trusting of, oh, say, someone like Mickey Forbes?"

Beck looked up sharply. "Why Forbes?"

"He fits the profile, don't you think? His mother is domineering and most likely has been all his life. Hal told me that Christina's been focused more on building up the community than either of her marriages. Maybe that extended to her child as well. Was he neglected, do you know? Did Christina bully her husband, demean him in front of their son?" She started to refill her glass, but under Beck's scrutiny only poured half a glass. "What do you really know about him, anyway?"

"I know he's a jerk, but that doesn't make him a murderer."

"Maybe. Maybe not." She put both feet on the ground and rested her forearms on her thighs, holding the glass between her knees. "Right now, we need to look at everyone as a possible killer. That's my point. We haven't been able to narrow the field at all, so we can't eliminate anyone. Whoever this guy is, he's flown under the radar for a long time." She held up a hand to silence the protest he was about to launch. "Yes, I realize he may not have gone to this extreme in the past, but I think that when we find him, we'll find that he's raped before. He's simply carrying that fantasy several steps forward."

"If that's true, why now?"

"Something's set him off. Something's changed in

his life. Maybe he's been passed over for a promotion. Maybe for someone like Mickey Forbes, for the sake of argument, it was the breakup of his marriage. I know everyone who is passed over for a promotion or who gets divorced doesn't turn into a serial killer. I'm just saying, these can be life-changing situations."

"So how do we smoke him out?"

"I'm still working on that."

"Well, don't try to fly solo on this one, okay?" He reached out and touched her arm. "I'd hate to see you become his victim."

"Oh, trust me, so would I." She shook her head slowly. "I have no intentions of ending up in one of his cocoons."

Beck looked at his watch. It was after midnight already.

"It's late. I need to get home and get some sleep so I can do it all again tomorrow." He stood and extended a hand to her. "Come on, I'll walk you to your cabin."

"That's okay. I can walk twenty-five feet by myself."

"I don't doubt it. But I want to be able to leave here and know for certain that I'll be seeing you in the morning."

She held up the bottle.

"You afraid I'll polish this off by myself, wake up with a hangover, and be unfit to report in tomorrow?"

"No. I'm afraid I might not be the only person who knows where you're staying tonight."

"You mean the killer—"

"You stirred him up, Mia. He may not be able to resist."

She gathered her things and stood.

"I admit I'm tired. I might as well turn in."

They walked across the grass to her cabin.

"Did you lock it?" he asked when they reached the door.

"Of course." She hoisted her bag up higher on her shoulder and dug in her pocket for the key, then unlocked the door. The lights were all still on, just as she had left them. "See? All's well."

"Good. Lock the door behind me, then get some sleep. We have miles to go with this case."

"Agreed. I'll see you in the morning." She closed the door halfway. "Thanks, Beck."

"Any time."

Mia closed the door and turned off the outside light, then went into the bathroom and caught her reflection in the mirror. Her hair was loose around her shoulders and her eyes were slightly rimmed in red. She stared at herself for a long time before going into the sitting room to find the bottle and the glass.

Returning to the bathroom, she rinsed out the glass, poured what remained of the bottle into the sink, and turned off the light.

Beck stood in the shadows until the only light still visible in the cabin was in the small back room. He shoved his hands into his pockets and walked across the grass to the chair in which she'd been sitting and turned it around to face her cabin.

Mia would have a fit if she knew he was there, but

he couldn't walk away knowing she might have set herself up. He knew she was strong and he knew she was capable—and armed. But there was also a chance her reflexes were impaired, and he couldn't shake the feeling that she'd painted a target on her back. He wasn't about to let anyone take aim on his watch.

He stretched his long legs out in front of him and eased back into the chair. Overhead the moon was full, and off in the distance a dog barked. He made himself as comfortable as he could in the wooden chair and waited for the sun to rise.

18

Mia poked her head into Beck's office at eight the next morning.

"Hey, I have some good news," she told him excitedly. "There was a message on my phone from JoJo."

"JoJo?" He frowned. Who the hell was JoJo?

"FBI JoJo who works magic with damaged tapes?" Mia sat in the chair closest to the door. "We sent her the tape that was found with the body we believe belongs to Holly Sheridan?"

"Right. JoJo." He suppressed a yawn. "Got a thing for one of your brothers."

"Andy, yeah. Anyway, JoJo couldn't restore all of it, but she's made a copy of what she has, and overnighted it to us. We should have it in a few hours." Mia leaned forward. "Beck, she said he called the woman *Holly* on the tape."

"Pretty much what we expected."

"She said it was really gruesome, what she could hear."

"I'm sure it was. The whole damned thing has been gruesome." He snapped. "It isn't likely to get any better."

"Sounds like someone got up on the wrong side of the bed this morning."

"You could say that." He rested an elbow on the edge of the desk.

"You okay?"

"I'm fine. Let me know when you get that tape."

"Sure." Feeling as if she'd been dismissed, Mia gave Beck a mock salute and went into the conference room where she'd set up a temporary office.

She'd just hung up the phone from a conference call with the agents who were tracking down the 2000 and 2001 victims when Lisa Singer stuck her head through the doorway. She wore what was apparently her summer uniform: khaki walking shorts accessorized by a holster attached to the front of her belt, and a short-sleeved shirt. Large round tortoise shell sunglasses sat atop her head.

"Morning, Agent Shields," she said.

"Hi, Lisa. Please, call me Mia. How was your weekend?" Mia asked, then laughed. "Oh. Right. What weekend?"

"Probably as much of one as we're likely to get until this is over." Apparently encouraged by Mia's friendliness, the sergeant came into the room carrying her coffee and a fistful of pink phone messages. "Have you handled a lot of cases like this before?"

"You mean serial killers?"

Lisa nodded.

"More than my share."

"It's so hard to understand how someone could be so horrible. So without a soul." Lisa shivered. "Do you ever get used to it?"

"If I did, it would be time to retire."

"Everyone in town is so jumpy about this, especially after last night's meeting." Lisa leaned on the back of one of the chairs.

"Everyone should be jumpy. We don't even have a lead on this guy."

"Well, I did have a thought. I was just on my way in to talk to Beck about it." She tucked a stand of hair behind her ear.

"Run it past me, too?"

"All of these victims have been young, you know? So I was trying to think of places around here where young people hang out." She grinned. "It wasn't that hard. There aren't many."

"But you thought of one."

"Maybe. There's a new gym out on the highway, in that shopping center? You don't have to buy a membership to work out there. You can pay by the visit, if you want. Chief Daley says one of his men spoke with them about Colleen Preston. She was a member. Mindy Kenneher was not and neither was Holly Sheridan— I checked—but they could have worked out there from time to time. I'm going to drive out there with their photos and see if anyone recognizes either of them."

"Great idea." Mia nodded. "Just make sure you don't put Chief Meyer's nose out of joint while you're at it."

"God forbid." Lisa rolled her eyes. "A couple of store fronts down from the gym, there's one of those gourmet coffee places. It seems to be a pretty popular place. I'm going to run in there, too, see if anyone remembers any one of the victims coming in, and if so, if they were with anyone."

"You ever think about the FBI, Lisa?" Mia leaned back in her chair and smiled. "We could use a few more like you."

"To tell you the truth, I used to dream about being in the FBI," Lisa admitted.

"What stopped you?"

"Oh, life. You know how things go." Lisa shrugged. "After college, I went through the police academy and did pretty well, got a job here, that was when Hal was still chief. I actually did apply to the FBI, though, back in the nineties. But then I met Todd, and, well, you know how it is. He was my dream man. I fell—he fell—we got married three months later."

"You met him here in St. Dennis?"

"No, we met in Chestertown. He had a fraternity brother who lived there. We ended up in St. Dennis because he used to summer here as a little boy and inherited some property from a relative. But don't think I'm complaining, I have no regrets. I've been happy here, I love my job. Loved working for Hal, and I love working for Beck. Love my family."

"That's great." Mia smiled again. "Great that you're happy with the choices you made."

Lisa smiled back. "I definitely am. I have a great husband, great kids, a great job. When I wanted to come back to work after the kids were born, Hal let me start back part-time on dispatch. When I was ready to go back out on the street, they hired Garland. Hal was great to work for, Beck is, too. He keeps pushing me ahead, you know? Encourages me to take courses, and any time there's some special extra class, he sends me. Someday, St. Dennis will be in a position to hire it's first detective, and I want it to be me."

"There's no reason why it can't be."

"I hope my boss thinks so, too."

"How does your husband feel about you being a cop?"

"I think secretly he'd be happier if I stayed home all the time and catered to him and the kids." She lowered her voice and added, "But what man doesn't, right? Todd's pretty cool about me being with the department, though he'd probably rather I had a nine to five. I think he liked it better when I was on the dispatcher's desk. The hours were more regular, but all in all, he's fine with it. We've adjusted."

"You are one lucky woman, you know that?"

"Luckier than anyone deserves to be."

Mia's phone rang and she reached for it.

"And one of these days you'll have to share with me the secret of how to get and keep it all."

"Anytime." Lisa waved and left Mia to take her call.

An hour later, Mia was back in Beck's office with a stack of faxed reports from Miranda Cahill, one of the agents assigned to track the 2000 and 2001 victims.

"Miranda says she can't find a listing for the victim in the city or any of the suburbs but she's still looking. She did speak with the investigating officer who sent her a copy of their electronic file. According to the statement the vic gave at the time, she and her friends were in the bar, there was a large group there and they were all milling around, dancing with some of the guys, that sort of thing. The guy she'd been dancing with—said his name was Jake—bought her a beer. Said the guy was really nice, polite, not pushy or anything, so when he suggested they take the beers outside so they could cool off, she didn't think twice. They left the bar through the rear door, opens onto the back of the parking lot. Said it was almost two, almost closing time, so there were fewer cars in the lot. Said one minute they were talking, the next minute, he had a knife to her throat and was shoving her into a car."

"So much for Mr. Nice Guy," Beck muttered.

"No fooling. Kept the knife to her throat the entire time he was raping her. The cop said she was real reluctant to go into detail about everything he'd done to her, so it must have been really bad."

"He get a description?"

"Late twenties, dark hair. Average height and weight. The cops said if they picked up every guy who fit that description, there'd be no one left on the beach." She shrugged. "Not much to go on. We're hoping Miranda can track down the victim and get a little more than that."

"And the other ones?"

"The victim from Columbus was contacted and she refused to discuss it. Said she spent a long time in therapy to put it behind her and absolutely was not going there again. Threatened legal action if anyone else called her. The third woman recently moved to Atlanta. Miranda is supposed to be meeting with her tomorrow. If her memory's good, we'll get a sketch artist out there as soon as we can."

"Great. Let me know what you hear."

"Will do."

"What do you think he'll do next?" Beck asked.

"Something to shake us up, turn up the heat," she replied without thinking. "Something to remind us that he's in control here, not us."

"Another ballsy statement."

"I'm afraid so."

"Shit." He rubbed a hand over his chin.

"My thoughts exactly . . ."

She turned to leave and saw Garland walking toward her with a package.

"Agent Shields, this was just delivered for you."

"Terrific, thanks, Garland." She took the package and held it up to Beck. "This must be the tape from JoJo."

He took a tape player out of his desk drawer and handed it to her.

"Let's see what's on it."

Mia plugged in the machine and slipped the tape inside, then pushed *play*. The static was thick initially, then some background noise could be heard. Then, a voice, pleading.

"Please don't hurt me anymore. Please don't . . ."

"It's almost over, Holly." The distorted voice said in a soothing tone. "Just a . . ."

The tape went silent, then they heard, ". . . don't want to die . . ."

"We don't . . ." silent . . . "we want, Hol . . ."

Another silent stretch, then, "Say good-bye, Holly. Tell them good-bye . . ."

"Mommy . . . Daddy . . . Eric . . ." the voice began to sob. "I love you . . ."

"Very nice, Hol . . ." The next section was garbled, then the static returned. Mia let the tape run out.

"Well, we know for sure it was Holly Sheridan," Mia told Beck after she turned off the machine.

"We already knew that." He stared out the window for a long time. Without turning around, he said, "Do we have to let them hear the tape? The Sheridans?"

"No. I don't know if it wouldn't hurt more." She thought it over. "Then again, if we catch him and he goes to trial, they'll hear it."

"*If* we catch him?" He turned back to her, his blue eyes narrowed and darkened. "Are you losing faith, Agent Shields?"

"My mistake. *When* we catch him . . ." She rose from her chair. "Let's just hope that happens before he makes that next bold move. Otherwise, we both know that someone else is likely to die . . ."

19

The mist rising from the marsh had settled a few feet above ground, but Hal knew as he walked along the edge of the field that by the time he reached the marina, it would be gone, burned off by the hot July sun. Which was fine with him. Hal had no problem with the heat.

For a man in his sixties, he was in fine shape, healthy and strong and no infirmities to speak of beyond the usual. A little arthritis here and a little there. Thinning hair. But for a man his age, he was in remarkable shape.

Still strong as a bull, he liked to say.

He'd retired reluctantly, but knew it was for the best. It was time to pass the office on to someone younger, someone better trained in all the latest law enforcement techniques, someone up on all the newest technology. Someone who could keep the police department in step with all the other changes that were taking place in St. Dennis.

Someone like Gabriel Beck.

Hal whistled as he walked down the stone steps toward the slip where the *Shady Lady* was tied. Beck had done just fine. And he, Hal, couldn't congratulate himself enough on having had the foresight to track

Beck down and talk him into coming back to St. Dennis and taking the job.

A gull swooped over his head and dove toward the water where some chum had been tossed overboard by a fisherman already on his way back into the marina.

"Calling it a day, John?" Hal called to the skipper who was backing his cruiser into its slip.

"Out since four and not a nibble. God's way of telling me to get back to work." The man waved as Hal passed by.

Hal chuckled and continued on down the wooden walk to where his boat was tied. He didn't really care if the fish were biting or not. *Fishing* was just euphemism for *lazing on the bay* on a day off, as far as he was concerned.

The new blue tarp covered the deck and the ropes were taut against the tide. Hal climbed aboard his craft and began to unfastened the tarp. He'd bought it just days earlier at Singer's and had spent an hour before last night's meeting fitting it. He'd been pleased to find it fit like a glove, just as Todd had promised.

That boy did know boats.

Hal had removed half of the tarp before he saw the thing on the deck. It took him several long minutes to react.

"Holy Mother of God." He backed away in horror. "Holy Mother of God . . ."

The body wrapped mummy-style in plastic was in even worse shape than Holly Sheridan's had been, but the killer had added a little something extra to make identification easier. He'd placed the victim's driver's license inside a plastic sandwich bag along with the tape.

"Considerate bastard." Beck leaned over the body and studied the photo ID through the layers of plastic wrap. "You think there's any reason to doubt this is in fact Mindy Kenneher?"

"I think I'd want something conclusive before I turned her over to the family, but the hair's the right color," Mia pointed out. "And why would he have Mindy's driver's license if he hadn't had Mindy?"

"Good point." Beck took his phone from his pocket. "Might as well give Rich Meyer a call, get him over here right away."

"We need some good crime scene techs, and we need them soon," Mia noted.

"I'd just as soon put Lisa on it. The fewer hands on this deck, the better," Beck said as he dialed. "Besides, Lisa's had a lot of training in lifting prints and she's damned good at collecting trace. We're going to be sending anything we find to your lab anyway. The only other option is to call in the state, and I'd rather leave them out of it. If I let Lisa process the scene, there's no one on board except you, me, Lisa and the ME. That okay with you?"

"It's fine with me. By the way, I told Lisa she'd make a great federal agent," Mia told him.

"Don't get any ideas, she's worth two of anyone else I have. Council's already approved her promotion to detective, thank you very much. We just haven't told her yet. Maybe not as glamorous as being a fed, but she likes her home life."

Beck stopped pacing when his call was answered. "Yes, this is Gabriel Beck in St. Dennis. I need to speak with Chief Meyer immediately . . ."

Beck finished his call, then immediately placed another one to his dispatcher.

"Garland, I need Lisa down here right away. Did you call her like I asked you to?" Beck began to pace again. "Well, try her again. Page her. Call her house. Maybe she stopped home for something and hasn't checked her messages yet . . ."

"Is everything all right, Beck?" Mia asked. "You look annoyed."

"I need Lisa and she hasn't called in."

"When I spoke with her early this morning, she said she was going out to that shopping center outside of town, the one that has the gym and the coffee shop. She was going to show around the photos of the three victims, see if anyone recognized one or all of them."

"Yes, I know where she went and why. She should still be answering her page. Garland said he's paged her twice without a response."

He glanced behind him at the showroom beyond the dock. "Duncan, call up there to Singer's and ask Todd if he's spoken with Lisa in the past hour or so. I need her now."

"Right, Chief." Duncan nodded and trotted off up the steps.

A crowd began to gather, and Beck spent the next fifteen minutes asking them all to leave. Garland re-

ported back to Beck that Todd Singer was out, showing a boat to a client, but was expected back any
time, and that Lisa had not been in the showroom
since it opened at nine.

An annoyed Beck sent Duncan back to the station
for an evidence kit, then walked over to Mia and said,
"Duncan should be back in a few minutes. We can get
started then."

"I'll be here." Mia nodded and wished she was
wearing something other than the new short, slim
skirt and shirt she'd picked up at Bling the night before. Not exactly what to wear when crawling
around a boat looking for evidence.

She opened her bag and searched her wallet for receipt for her purchases, and hoped the shop's phone
number was printed on it. It was, and she dialed the
number on her cell phone.

"Vanessa, it's Mia . . . yes, thank you, it was fun. I
would definitely love to come back. Listen, I . . . yes,
I love the outfit, as a matter of fact, that's why I'm
calling." Mia explained what had happened, where
she was, and what she was going to have to do.

"So I was wondering, if those cute jeans that I was
looking at are still there, if I could run down and pick
them up, they're more suitable to what I have to do
this morning than what I have on. No, no, I wouldn't
ask you to do that . . ."

Mia paused, considering Vanessa's offer to run the
clothes over for her.

"On second thought, I would appreciate it enor-
mously, if it isn't going to put you out too much. It
would save time. Thanks, Vanessa. No, I have no

preference. Any shirt is fine, the simpler the better. Just a basic T-shirt would be best."

Mia thanked her again, and dropped the phone back into her skirt pocket.

"Odd time to be clothes shopping," Beck said.

"I really wasn't prepared for this. We can't get onto the boat until we have the equipment, so in the interim, I thought I'd change. Vanessa has offered to run over with a few things I tried on last night but didn't buy because I didn't expect to need them. It won't hold us up. I'd just be more comfortable climbing around on the deck of that boat in something other than a skirt."

He glanced at her abreviated hemline. "Good call. I'll meet you on deck when the ME gets here."

Beck set off after Hal, who was carrying two orange cones across the parking lot to block off the entrance in an effort to keep out the gathering crowd of spectators.

Mia paced along the dock, watching for Vanessa.

"Well, wasn't someone saying last night that this guy was going to make a bold move soon? I'd say this qualifies." Susan joined Mia on the dock.

They both turned to watch the Cameron cruiser pull into the lot. Chief Meyer got out of the car, and caught up with Beck. They spoke briefly, then walked toward the boat.

"It was a surprise." Mia nodded, as the two men passed her silently. "But this isn't quite what I was expecting."

"Are you kidding? This is about as ballsy as they come," Susan insisted. "Ballsy as leaving the other body in Beck's car. And just as much of a jab at Beck, if you ask me."

"Because Hal is the former chief of police?"

"That, sure." Sue nodded. "And because Hal is Beck's father."

20

Mia stared in silence at Sue.

"Ah, I take it you didn't know that?" Sue asked.

"That Hal Garrity is Beck's father?" Mia shook her head. "No. I had no idea."

"I forgot that you're not from here. It certainly isn't a secret."

Mia looked over her shoulder to the end of the parking lot, where Hal was blocking off the drive, then glanced back at Beck, who stood on the deck of the *Shady Lady*. The two men stood in exactly the same position, right hand on right hip, and though impossible to see their faces, even from a distance, the similarities in their body builds were unmistakable. Mia wondered why she hadn't noticed it before.

Several people were gathered on the opposite side of the building that housed Todd Singer's showroom. On his way back from the station, Duncan stopped to turn away the curious, except for Vanessa Keaton. Apparently crime scene tape wasn't intended to keep out members of the chief's family.

Or maybe it was just that Duncan had a thing for Vanessa, Mia thought as she watched the officer's eyes follow the pretty young woman along the boardwalk.

"Mia, here are your things," Vanessa called to her. "God, does this thing just keep getting crazier and crazier or what?"

"It's pretty crazy, all right." Mia met her halfway.

"How is Hal? Is he okay?"

"I think he was a little shaken up. As anyone would be."

"Is it that woman from Cameron?" Vanessa handed Mia the bag she'd brought from Bling.

"It could be her," Mia nodded, not wanting to discuss what they'd found on the body until they were certain. "We're not positive. Chief Meyer is on the boat now with Beck."

The sound of tires crunching on stone drew their attention.

"I see Dr. Reilly is here already." Vanessa nodded in the direction of the van that had just arrived. "I'll bet she never expected anything like this when she moved to St. Dennis from Baltimore."

"She's been kept busy, that's for sure." Mia looked around. "Where's a phone booth when you need one?"

"What?" Vanessa frowned, then laughed. "You mean to change?" She pointed up the rise to Singer's. "Todd has a ladies' room. I'm sure he won't mind if you use it to make a quick change. Come on, I'll walk up with you."

"Thanks again." Mia looked back at the boat, where Beck was still talking to Rich Meyer. If she hurried, she could change and get back to the dock before he even realized she was gone.

She fell in step with Vanessa.

"If that is the woman from Cameron, why do you think he left her in St. Dennis?" Vanessa asked as they walked toward the boat showroom.

"I'm thinking he's taking another shot at Beck," Mia said. "Leaving the body on your dad's boat was just another way of making it personal."

"My . . . ?" Vanessa smiled. "Oh, Hal's not my dad, he's Beck's. We had the same mother, different fathers."

"I am so sorry." Mia flushed with embarrassment. "I shouldn't have assumed . . ."

"Hey, you're not the first person who wasn't aware we're half-siblings. It's okay. We've never referred to each other in terms of fractions."

"I apologize, all the same. Someone just mentioned that Hal was Beck's father . . ."

"I would love to have had him for a dad. I never really knew my own father. He and my mother split up before I was born."

Vanessa stopped in mid-stride.

"They do walk alike, don't they?" Vanessa nodded toward the parking lot. Hal was taking more orange cones from the back of a pick-up truck that had just pulled up and setting them around the end of the lot.

"They do. I'm surprised I didn't figure it out." Mia told her. "I'm usually pretty observant."

"How would you know? Beck doesn't call Hal, 'Dad' and they have different last names." Vanessa smiled. "The funny thing is, they are so much alike in so many ways, and yet they didn't even know about each other until Beck was . . ."

Vanessa slowed her pace. "If you didn't know

about their relationship, you probably haven't heard the story."

Mia shook her head, no.

"You could be the only person in St. Dennis who hasn't. Hal was living here when it happened. He'd grown up here, came back after college and stayed. Maggie—she's our mother—met Hal in Indiana, when he was playing minor league baseball. She was eighteen and he was in his early twenties, I think. Anyway, she met him when he came into her parent's restaurant. She was engaged to someone else, but apparently that didn't stop her and Hal from falling in love. Then the unthinkable happened."

"She got pregnant."

"Yeah, well, that, too. But before she even knew about that, Hal was drafted into the army and ended up in Vietnam. He didn't know about Beck, and because her parents were having a hissy, they forced Maggie to marry the guy she was engaged to."

"Did he know . . . ?"

"About Beck? Yes. Said he didn't care, he loved Maggie, wanted to marry her anyway, he'd treat Beck as if he were his own, yada yada."

"I take it he didn't?"

"He tried. But frankly, I think Maggie must have been miserable. Her brother—my Uncle Jack—told me that her husband really loved her but couldn't make her happy. I guess she just couldn't love him. They didn't stay married long, less than a year. She took Beck and moved to Chicago and stayed with a cousin for a while, I don't really know the whole story. Maggie doesn't talk about that time in her life very often. She remarried—my father—when Beck was about twelve or thirteen. About a year later, she found out she was pregnant with me, but by that time, she'd left that husband, too. Beck was supposedly a real wild child, so she tracked Hal down and drove Beck to St. Dennis. The way I heard it, she walked right up to Hal's door one night and rang the bell, and when Hal answered it, she said something like, 'I can't do a damned thing with him, so you're going to have to take it from here.' "

"Just like that?"

"Just like that. Handed over Beck's birth certificate and just walked away."

"Wow. That's hard to believe."

"Not if you knew Maggie." Vanessa watched Beck approach them, and she lowered her voice. "Frankly, I always thought he was the lucky one . . ."

Mia looked at her, a puzzled look on her face.

"She kept me." Vanessa walked up the steps and opened the door to the showroom, leaving a stunned Mia to follow.

"I guess I should have expected it, but I really didn't think he'd make his move so quickly." Beck stood over the body, Viv Reilly on one side, Mia on the other. Rich Meyer stood on the dock, watching. He was fairly sure the body was that of his neighbor's child, and did not want to be on the boat while evidence was being collected.

"Well, you said bold, he wanted to show you bold," the ME said.

"That was my initial reaction, too. But I'm not so sure . . ." Mia told them.

"Not sure about what?" Beck asked.

"Not sure this is it. The big move. I'm wondering if this isn't more like wagging a finger in your face. I expected something . . . I don't know, more dramatic." Mia frowned.

"I think for Hal, finding a dead naked woman wrapped up like a sandwich on the deck of his boat was pretty dramatic," Beck said.

"I'm sure it was. This just feels like, I don't know, staging, maybe. I could be wrong. Let's hope I am." She slipped on the plastic gloves and said, "Where would you like to start?"

"Is it beneath an FBI agent to dust for prints?" he asked. "Do you have a problem playing CSI?"

Mia made a face and grabbed the kit from his hands. "Are you kidding? I can dust with the best of them."

Beck vacuumed the deck but wasn't willing to bet that anything of any use would turn up in the bag. Though he was hoping for some fibers or hair, he wasn't optimistic. Just as he wasn't hopeful Mia would find any prints that would lead them anywhere. He was certain the killer spent as little time on the *Shady Lady* as possible, wore gloves and left nothing of himself behind. Just as he'd left nothing of himself on the other bodies they'd found.

"Crafty son of a bitch," Beck said under his breath.

"What?" Mia stood up and turned around.

"I said he was very careful."

"You betcha'," she agreed. "So far, I've found

prints on the railing, but I'll bet my life savings they're Hal's. Or maybe one of ours—yours, Viv's, mine, Meyer's, even. This is what you grab onto when you're hopping onto the boat. I did it myself. But there's no way this guy would be careless enough to leave a print. My guess is that he wiped down anything he may have touched."

"People watch too damned much TV," he said. "They think they know how to clean a crime scene as well as any cop. And in many cases, they do. This guy, for one. I don't see a damned thing. Not even a footprint. I'm betting he came on board in his stocking feet."

He stood and waved to the ME.

"Might as well do your thing, Viv."

"Give me just a minute more," Mia told him. "I think we need to check the cabin."

"I'll do that." He removed the powder and brush from the kit, but hesitated at the tape.

"You finished with this?" he asked, holding it up.

"I will be in a minute. I'm afraid I've gotten all I'm going to get." She stood up and rubbed the small of her back, then reached for the tape. She lifted the impression from the last bit of railing, then transferred the image to a fingerprint card. She handed the tape back to Beck.

He took it with him into the cabin, and when he emerged ten minutes later, he had a small stack of evidence cards under his arm.

"This should do it," he told Mia, "though I suspect most of the prints we have belong to Hal."

"We can print ourselves when we get back to the

station for elimination, but I'm sure you're right."
She began to repack the kit. "I certainly don't expect
any surprises."

"Did you take any prints from the tarp?" Beck
asked.

"No." Mia straightened up. "I'll do it now."

"What do you use here for fabric? Ninhydrin, silver nitrate . . . what?" She poked into the kit and
found the silver nitrate. "Ah, silver nitrate, it is."

She looked up from the large black bag and asked,
"Want to give me a hand? You spray, I'll photograph?"

"Sure."

She took the camera from the bag, then stepped
back so Beck could get what he needed. As he sprayed
the solution on the canvas tarp, several reddish-
brown prints appeared, which Mia photographed immediately, before they faded in the hot sun. When
they were finished, Beck packed the evidence they'd
gathered along with the camera, and carried it onto
the dock. Since he'd walked to the scene from the municipal building, he'd have to carry it back with him.

"She's all yours, Viv," he told the medical examiner.

"Thanks, Beck." A somber Vivien dropped onto
the deck with one of her assistants.

"I'm going back to the office." Beck turned to Mia
and held up the evidence bag.

"I'll walk back with you." She stood back and
watched respectfully as Vivien directed the careful
transfer of the body from the deck of the boat into a

body bag. "There really isn't anything to do here except wait for the press to show up."

She fell in step with Beck, but stopped halfway across the parking lot.

"Crap. I changed in the ladies' room at Singer's and left the bag with my other clothes there. Give me a minute to run inside and grab it?"

"Can you make it fast?"

"Sure." Mia jogged up to the door and went inside.

She was back in less five minutes. Beck started walking as soon as he saw the door open, so she had to hurry to catch up with him.

"Sorry, Todd was there. I hadn't met him before. I told him you were trying to get in touch with Lisa, but hadn't been able to. He said the last time he spoke with her was around an hour ago, but her phone was having trouble keeping a charge, said the battery needed to be replaced. Said he's taking their kids to his sister's in Annapolis today to spend the week and he checked in with Lisa to make sure their bags were packed and ready to go, since they'll be leaving before she gets home from work."

"I guess Lisa will just head back to the station when she's finished. In the meantime, we'll take a look at these prints."

"You expect to find anything that will point us in the right direction?"

"No. But I want to make certain, get that piece out of the way."

They completed the walk to Kelly's Point Drive in silence. When they reached the building, Mia held the door for Beck, and once inside, he stopped to exchange a few words with Garland and Mia went directly to the conference room.

The first thing Beck did when he reached his office was check the fingerprints Mia had lifted from the boat against the prints he had on file for Hal. As suspected, the majority of the prints matched. He printed himself and checked against the remaining prints, and found two that matched his own. That left two other prints unmatched.

He went into the conference room and asked Mia for her prints. One matched a print that was lifted from the rail, which made sense. She'd grabbed onto it as she'd jumped to the deck that morning.

One down, this one from the tarp.

He was packing up envelopes holding the cards with the matched prints when Hal came in.

"You okay?" Beck studied Hal's face.

"Damnable thing, Beck." Hal shook his head and lowered himself into the nearest chair. "Damnable."

"I asked if you were okay."

"Yeah." Hal got up and walked into the kitchen. "Want water, soda?"

"Nothing, thanks."

Hal returned for a moment and stood in the doorway taking the lid off a bottle of spring water. He took a long drink, then asked, "You hear from Lisa?"

"No. She must have found someone at the gym who recognized Holly Sheridan or Mindy Kenneher, maybe she's taking some statements." Beck tapped his fingers on the desk. "Todd told Mia that Lisa's having trouble with her phone losing the charge. Which would explain why she's not getting our calls."

"Damn cell phones. I'm forever forgetting to recharge my phone, then it makes that beeping sound in the middle of the night to remind me. Drives me nuts." Hal nodded in the direction of the evidence envelopes on Beck's desk. "You find anything there worth mentioning?"

"No. Most of the prints are yours. One print is Mia's, a couple are mine, probably from last week when we took the boat out. One print from the tarp doesn't match any of us."

"Todd's, most likely. He sold me the tarp, he would have handled it. I can stop out later and get his prints, just to make sure, but I'd bet money they're his."

"He said something about driving their kids over to his sister's in Annapolis today. You might want to try to catch him before he leaves."

Hal glanced at the wall clock. "I'll do that now. I want to talk to him anyway. He's been after me for the past couple of years to sell him the *Shady Lady*. After today . . . well, I think I'm going to be looking for another boat. Doubt I'd ever set foot on that deck without seeing that poor girl, all wrapped up like that."

Hal stood with his hands on his hips.

"God damn him, why'd he have to choose my boat?"

"He's taking another shot at Beck," Mia said from behind him.

Hal turned to her and asked, "Why?"

"I've been thinking a lot about that. Maybe he's just pissed off and this is his way of giving him the finger. He's showing you how clever he is, how slick, that he can get that close and still elude you. It was a risk, both times—leaving one body in Beck's car, and another on your boat, Hal. Risk is essential to him, it's vital." She sat on the arm of the chair so she could face both men.

"Why?" Hal asked again.

"It ups the stakes." She shrugged. "Then again, it could be something deeper than that, something far more personal."

Beck leaned forward, his arms resting on the desk. "Dr. McCall said that, too. That she thought it could be personal."

"Maybe somehow he holds you responsible for whatever kicked this off, and he's sharing the spoils with you. Laying the victims at your feet, so to speak. 'See what you made me do.' "

Beck ran a hand over his face. The expression on his face was pure anguish.

"If I thought for one second that something I did or said somehow kick-started this madness . . ."

"No, no," Mia told him, "don't buy into it. Whatever his thinking is, it's strictly his choice, all the way. He has to explain his choice to himself, remember, he has to have an excuse that permits him to do these things. His thinking is twisted. He could just as easily be mentally pointing the finger at Mother Teresa or Madonna. Whatever it is, it only exists inside his mind."

"So he rationalizes . . ."

"Absolutely. He has to. He has to justify his actions to himself. And remember, I'm just speculating. We don't know that you have anything to do with his motive."

"But your gut tells you . . . what?"

Mia thought it over for a moment before replying. "If he'd left the second body someplace else, I'd say the first time, leaving one of his victims in your car was a tweak."

"But . . . ?"

"But . . . leaving this one on Hal's boat . . . I'd have to say, yeah, it's more personal."

"Maybe it's because I was the chief before Beck," Hal said. "Maybe it's something to do with that, something to do with not liking the police."

"Maybe. Or maybe it's because you're his father." She looked from one to the other.

Beck stared at her without comment for several seconds.

"Bastard," Hal said and started out of the room. "I'll be at Singer's if you need me."

Mia turned to Beck. "If that trace is ready to go to the lab . . ."

"How did you know?" He asked when Hal was gone.

"Someone mentioned it," she replied.

"Why?"

"In reference to why the body may have been left on Hal's boat. Does it bother you?"

"Not really." If he did, he'd already dismissed it. "I'm going to run out to the gym outside of town and see if Lisa's still out there. She might have found some witnesses to interview, and I want to tell her about finding Mindy before she hears it on the news. Want to come along?"

"Sure . . ."

Mia drove, Beck's Jeep still being impounded. He'd been meaning to call for a rental, but kept forgetting.

On their way out of town, Beck said, "By the way, I had a chance to go over the cell phone records for both Mindy and Colleen."

"I take it there was nothing of any great use." Her eyes shifted from the road to him and back to the road. "Assuming you'd have told me if there had been."

"A few calls to a number that turned out to be . . ."

"Let me guess . . . untraceable."

"Right. Damn those prepaid phones."

"I wouldn't have expected anything less from this guy. He's certainly not stupid enough to call his victims from his home or work phone. Though that would have been nice."

She turned onto the highway. "You're going to have to tell me which way to go here."

"Straight, then make a right at the second light into the shopping center, maybe a mile down the road."

"How about the victims' computers?"

"Nothing. I had hoped we'd find there was some Realtor's website that one or both of them had visited, but there was nothing like that, and nothing out of the ordinary. No e-mails from a Realtor—legit or otherwise—or from any of the same contacts. Nothing that rang any bells whatsoever."

He pointed up ahead. "The shopping center is at the next light."

She put on her turn signal and pulled into the parking lot.

"Stay to the left," he told her. "The gym is the last building."

"I see it." Mia drove around and parked in one of the spaces right out front. She got out of the car and glanced to her right.

"Is that Mickey Forbes's sporting goods store?" she asked.

He nodded and pointed to the gym.

"First things first," he said.

"I was just wondering if he was working today, if he'd seen Lisa." Mia followed Beck through the automatic doors leading into the gym. "He splits his time between here and the car dealership, right?"

"Yes, but I don't know when he's where." Beck walked up to the reception desk. "I'm Chief Beck."

The young woman behind the desk looked from Beck to Mia. "Can I help you with something?"

"One of my officers was planning on stopping out here today. I had someone call as a follow-up a little while ago. He was told she'd been here."

"Sergeant Singer." The girl nodded. "She was in a few hours ago."

"Do you know if she spoke with anyone here?"

"She spoke with me. She had pictures of those women who were killed, the two who weren't members but who worked out here sometimes," the receptionist told him in a hushed voice, as if almost afraid to speak of the dead.

"You recognized them?" Mia asked.

"Sure. The older one, the one who worked at Sinclair's Cove? She used to come in and only use the treadmill. Never did anything else. The other girl, the one from Cameron, Mindy? She came in a few times, she tried everything a few times before asking for a form to apply for membership. She never did bring it back, though."

"Did you ever see either of them together?"

"No."

"Did you know Colleen Preston?"

"Sure." Her face grew sad. "Everyone knew Colleen. She was real friendly. No one could believe what happened to her. It just made us all sick."

"Did you ever see her with either of the other two girls? Or with anyone? Any of them work with one of the personal trainers?"

"No. Sergeant Singer asked the same thing. I never saw Colleen with anyone. She just came in after work, did her thing, then left. The other two were just sort of sporadic."

"Did you notice what time Sergeant Singer left?"

"Sometime this morning, but no, I didn't notice the time."

"I guess you didn't see her leave the parking lot?" Mia asked.

"No, but you could ask over at The Coffee Counter." Karen pointed out the door. "She said she was going to stop there."

"Thanks," Beck said. "You've been very helpful."

"It's so horrible, what he did to those girls." A frightened look came over the young girl's face. "Do you think you'll catch him soon?"

"We're doing our best," Beck told her.

"Me and my friends, we're scared to go out at night," Karen confided.

"Good," Beck told her. "If you're not scared, you won't be cautious. And being cautious could mean the difference between . . ."

The girl's eyes widened.

"What he means is, it's better to be safe than sorry. Stick with your friends and stay together if you go anyplace," Mia told her, and nudged Beck toward the door. "Thanks again. You've been very helpful."

Once outside, Mia asked, "What were you trying to do, scare the living shit out of her?"

"Yes. She should be scared."

"But not paralyzed with fear." Mia pointed up ahead. "There's The Coffee Counter. Maybe we'll find Lisa at some small table, knee-deep in an interview and strung out on caffeine and donuts."

"With luck." He pushed the door open and held it for her to follow him inside.

The shop was small, with a long counter lined with a dozen stools, a second smaller counter where orders were given and filled, and yet another long counter with more stools. There were two tables for four, and two tables for two near the front windows. A glass case held a variety of scones, donuts, and croissants. A middle-aged man stepped from behind the counter and waved to Beck.

"Chief, how's it going?" He greeted Beck, and nodded in Mia's direction.

"Not so good, Steve."

"Yeah, I gathered." The man nodded.

"Steve, you see Sergeant Singer today?"

"She was in earlier. Asking about those girls who got killed and wrapped up." He shook his head. "That's some bad business, Chief."

"The worst. Listen, did you notice what time she left the shopping center?"

"No, sorry. We were talking about those girls for a while—they'd all been in here, one time or another. She had a bunch of questions, you know, did I remember them, did I ever see them with anyone, or talking with anyone, that sort of thing."

"What did you tell her?" Mia asked.

"I said I never really noticed who they were with. I mean, the way we're set up here, people are always talking to one another, and half the town is in here at one point or another on any given day. One of the reasons I set it up like this, nice way for folks to meet, you know? Sort of encourages conversation. People sit next to strangers, you never know who you're going to meet."

Mia and Beck exchanged a long look.

"Thanks, Steve." Beck started toward the door.

"You might stop over at the Goal Post and see what time she left there," Steve called to him.

Beck turned around and asked, "The Goal Post?"

"Yeah." Steve nodded. "I told her that one of those girls—the little blond one, the girl from Cameron—had a big bag of stuff with her one time. I asked her if she wanted me to put it behind the counter while she had her coffee, the place was real crowded, and the shopping bag didn't fit under the stool. She handed it over to me and I put it on the floor, right back there." He pointed to the far counter. "I saw the name on the bag. The Goal Post. So when the sarge asked me about the girls, I told her she might want to try over there. See if anyone remembers her."

"Thanks a lot, Steve, you've been a big help." Beck pushed the door open and stepped outside. When Mia joined him on the sidewalk, he said, "Funny, I don't remember Mickey mentioning that one of the victims was a customer of his."

"He may not have known." Mia hurried to catch up with him. "He may not have been in the store when Mindy was doing her shopping."

"You'd think the clerk who waited on her would have remembered and would have mentioned it to him, and that he'd have mentioned it to me." They reached the sporting goods store. "Let's see what he has to say about it . . ."

They entered the store and went straight to the back. A young sales person in a white polo shirt and black soccer shorts approached them.

"Can I help you?"

"We'd like to speak with Mickey Forbes," Beck told him.

"I'm sorry, he's not in this afternoon. He owns the car place down the road, Bay Motors? Would you like me to call and see if he's there?"

"Was he in this morning?"

"Well, earlier, for about an hour, but . . ."

"How about a policewoman, in uniform?" Beck asked curtly. "Was she in?"

"This morning, she was asking . . ."

"Who'd she talk to? You? Or Mr. Forbes?"

"Both of us." The young man looked confused.

"She asked us both about one of the women who got killed, wanted to know if we remembered her. I didn't. Mr. Forbes, he said he didn't, either, but he'd have someone check to see if there were any credit card sales to her and he'd give her a call if he found anything."

"And the officer left the store?"

The sales clerk nodded.

"And Mr. Forbes? How long after did he leave?"

"I don't know, a few minutes, I guess."

"Thanks. Make that call for us now, please." Beck pointed toward the phone.

The clerk did as he was told.

"He isn't there," he told Beck, his hand over the receiver. "Do you want to leave a message for him to call you?"

"Yes. Chief Beck. St. Dennis P.D. He knows how to find me."

Beck turned and left the store.

"Thanks for your help," Mia called to the clerk as she caught the swinging door.

"Now what?" She caught up with Beck at her car.

"Now we track down Mickey Forbes and see what else he knows that he hasn't told us."

21

"Vanessa, any chance you might have seen Mickey Forbes today?" Beck had dialed her shop as soon as he got into the car. He leaned back against the headrest and exhaled loudly. "When was that?"

"Where did you go?"

"What time did he leave . . . ?"

From the driver's side, Mia could hear Vanessa's protest.

"Because I need to talk to him, that's why. Where did he go when he . . . Thanks. And Ness? Stay clear of him for a while, okay?"

Mia figured his ears were still ringing after he hung up the phone.

He caught her glancing in his direction, and said, "What? You think I was a little heavy handed? She's my sister, and he's . . ." He paused.

"He's what? A guy who's interested in her?" She stopped at the light. "It's obvious from your conversation that she was with Mickey this morning."

"They had lunch at Lola's." Beck rubbed his chin. "She said he got there around noon and left about an hour and a half ago. Went back to the car dealership."

"So which way?" she asked. "Should I make a

U-turn or go straight? I'm assuming you still want to talk to Mickey."

"Yeah. Take a right at the next light . . ."

Mickey Forbes was front and center in the showroom when they arrived.

"Hey, Beck. I just got the message you called. Let me guess . . . you're in the market for something to replace that old Jeep of yours. I just got a really nice Saab in on Friday, guy traded it in for a Jag. It's right over . . ."

"I'm not looking for a car, Mickey." Beck lowered his voice. "Is there someplace where we can talk?"

"Sure. Right on in here." Mickey pointed toward an open door. "How's it going, Agent Shields? Nice wheels you have there, Lexus is a fine car . . ."

Mickey ushered the pair into his office and closed the door.

"What's going on, Beck?" Mickey sat on the edge of his desk.

"I understand that Mindy Kenneher, one of the victims, was a customer of yours," Beck said. "How come I had to hear that from Steve at The Coffee Counter, and not you?"

"I wasn't aware of it myself." Mickey shrugged. "I just heard about that this morning, from Lisa. She said Steve told her about that girl coming in one day with a bag with our name on it. I told Lisa I'd have the store manager go through all the sales slips starting back in April so we could see who waited on her."

"You can tell that?" Mia asked.

"Yeah. I'm afraid my system is a little old fashioned, but there's a method to my madness. We hand write our slips, whether it's cash or credit, so that we have a record of the customer. That way, we know what they bought and when."

"What do you do with that information?" she asked.

"The names all go on a master list for sales, promotions, that sort of thing. If we know someone has bought a lot of fishing gear, for example, when we have something special, we give him or her a call. We try to keep our service specialized, you know?"

"And what did Mindy Kenneher buy?" Beck asked.

"We don't know. My manager was scheduled to be in at two, but I spoke with him and asked him to get in as soon as possible and asked him to make finding her slip his priority. I told Lisa I'd give her a call as soon as I had something. She said she'd want to talk to the salesperson, maybe they'd remember if someone was with her at the time."

"I need you to call everyone in and ask them to take a look at the photo."

"Sure, Beck, but my staff always turns over at the end of May. I lose all the college kids who work here part-time during the school year when they go back home. I don't hire part-timers again until the fall, so I don't know that they'll be much help."

"What time did Lisa leave The Goal Post?" Beck changed the subject. He'd have to wait for the sales slip.

"Around eleven, I think it might have been. We were just about finished talking when her phone starting ringing. She just said for me to call her as soon as I had something, then she answered the call and left the store."

"Any idea who she was speaking to?" he asked.

Mickey shook his head. "No idea. I didn't hear her say a name."

"Did you see which way she went when she left the store?"

"No, I had an appointment to meet a customer at eleven, so I left pretty much when she did."

"Thanks." Beck stood abruptly.

"Sure." Mickey looked from Beck to Mia, then back to Beck. "Is there something else going on here that I'm not picking up on?"

"Nah. Nothing else going on, Mick."

"Is Lisa all right?"

"Is there a reason she wouldn't be?"

"No. I just . . . you're asking all these questions about her, that's all."

"Nice of you to be concerned."

"Hey, we're old friends, me and Lisa. We go back a long way, Beck."

"Right." Beck opened the door. "Don't forget to call me as soon as that slip turns up . . ."

Beck and Mia walked to her car in silence. She put the key in the ignition, then turned to him and said, "You think he's a suspect."

"Until I know better, everyone's a suspect." He snapped his seatbelt.

Beck stared out the window for several minutes while Mia drove, then took his phone from his pocket and dialed.

"Hal, did you speak with Todd? Has he heard from Lisa?"

Mia braked to avoid hitting the car ahead of them which had made a left turn without signaling.

"When you're done there, I want you and Duncan to make another search of those abandoned buildings down around the river. Make it every abandoned or empty place in town. And get Garland to run a list of the properties and their owners. Thanks . . ."

He hung up and seemed lost in thought.

"So, what did Hal have to say? Has Todd heard from Lisa?" She slowed as the cars in front of her began to stop.

"Hal said he caught Todd just as he was leaving to pick the kids up from the babysitter to drive them over to his sisters. He said they do this every summer. His kids stay with the aunt and uncle and cousins for a week or so, then everyone goes to the grandparents for a week. Todd's parents own a very jazzy horse farm. According to Lisa, it's really a showplace. Acres and acres of farmland, dozens of horses. They breed thoroughbreds." Beck reached for the radio dial, then stopped. "Would you mind some music?"

"No, go ahead. Anything is fine." She rolled down her window and stuck her head out. "Looks like there's some road construction up ahead. Everything's stopped."

"Damn, I forgot they're repaving this section." He looked around. "We're stuck now. The last turn off was about a quarter mile back."

"So what else did Hal say?"

Beck scanned through several stations until he found something he liked. "Todd told Hal he'd just spoken with Lisa right before Hal got there. Said the connection was really bad and all he understood was that she was interviewing some witnesses and she'd be back to the station when she was finished to write up her reports. Then he said the call cut off."

"Sounds like Lisa needs a new phone."

"I guess so. The important thing is that she's okay."

"Did you think she wasn't?"

"I don't know." He thought it over for a few seconds, then said, "I guess knowing how this guy is— how clever and how slick—for a while there, I felt as if she'd disappeared, too. It was just a bad feeling I got when no one was able to contact her. She's a really good cop, like I said."

"And a good friend, I'd guess."

"Yes. She's a good friend." He nodded. "She was the first woman officer Hal hired. She was here when I started."

"Do you think she resented that you were brought in over her?"

"Lisa?" He seemed surprised by the question. "No. She didn't want the job, made no bones about it. Her kids were still real young then, and she's always made them her priority. The kids and Todd, that's what she lives for. She loves the job, there's no doubt in my mind, but it's always been second for her."

"Smart woman."

"Very." A song came on that he apparently didn't like, because he started scrolling through the dial again. "I think the only person who resented me for a while was Duncan. I think he's always wanted to be chief, but he's never really reached that level of competency, you know what I mean? Administratively, that is. He's a good cop but a piss poor record keeper and as Hal said, he just isn't a leader. He's come around since then, though. We get along just fine now."

"You must have been a police officer somewhere before you came to St. Dennis," she said, craning her next to see if any of the cars were moving. They didn't appear to be. "You must have proven yourself to have even been considered for the job here, even if. . . ."

"Even if my father was the retiring chief and head of the search committee?" He finished the sentence for her. "Yes, I'd been in law enforcement for years."

He seemed reluctant to say more, but Mia was curious and persistent.

"Where?" she asked.

"I was with the Newtown police department here in Maryland for six years, and before that I was in the service."

"Which branch?"

"What difference does it make?"

She smiled. "That means Special Forces."

He turned up the radio and acted as if he hadn't heard.

"So which was it?" she asked.

"You don't give up, do you?"

"Only when I absolutely have to." She slanted a glance at him, but he ignored her. "So what about these abandoned places you told Hal to look into?"

"St. Dennis is full of them. Down by the river, there are some old oyster shacks, some old buildings where boats were built and stored about a hundred years ago. They were used for different things through the years, then were boarded up. They're pretty ramshackle, for the most part. On the other side of town, we have an area that's about to be up for renovation. There are a few places that have been vacant for a while. The owners are waiting for the right market to sell, I guess."

"Sounds like the perfect place to keep a woman chained up."

"We did check them out last week, but only from the outside, so I want to take a closer look. If I wanted to keep someone hidden for a few weeks and not attract any attention, I'd be thinking hard about one of those buildings."

"And you think he's keeping them in St. Dennis?"

"Pretty certain. Daley and Meyers have said they've searched high and low in their respective towns, and nothing's been found. Of course, neither Cameron nor Ballard has the number of vacant buildings that we have."

"Why is that?"

"They're newer towns. St. Dennis is a couple hundred years old. Our buildings have been around longer, and some of them have been used for different purposes over the years. We've gone through a period of renovation and restoration, and now we're being discovered, so the old properties are increasing in value. And the other towns are not built on the water, the way we are. For generations our people made their living from the bay, so it follows we'd have old buildings near the water that are no longer being used because the businesses they served are gone." He seemed to think that over, then added, "There are some old crabbers' shacks out near the bay, past Sinclair's Cove. I think I asked Duncan to look into them but I don't remember that he said he did."

He took out his phone as the traffic started moving.

"Garland," he said, "I need Duncan. Is he around? Find him for me, please. And call the mobile phone service. It looks like Lisa needs an upgrade."

"Well, that should make Lisa happy. Getting a new phone, that is."

"Hey, I live to please." He played around with the radio dial for a minute, then said, "She's almost like a sister to me, maybe even more like a sister than my sister. I've actually known Lisa longer than I've known Vanessa."

"That must have been quite a surprise," Mia said, "finding out you had a sister."

"When it comes to Maggie, anything is possible. That woman is always full of surprises."

"Like bringing you here unannounced to Hal?"

"Yeah, that was a good one," he said dryly. "Pissed me off more than you could imagine, her dragging me here, never saying a word about where we were going or what she intended on doing. Just telling Hal that I was his problem, turning heel and walking away, leaving me standing there . . ."

Even now, years later, the pain in his voice and in his eyes was unmistakable.

"Looks like it turned out okay, though. With Hal, I mean."

"Only good thing she ever did for me." He nodded. "Still, you have to have something seriously wrong with you to do that to your own kid."

"But in the end . . ."

"In the end, it was the best thing that could have happened to me. She really couldn't handle me. And I guess that last time I got into trouble was the last straw, as far as she was concerned. And Hal was a terrific dad. Just took to it straight away, never questioned for a second whether I was his or not. Here he was, a small town cop, living alone . . ."

"He never married?"

"Nope. Always said the only woman he ever loved was my mother." Beck shook his head as if the thought was incomprehensible to him. "How crazy is that?"

"She must have had something going for her. Hal's no fool."

"Yeah, well, he is when it comes to Maggie. I swear, if she walked back into St. Dennis today, he'd let her."

"She must have had a reason to do what she did, Beck."

"Oh, she had a reason, all right. Her new husband didn't like me." His face hardened. "And I guess when you have to decide between your kid and your meal ticket, your stomach is going to win out every time. At least, for some it will."

"This new husband, he was Vanessa's father?"

"Right. One mean son of a bitch."

"But Vanessa told me they split up before she was born."

"Guess he didn't like kids, his or anyone else's."

"Was he abusive?"

"Abusive?" Beck frowned. "What made you ask that?"

"I don't know." Mia shrugged. "I was just thinking, she brought you to Hal right after she married this guy. Then, before she even had Vanessa, she split with him. Maybe she was trying to protect you. Both of you."

"And her reason for sending Vanessa out here?"

"Maybe she just thought it was time you got to know each other."

"More likely she was trying to get Vanessa out of her hair."

"Vanessa was an adult when she showed up here in St. Dennis."

"Maybe having a daughter in her twenties was cramping Maggie's style. Who knows what goes through that woman's mind?" He shook his head. "I for one don't want to know."

Mia was thinking that Beck very much did want to know, but she figured it wasn't her place to point that out. Instead, she said, "So where to now?" as they headed back into town.

"It's late afternoon. Just drop me off at the station," he replied. "Are you staying at Sinclair's Cove again tonight?"

"No." She shook her head. "But it would probably make sense if I did until the case is solved. I think when I get home tonight I'll pack enough things for a few days."

She turned on to Kelly's Point Drive.

"Just pull into the lot and take off, why don't you? Get a jump on the traffic," he suggested. "And maybe by the time you get here in the morning, we'll know what Lisa and Duncan have been up to all day."

"If you're sure . . ." She stopped in front of the door.

"Positive. Go on home." He gave her arm a quick squeeze, then opened the door and got out. He leaned into the car and added, "I was in the army."

"Delta Force," she said softly.

Beck smiled and said, "Get a good night's sleep."

"Will do." She waved and he slammed the door.

Looking forward to a night in her own bed, Mia headed for the highway, the Bay Bridge, and home.

22

He knelt in the shadow of a hydrangea that badly needed a good pruning, though its overgrown state was perfect for hiding him from the road. Not that he expected anyone to come by. This was, after all, the middle of nowhere.

At least, that was how it seemed. He couldn't believe his luck when he first saw the house. He'd never have expected someone like Mia to live in a place like this. For one thing, it was probably the ugliest bungalow he'd ever seen. For another, it was pretty isolated. The road wasn't even paved, for Christ's sake. Who lived on dirt roads these days?

It was enough to make a man believe in fate.

He laid the small leather case upon the ground and took out a small implement with a very sharp cutting blade. He crouched lower to better see the basement window, and began to cut along the outside edge of the glass. With luck, he'd be able to force it to fall on the outside in one unbroken piece, neatly and quietly.

As he painstakingly ran the blade along the perimeter, he reflected on just how lucky a man he was. He couldn't believe his good fortune to have been passing the gas station at just the moment when the pretty

FBI agent was filling up her car at the tank. He'd pulled in to the parking lot across the street, and watched to see in which direction she'd drive off. When he realized she was headed for the Bay Bridge, he thought, what the hell, he'd follow her and see where she was going. He figured she was going home, and knowing where she lived and how to get there could only be a good thing as far as he was concerned. Just that afternoon Mia Shields had moved to the top of his *to-do* list.

He'd followed her carefully and from a distance, and there were only a few hairy moments when he'd thought he'd lost her. He'd had to be particularly cautious once she turned off the highway, because any car traveling too close would surely be noticed. When she made that last left turn onto this narrow unmarked road, he'd gone straight, figuring she'd spot him immediately, though he was fairly certain she wouldn't recognize the car he was driving. Better to wait, he'd told himself, give her time to get to wherever she was going, then take a spin down that lane and see what was what.

He'd waited five minutes, then followed the dirt road past the lone house on the corner, the only one before the woods began to close in on both sides of the road. Then came a clearing, and several hundred feet down on the right sat this little house. From the edge of the woods he could see that the lights were on, and as he drove by—without slowing, without even *looking* just in case she happened to glance out the window—he saw her shiny black Lexus there in the drive. He kept going until he came to a second clearing, then pulled off the road. He sat for a few minutes, debating what to do. He was tired—after all, he'd been a very busy man today. But this was an opportunity he couldn't pass up. Lucky for him, he still had all his equipment in the trunk.

He got out of the car and walked down the road, taking care to stick to the woods, in the event another car should come by. He looked overhead and made a wish on the first star he saw winking down at him.

Another good sign, he thought to himself. *I guess this was meant to be.*

He paused at the spot where the woods ended and he studied the house. Surely the doors would all be locked, and the windows on the first floor as well. He'd just have to find another way in. He kept to the deepest shadows and stood parallel to the porch. He could see her moving about in the kitchen, so he sat on a tree stump for a while, just watching her. After about twenty minutes, she disappeared, and moments later, he saw the lights on the second floor go on.

Ah, her bedroom, he thought, and licked his lips. He continued to stare, but she didn't reappear.

He walked back to the car and opened the trunk, and took out a small bag. After checking its contents, he walked back to the house and went through the shadows directly to the basement window.

This would be the best place, he told himself, noting that her car was parked in such a way that even if someone were to drive past, even if they could see through the leafy hydrangea, he'd still be hidden from view.

Perfect.

And there'd be no better place to keep her for a few days, he was thinking, except that she'd be missed and someone would come looking for her. Damn. He'd have loved to play house here for a while.

For once, the water pressure in the shower was fairly decent, and Mia turned it to the maximum setting. She'd have to remember to mention the inconsistent pressure to Connor the next time they spoke. He might want to look into that. Of course, for him, it might not be an issue. For her, having the pressure dip while she had a head full of shampoo was pretty annoying.

She finished rinsing, turned off the water, and stepped out of the shower. She towel dried her hair, then dried off the rest of her. She wrapped up in her favorite robe, then turned on the hair dryer. Sitting on the edge of the small stool, she turned her head upside down and brushed her hair until it was almost dry. When she finished, she turned off the dryer and went into the bedroom. She'd gone three steps when she heard the footfalls on the steps.

She froze where she stood. Her gun was in her bag, on the opposite side of the room. She'd never make it in time.

"Mia?" A voice called from the top of the stairs.

"Damn you!" she shrieked. "Damn it, Connor, that's the second time you did that to me. Would you please announce yourself before you come up the steps all stealthy-like and scare the living shit out of me!"

"I called to you a couple of times," he told her from the other side of the door, "but I guess you didn't hear me. I was halfway up the steps when you turned the dryer off."

"Well, go on back down, give me a minute to get dressed."

"Hey, I'm sorry. Really." She heard him retreat, taking the steps two at a time. "I'll be in the kitchen, making dinner. You haven't eaten yet, have you?"

"Not really. But it had better be a pretty damned fine dinner to make up for the scare you just gave me."

"I'll do my best."

"And Connor . . ."

"Yeah?"

"We have this new invention here. You've been out of the country, so you may have missed it. We use it to communicate with other people." She opened the door and yelled, "It's called a telephone."

She dressed quickly in a short-sleeved sweatshirt and a pair of cut-off jeans and looked under the bed for a pair of flip flops.

"There's some cream cheese and pepper jam and crackers there on the counter." He was at the sink with his back to her when she came downstairs. "And I poured us each a glass of wine."

"Thanks." She gave him a quick hug from behind. "I am happy to see you, but you have to stop doing that."

He laughed. "I swear, I didn't intend to sneak up on you. Believe me, if I had . . ."

"Yeah, I know. I wouldn't have heard you until you were standing right behind me." She grabbed the wineglass and raised the glass to her lips, then sat it quietly on the counter. She opened the refrigerator, noted the supply of food he must have brought with him, and took out a bottle of club soda.

"What are you making?" she asked as she got another glass and filled it with ice and soda.

"Just something simple." He smiled, looking more relaxed than she'd seen in a while. "Salmon, roasted red potatoes, carrots and zucchini. Some fresh figs for dessert."

"That's your idea of a simple dinner? It's way more than I make for myself."

"That's because you can go out and get a great meal whenever you want one. These days, I have to come back to the Chesapeake or go to Essaouria for great fish."

"I don't even know where that is."

"Essaouria? It's a city on the coast of Morocco." He checked the oven's temperature and unwrapped the fish. "There's a hotel in an old villa there owned by some friends of mine. It's where I stop when I'm on my way . . . here and there. They have a chef there who ranks with the best in the world."

"Then why isn't he in Paris, or London? Or New York? Some place people have heard of."

Connor laughed again and juggled three lemons playfully. "He loves the city, loves Morocco, loves the villa. Everyone who goes there loves it. It's beautiful, it's peaceful, and yet it still has that hint of danger that you expect to find in Morocco."

"I'll put it on my list of places to visit."

"Let me know when you decide to go and I'll meet you there." He lined the lemons up on the counter and started to chop up garlic.

"You go there a lot?" She scooped up some pepper jam and cream cheese with a cracker.

"As often as I can."

She finished off the cracker, chewed, swallowed, then asked, "So who is she?"

"Who is who?"

"The girl you keep going back to Essau . . . what was it?"

"Essaouria." He smiled over his shoulder.

"So who's the girl? Who do you go there to see?"

"Like I said, I have friends who own the villa and . . ." He shrugged.

"Don't be evasive. I know when you're conning me." She smiled and added, "Pun intended."

He made himself busy, concentrating on the task at hand, chopping green onions and garlic and opening the jar of chutney.

"There's no one."

"How come?"

"No time these days." He continued chopping, his eyes on the onions as if they held the secret of life. He stopped after a few moments, took a sip of his wine and said, "There is one woman . . ."

"Aha! I knew it!"

"I barely know her. I met her once—the last time I

was there, at the villa. She's American. An archaeologist."

"And . . ." Mia urged him on.

"And I don't know much else about her."

"What's she look like? Start with that."

"She's blond. Pretty. A little shorter than you." He appeared to be considering the question. "She looks fragile, but she can't be, all the time she spends in the field."

"Hair?"

"Short, kind of choppy." He smiled. "Not like stylish choppy, like Livy Bach's." He named a fellow agent who was always at the top of the style game. "Just . . . choppy. As if she did it herself in the field. Which she probably did."

"Eyes?"

"Blue." He responded without hesitation, making his cousin smile.

"Well, who does she look like?" Mia asked. "Does she resemble anyone we know?"

"She just looks like herself."

"What else do you know about her?"

"I don't know a whole lot else." He shrugged. "Except that she spends a lot of time in the Middle East. Turkey, Afghanistan, Pakistan. She was cataloguing some digs or something."

"Isn't that dangerous for a woman in that part of the world these days?"

"From what I've learned about her, she's well respected. She's considered an expert in several fields of interest, I do know that. And she's written a lot, been published, has lectured at some of the major universities here and in other countries."

"Where did you hear all that?"

"From Magda. She and her husband own the villa—and knows her pretty well." He turned and grinned. "And from the Internet."

"You did an Internet search on her? You must be interested." Her eyes twinkled. "What else did you find out about her?"

"Mother's an anthropologist, father's an archaeologist, as is one of her brothers. Oh, and her grandfather was as well. He was famous, discovered some ancient lost city."

"Sounds like quite a gal. Have you made your interest known?"

He shook his head. "There really hasn't been an opportunity. But one of these days . . ."

"How do you know she isn't involved with someone else?"

"Magda would have told me. She's always trying to fix us up."

"Why don't you let her?"

"The time hasn't been right."

"Don't you ever get lonely?" Mia asked.

When he didn't answer, she said, "I do."

"I guess that explains the line-up of wine bottles near the back door."

"Those are from the entire time I've lived here," she told him, "and they're still sitting there because this house is so far out in the fucking sticks no one's even heard of recyling."

"Just seems like a lot of wine for one small person." He turned and she raised the glass of seltzer to him in salute. Seeing it, he said, "So, would you want a little lemon with that?"

She laughed and held out the glass. He cut a small wedge from the lemon and dropped it in.

"Before you ask," she said, "yes, I was starting to depend on the wine to help relax me at night. Too much so. I thought maybe I should try to cut back, you know. Before I had a problem and couldn't cut back on my own."

"Can you?"

She nodded. "Yeah. But I think if I waited much longer . . . maybe not."

"Demons? Ghosts."

She nodded. "A little of both."

"Want to tell me about them?"

"You already know about them." She leaned on the counter. "You know their names."

"Let them go, Mia." His face tightened. "Brendan's in hell, where he belongs. Let him stay there. And Dylan, well, there's nothing anyone can do to bring him back. We all have to move on, get past it. You, me, Annie . . ."

"Does it bother you, that she married someone else, Con?"

"The idea of it did, until I got to know Evan. He loves her. It isn't her fault that she didn't get to marry Dylan and live happily ever after. She's a good person and one of my best friends. She deserves to be happy. So no, it doesn't bother me. At least, not anymore."

He wrapped up the unused onions and returned them to the refrigerator.

"You have to stop hiding behind dead bodies, Mia."

"What does that mean?" Mia frowned.

"That means, stop using your work as an excuse for not having a life." He turned to face her. "You didn't do anything wrong. Stop punishing yourself for what Brendan did. You were not your brother's keeper, kiddo."

"You're a good one to talk." She put the glass down on the counter and crossed her arms over her chest.

"What's that supposed to mean?"

"Don't think I don't know why you keep running all the time, Con. Don't think I haven't noticed that you volunteer for every dangerous assignment that comes along."

"I've been trained for it." He went back to work on the fish. "And I do it better than just about anyone else."

"Don't you ever ask yourself why?"

"No."

Mia studied his back, and recognized the tension in the muscles of his neck. He'd been the intended target that night, and his brother had died instead of him. Surely his burden of guilt was greater than hers. If she could learn to work her way out of hers, perhaps in time he could as well.

She decided to let it go.

"I'm having dinner with Andy and his new girl-friend next week."

"Andy has a new girlfriend?"

"Dorsey Collins, you know her? She's terrific. She's with the Bureau. They're IN LOVE." Mia smiled. "Maybe you can join us if you're still here."

"I'd love to," he told her. "If I'm still here."

"So when did you become such a gourmet?"

"When I started traveling so much. Now when I'm home, I want to stay home. I want to be comfortable and well-fed. If I want to eat well at home, I have to do it myself."

"Yeah, well, if you were serious about being comfortable, you could have bought some furniture that had a little spring to the cushions."

Mia leaned past him to the counter and turned down the radio. She'd left it on when she'd gone upstairs to shower.

"Now, maybe we can talk without shouting." She leaned on the counter and sliced a cracker through the cream cheese on the plate, careful to scoop up a little of the hot pepper jelly before popping it into her mouth.

"Whoa, that's a little spicier than you usually . . ." She stopped mid-sentence. Connor had turned around, and was tilting his head as if listening to something, a look of concerned curiosity on his face. "What is it?"

"The alarm's been tripped." He stood stock still, listening.

"I didn't set an alarm," she whispered.

"I did. It's a sensor and it's always on unless I disable it."

"Great. When were you going to tell me? What if I'd tripped it?"

"You wouldn't have. Unless, of course, you were trying to break in through one of the basement windows." He lifted his jacket and took out a small, lethal looking handgun.

"Connor, I don't hear anything."

"I imagine you don't." He opened the basement door silently, and descended.

Mia ran up the steps as quickly and as quietly as she could, grabbed her own Sig Sauer from her purse, and came back down. She stood at the top of the steps, listening.

She was about to call his name when she heard glass shatter. She ran down the steps and stopped at the bottom to get her bearings.

Connor stood at the window that faced the driveway, broken glass at his feet.

"Get John Mancini on the phone," he told her. "It looks like we've had a visitor . . ."

He looked over his shoulder to meet her eyes. "But I don't know if he was looking for me, or looking for you . . ."

"Who'd be looking for me?" She frowned.

"I don't know. But I do know that only three people know I'm here in the country, and two of them are in this room."

"The third being John."

"Right. So give him a call, and tell him we need a little backup here ASAP."

He started up the steps.

"Where are you going?" She paused in mid-dial.

"I'm just going to take a look around outside." He grabbed a large flashlight from an old wooden workbench and headed up the stairs. "You need to think about what it is you're working on right now, and why someone might want to take you out of the game."

23

Mia listened as the phone rang and rang. Finally, a gruff, "Yes?"

"Beck?"

"Yes."

"It's Mia. Listen, I'm going to be late today. Last night . . ."

"Let me guess. You couldn't get to sleep on your own, so now you're hung over?" His voice held an edge she had not heard there before. "Can't clear your head this morning?"

"I'm going to pretend you did not say that."

"Is that all? Is that what you called for?"

"I just wanted you to know I was going to be late. This was supposed to be a courtesy call, Beck, but I guess you'll see me when you see me." She fought back an urge to curse. It had been a very long night. "How's that for courtesy?"

"Lisa's missing," he said tersely.

"Missing? What do you mean, she's . . ." The words caught in her throat. "Missing? You mean . . . *missing*? You think . . . ?"

"Yeah, Mia. I do. And if you'd answered your phone last night, or maybe checked your voice mail once in a while, you'd already know. So you can un-

derstand why right now I'm not particularly sympathetic to how you feel this morning. I think you need
to get some help if you plan on staying in this line of
work."

The line went dead. She barely noticed.

If the killer had Lisa . . .

She grabbed her bag from the kitchen counter and
hurried outside. Checking for messages on her cell.
Damn. Four missed calls. Two new voice mail messages. She played them back, listening to Beck's terse
voice as she searched for Connor.

A half-dozen agents had been combing the woods
and the fields and every square inch of ground around
the house. So far, they'd found tire prints down the
road and some impressions next to the basement window, but little else.

"I have to go," she told Connor when she found
him hunched over the tire marks, supervising the
young agent who'd drawn the job of photograph-
ing and casting the tires. "I have to leave for St. Dennis."

"Not a good idea, Mia." Connor straightened up.
"We still don't know who was coming after who and
why. It could very well be someone connected to
the case you're working on there, making a move on
you."

"Doesn't matter. If he makes the mistake of coming
after me, he'll wish he hadn't."

"Brave words, little cousin." Connor turned his
full attention to her. "Mia, what's going on?"

"This killer . . . he abducts women and keeps them
someplace. Keeps them alive, rapes them, tortures

them. When he's finished with them, he kills them by
wrapping them up in plastic wrap and watches them
suffocate."

"Jesus."

"Right. Well, he's killed three women that we
know of. And apparently, yesterday he took a fourth
victim. She's a cop, Con. I was just starting to get to
know her. I like her. Just yesterday she was telling me
how happy she was, how she married the man of her
dreams and has this perfect life. And just hours later,
she was gone." She cleared her throat. "I have to go.
You don't really need me here."

"You have someone there who'll watch your back?"

"Beck." She called over her shoulder as she started
down the road. "The chief of police in St. Dennis.
Beck will watch my back . . ."

Mia hustled through the glass doors off the lobby
of the St. Dennis municipal building and into the
miniscule area that served as reception for the police
department. Garland watched her approach, a look
of surprise on his face.

"That's a different look for you," he said.

She looked down at her cutoffs and realized she
was still dressed in the same shorts and T-shirt and
flip flops she'd put on the night before.

"Yeah, well, it's been a busy night." She pointed to
Beck's office. "Is the chief in?"

"He's in, but he's downstairs in one of the interrogation rooms."

"St. Dennis has interrogation rooms?" She
frowned. "You have a holding cell, too?"

"They're pretty much the same room," Garland admitted. "We don't hold prisoners here. If we arrest someone, we usually take them right to the county facility, or over to Ballard, if it's only going to be for the night. We've never had cells here."

"Who's he interrogating?" she asked.

"Mickey." Vanessa stepped through the open conference room door. "Beck's questioning Mickey. He thinks he has something to do with Lisa being missing."

Vanessa's eyes were clouded with tears.

"He won't let me come down there." Vanessa pointed to the steps. "You go on down there and tell him that Mickey couldn't have had anything to do with anything."

"Vanessa, maybe you should go on back to the store." Mia took her arm and tried to steer her gently in the direction of the lobby. "I'll have Beck give you a call when they're finished downstairs, okay?"

"You don't understand, Mia." Vanessa lowered her voice to a whisper. "Beck really doesn't like Mickey at all."

"Trust me. That won't have a thing to do with it. Beck is too professional to allow his personal feelings to influence an investigation." She hoped. No, she knew. Beck was a cop first. "Look, how about if I check downstairs, see what's what. I'll stop over at the shop later, all right? I'll keep you in the loop, I promise."

"Okay." Vanessa nodded.

"Vanessa, are you in love with him? With Mickey?" Mia couldn't help but ask.

"No." She smiled weakly. "But we're friends. He's not capable of doing . . . whatever Beck thinks he might have done. Mickey's had a hard year, with his wife leaving him and all that, but he's a good guy, Mia. He really is."

"I'll keep that in mind." Mia nodded. She watched Vanessa head for the door. "Vanessa," she called out and the young woman turned. "Do you know why she left him? Mickey's wife?"

Vanessa nodded. "She was offered a job with some big hospital in Philly."

"What does she do?"

"She's an E.R. doctor. After the kids were born, she worked part-time, mostly weekends, but then, I guess it just wasn't enough for her. According to Mick, she sent out applications to a bunch of hospitals without telling him, then when she got an offer she liked, she just told him she was leaving and taking the kids. Sad, huh? To just walk like that?" Vanessa shook her head. "Talk about dropping a bomb into someone's life . . ."

"Yeah." Mia nodded. *That would certainly qualify as a life-changing experience . . .*

She knocked on the door, then opened it without waiting to be invited in.

"Beck." She walked into the room as if she'd been expected. "Mickey."

"Agent Shields." Mickey, his eyes dark and angry, glared at her from across the room. "I was just leaving. Unless, of course, the chief here has any more questions . . . ? I am free to leave, aren't I?"

"You're free to leave. Just don't leave town."

Mia stepped back as Mickey passed her on his way out. He stopped in the doorway and looked back at Beck.

"I don't know anything about Lisa Singer being missing, Beck," Mickey said softly. "I swear it on my kids' lives. For Christ's sake, she was my friend."

Beck appeared to have not heard. He neither turned to the door nor did he look up when Mia closed the door after Mickey left the room.

"What's the latest on Lisa?" she asked.

"Same as yesterday. Gone without a trace."

"I ran into Vanessa upstairs."

"She needs to keep her distance from Forbes right now."

"Do you really think he has anything to do with Lisa's disappearance?"

"As far as we know, he was the last person to see her, to talk to her. Until we find someone who saw her after he did, he's our best bet."

"It doesn't feel right."

"Why not? You said yourself he fits the profile."

"I just don't think he's all that smart. I think our killer is much smarter, slicker. He's more sophisticated. Mickey's like, oh, like a big goofy pup. There's nothing playful about our killer."

"Maybe he's smarter than he looks, Mia. Maybe that's a ruse."

"If it is, he's damned good at it." She sat down across the table from Beck. "Beck, I'm really, really sorry that you weren't able to get in touch with me. I left my phone on the kitchen counter and unfortunately, forgot about it. I can't tell you how sorry I am about Lisa. And that I wasn't here for you. Personally and professionally."

He nodded slowly. "It was a long, sad night, Mia."

She reached across the table and took his hand in both of hers. "Start from the beginning. Tell me everything . . ."

"I stopped out at Singer's house around six, but there wasn't anyone there. I stopped at the showroom, but Jay said Todd hadn't gotten back from taking the kids to Annapolis, that he'd called and said he was staying to have dinner with his sister and her family. Then Todd called me at home around eleven. Said he'd just gotten back and Lisa wasn't there. He wanted to know if she was working overtime. I got in my car and I drove up and down every street in town, looking for her car. I called in Hal and Susan and had them search for her, too. This morning I put everyone on it. If she's in St. Dennis, she's hidden pretty damn well."

"Those old buildings you were talking about yesterday . . ." She disengaged their hands.

"Funny you should bring that up. He held up a stack of computer printouts. "Three of the buildings were open—not secured in any way, and they were searched overnight. Oh, there were signs someone had been in them, but it was most likely kids. There were a few comic books, some empty beer cans. Cigarette butts, that sort of thing. There were a few that were pretty well boarded up, though. Hal had someone in records check them out. You'll never guess who they belong to."

"Surprise me."

"Hamilton Forbes." Beck shoved the list across the table. "Mickey's father."

"So you went inside and found . . ."

"Nothing, yet." Beck looked at his watch. "Once Ham knew we'd brought Mickey in and why, there was no point in asking for the keys. He went ballistic."

"I imagine his mother didn't appreciate it much either."

"Christina?" Beck scoffed. "She was the one who insisted Mickey come and talk to me. She says he couldn't possibly have anything to hide, so there was no point making it look as if he did by making him hide behind the family lawyer. She also demanded that Ham hand over the keys to all the properties he owns, which he is refusing to do. So the two of them are at each others throats again."

"And in the meantime, Lisa's still missing."

"Yes." He looked at her with weary cop's eyes. "Lisa is still missing."

"I'm assuming you asked for a warrant . . ."

"I'm just waiting for Hal to get back here with it." He nodded. "I swear to God, if I find a trace of her in any of those buildings . . ."

He pushed back from the table and out of his chair.

"She's a good cop, Mia. One of the best. She's a great mom—she's devoted to her kids, devoted to

Todd . . ." He raked a hand through his hair. "If that bastard has taken her, I swear to you . . ."

"We'll find her, Beck. We'll turn St. Dennis inside out if we have to, but we'll find her."

Duncan buzzed in on the intercom.

"Chief, Hal just called in. Judge Enoch signed the warrants. He said he's on his way down to the river and he'll meet you at the old crabbers' lodge."

"Thanks." Beck headed for the door. "Let's do it," he said to Mia.

She reached for her keys that she'd tossed on the table and followed him up the steps and out the door.

"Garland, call Susan and tell her to stick to Mickey Forbes like a burr on a dog." Beck and Mia passed the dispatcher's desk in a blur. "And find Duncan. He should have been in by now . . ."

Beck stopped outside the front door and cursed.

"What?" Mia asked.

"I meant to call for a rental car. I keep forgetting."

"Where's your cruiser?" She gestured for him to follow her.

"Hal has it. He loaned his car to his brother, Phil, who's on vacation, so I let him use mine. It was actually his, you know?" Beck waited for Mia to unlock the Lexus. "When he was chief. He picked out the options, he ordered the car. Whenever I drive it, I feel like a kid who's borrowed his . . ."

"His father's wheels?" She slid behind the wheel. Without waiting for him to comment, she added, "Nice of you to let him continue to drive it."

"He got shot when he was in 'Nam. Upper left

thigh. He likes to pretend it doesn't bother him, but if he's on his legs for too long, I know it hurts. So I'd just as soon have him use the cruiser. I like to walk around town anyway."

"Which way am I going?"

"Go left on Charles, then straight out to the highway. There are several roads leading down to the river. The old buildings Ham Forbes bought are all within walking distance from each other. One used to be a boat house, another was used by the crabbers who worked the bay. I forget what the third one was used for. Hopefully, not chaining up women and torturing them."

She drove through town, past St. Catherine's Church, the oldest church in town, with it's white spire and rustic cemetery.

"Listen, Mia." Beck shifted uncomfortably in his seat. "About this morning. I'm really sorry for what I said to you on the phone. It was inexcusable. It's none of my business what you do on your time or on anyone else's."

"It's okay. I know how worried you are about Lisa. And it isn't as if I hadn't set myself up for that sort of reaction." She tried to smile. "Ironic that I'd spent the night guzzling club soda instead of my usual beverage of choice. Which, given the way the night turned out, was probably a pretty good thing."

"What do you mean?"

"My cousin Connor came home last night. He was making us dinner when he realized some sensor he'd set in the basement windows had gone off. Guys got ears like a Doberman. I never heard a thing."

"You mean the security alarm went off?"

She nodded. "When we went downstairs to look, we found that someone had been cutting away the glass in one of the basement windows."

"Someone tried to break into your house?"

"Connor's house. We're not sure what they were after." She bit her bottom lip. "He thinks it couldn't have been him, because he says no one knew he was back in the country."

"Which leaves you."

She could feel his eyes on her.

"Why would someone be after you?"

"I don't know that anyone was." She kept her voice steady and her eyes straight ahead. "It could have been just a random burglary."

"Do you believe that?"

"I don't know." She shrugged. "Connor doesn't."

"So that's why you were late."

She nodded.

"Jesus, I feel like a real jerk," he said. "Giving you so much shit about not answering my calls . . ."

"Hey, it's okay. Given the circumstances, you were entitled to be a little testy."

" 'A little testy' is very kind." He touched her shoulder. "Why didn't you call me?" he asked softly.

"Everything just happened so fast. One minute, Connor and I were in the kitchen, getting dinner ready, the next minute, he's flying down the steps with his gun in his hand. Before I knew it, the troops started arriving. Besides, there wasn't anything you could have done from here."

"You had some backup?"

"Our boss sent five or six agents out to process the scene. There were some prints near the basement window where the prowler had been kneeling, I guess while he was cutting away the glass. Then they found some tire prints down the road, which they casted and are trying to match."

"I'd be interested in knowing what kind of tires they were. They're going to try to match them to a vehicle, right?"

"They'll try. Sometimes tires are too generic to get a good match, but other times you get lucky. We had a case last year where we caught a kidnapper by tracing the tires he'd just bought for his van. The treads were so deep, we knew they had to be relatively new, and there were only three places in the area that sold that particular type of tire. We had the guy in less than a day."

"What happened to the victim?"

"It was already too late for her," she said simply.

"Take the next left."

She turned onto a one-lane gravel road that led into a wooded area beyond which she could see the river.

"I have an APB out on Lisa's vehicle, and I've notified the other local agencies and the state. But I want to call in your people to help find her."

"Done." She picked up her phone from the console and tapped in some numbers.

While the phone was ringing, they entered a clearing. A long clapboard building, its paint faded and peeled down to the grayed wood, stood off to their right. The St. Dennis cruiser was parked alongside the building, and Mia pulled up next to it. Beck got out and met Hal halfway between the two vehicles.

"Put me through to John if he's in, please," Mia said when Mancini's secretary answered the call. "And if he isn't there, please find him."

24

Beck pushed open the door of the old building and stepped inside onto ancient chipped linoleum that at one time might have been red. Beneath his feet the floor sagged noticeably, and the stale humid air smelled of wood that had long since gone to rot. A wasp flew repeatedly at a dross-covered window and somewhere down the dark corridor in front of Beck, something scurried along the ground.

Mia finished her call and went into the building a minute or two later. She raised her sunglasses to the top of her head so that her eyes could adjust to the light. From up ahead, she could hear footsteps—Beck's and Hal's—and when she came to a large square room, she stood still to place the others. Off to the right, her senses told her, and she followed, treading carefully on the weak floor.

"Jesus God in Heaven!" Hal seemed to choke with pain.

"Oh, God no."

"Beck!" Mia called to him as she ran, following their voices.

"Sweet Holy Mother of God." Hal was transfixed before the figure that lay sheathed in shiny transparency on the bed.

"Is it . . ." Mia stepped closer. "Oh . . . oh, no . . ."

A stone-faced Beck turned his back on the abomination on the bed and opened his phone. "Garland, find out where Todd Singer is. It looks like we found Lisa. And get Dr. Reilly on the line . . ."

Mia stood with her hands in the pockets of her cut-off jeans, watching the scene unfold. News had spread quickly through the community—complements perhaps of an overly excitable EMT—and before anyone realized what was happening, the anguished husband had arrived and attempted to rush inside the building.

"Where's Lisa? Where is my wife?" Todd had cried, and it had taken both Hal and two newly arrived officers from Cameron to subdue him.

Mia remained apart, studying the scene, taking it in, mulling it over, even as Hal accompanied a distraught Todd Singer to the ambulance where he was given oxygen. When Beck finally emerged, after having secured the crime scene, Mia walked over to him.

"Beck, I'm so sorry. I can't even begin to imagine what you're going through right now." She put a hand on his arm, and he pressed his own hand over hers.

"Thanks." His eyes were murderously dark and haunted. "When I find this bastard . . . when I get my hands on him . . ."

"Look, I understand how upset you are, I know you were friends. I want to get this guy, too. But I need to talk to you." Her hand still on his arm, she led him close to her car. When they were out of hearing range, she said, "Beck, this doesn't feel right."

"What do you mean, doesn't feel right?"

"He just took her yesterday, and she's dead already? That's not his thing. For him, this is all about the power, all about humiliation. Why would he kill her right away, before he'd made her suffer?"

Beck met her eyes momentarily, then looked away when the ME's van pulled up.

"Maybe she fought him off, he got pissed . . ."

"He likes it when they fight back. He wants that. Because he knows that it doesn't matter, in the end, he's going to win." She lowered her voice. "There's something really wrong with this scene."

"Who else would it be?"

"Oh, I think it was him, all right. But why bring her here? It obviously isn't the place where he brought the others. We know he must have a place where he takes them . . . keeps them. Tortures them. We've been all through this building. There's nothing here. So why did he bring her here?"

"What are you thinking?"

"I think he killed Lisa to get her out of the way. I'm pretty sure we're going to find she wasn't suffocated the way the others were. I think she was probably dead when he wrapped her up."

"We won't know for certain until Viv is done with the body." Beck's eyes clouded as he watched the ME's assistant bring out the gurney holding the body, encased in a dark blue bag.

A hush fell over the small crowd that had gathered. The only human sound was Todd Singer's sobbing.

"Beck, maybe something someone told Lisa yesterday tipped her off to something the killer didn't want anyone to know about. Somehow he figured out that she knew and needed to keep her from telling anyone else."

"That would make sense. It's the only thing that does." He stood with his arms folded, looking beyond her to where Lisa Singer's plastic-encased body was being gently loaded into Vivien Reilly's van. He turned and waved Hal over.

"I want Mickey Forbes picked up now and brought in for questioning. Now. Keep him there until I get there."

He turned to Mia. "I'm going with Viv. I'll meet you back at the station."

Mia nodded, understanding that his accompanying the medical examiner was as much to make sure his friend's journey wasn't made alone as to be there when cause of death was determined.

"Sue, make sure Todd gets home all right. Give Jay a call and have him meet you over there so the guy's not alone."

Beck started toward the van, then looked over his shoulder at the three of them: Hal, Sue, and Mia.

To no one in particular, he said, "Has anyone heard from Duncan?"

25

Mia was waiting when the first of the FBI crime scene techs arrived. As she showed them where the body was found and walked them through the building, the more she was convinced that Lisa's death had been, for the killer, a matter of necessity rather than the fulfillment of a fantasy.

"We've been dealing with three crime scenes for each of our victims," she explained to Trish Sterling, one of the first techs on the scene. "The place where he's held them, the place where he killed them, and the place where he disposed of them. In this case, however, it appears we may have all three scenes in one. Most unusual for this offender."

"We'll see what we can find for you," Trish told her as she slipped the plastic booties over her shoes.

Mia pointed to them and said, "Unfortunately, you're going to find a lot of footprints in there. The chief, the former chief, me . . ."

"And no one covered up?" Trish frowned.

"The ME and her guys did. The others . . . we didn't realize we were entering a crime scene."

"Well, you, Shields, have sure kept us busy for the past . . ." Trish looked at her watch. "Looks like eighteen hours or so."

"You were over at Connor's?"

"Yeah." Trish nodded. "When this call came in, I figured I'd take this one, since I was the closest tech."

"Aren't you tired?

Trish grimaced and asked, "Aren't you?" She gathered up her evidence kit and started toward the building. "It was worth it to see your cousin Connor in the flesh. I've been hearing about him for years. Nice when reality lives up to the myth . . ."

Mia watched as several other techs prepared to enter the building. To the last man, she gave her card. "Here's my cell number. Give me a call when you're finished here."

She drove herself back to St. Dennis, the radio off and the windows down to blow out the hot stale air that had been building up since she arrived at the old building earlier in the day. Her stomach reminded her that she hadn't eaten a thing but she had no appetite. That Lisa, of all people, had become a victim made her weak in the knees. Lisa, who had everything, who had so loved her life . . . it just seemed so unfair. Why, she wondered, was Lisa targeted? What had she learned?

Beck suspected that Mickey Forbes was the man they were after. Maybe he was right. He had the opportunity, he had access to the building, and if in fact he'd killed the other women, he would have had a motive, with Lisa asking so many questions right there in what was essentially Mickey's own backyard. If he had been in the company of all of the victims, either at the gym or at the coffee shop or both, sooner or later, someone might have remembered and start putting it all together. Perhaps someone already had, and Lisa had figured out who that someone was. Maybe Lisa had been on her way to speak with that person. Maybe she'd told Mickey before she left the Goal Post . . .

"Maybe," Mia whispered. "Maybe . . ."

She parked in Beck's reserved spot out front of the municipal building and went inside. After the heat of the day, the air conditioning refreshed her. She waved to Garland on her way in and went straight to the kitchen, hoping to find something with some sugar in it. There were three Cokes left, and she took one.

"Garland, have you heard from Beck or Duncan yet? Anyone?" She asked as she popped the lid off the soda can.

"Beck's still out with Viv. He called a few minutes ago and said he thinks he won't be much longer. Hal just picked up Mickey. Sue is still over at Singer's, she said Jay Gannon is on his way over to stay with Todd for a while and as soon as he gets there, she'll be in." Garland's eyes were rimmed with red, as she suspected her own might be. "Do you think it's him? Mickey Forbes?"

"Don't know." She nodded. "Let's see what he has to say, once we get a chance to talk to him."

"Hal says he's lawyered up already."

"Doesn't surprise me."

"Damn this son of a bitch, whoever he is. Of all people . . . *Lisa* . . ."

"I know." She walked behind him and gave his shoulder a squeeze.

"It just sucks that it had to be her," he choked.

_"It sucks that it has to be anyone." She gave his shoulder one last pat and headed back to the make-shift office she'd set up in their conference room.

Mia was debating what to do next—where would she be most useful?—when Connor called her cell to give her an update on the near break-in at the house.

"The techs are done and gone," he told her. "They're going to run the tire prints to see if they can find a match there. That's about the only useful bit of evidence they were able to find. The ground wasn't soft enough to give us good shoe prints."

"So what are you going to do now?"

"I'm going to hang out here for a while, replace the glass in my basement window, and just enjoy being home for a while. You?"

"I'm going to stick here until this is done. A couple of the techs who were at your house were pulled over here, and they're still working the scene."

"Then your friend . . ."

"Yeah."

"I'm sorry, Mia. It's hard enough when it's a stranger, but when the victim is someone you know . . ."

She knew they both had the same "someone you know" in mind.

"Mia? You still there?"

"I'm here." She hesitated, then lowered her voice to a near whisper. "Connor, I don't know how much longer I can do this."

"You need a break, sweetie. It's been a very intense few years with little time off for good behavior. Take some now," he counseled. "Walk away if you need to, for as long as you have to. Forever, if that's what's right for you."

"I'd feel like a traitor," she confessed. "Everyone in the family has been with the Bureau . . ."

"Fuck the Bureau." His voice was firm. "You don't owe the FBI a thing. Look, even your brother Grady had enough sense to know when to leave. You really think he'll ever be back?"

"He lost everything he cared about—at the hands of his own brother."

"Well, it seems to me that as protective as you are toward Grady, you could spare a little of that compassion for yourself."

When she didn't say anything, Connor told her, "Take some time off, Mia. As soon as this case is over, find a place where you feel at peace and sort things out for yourself. Figure out what's best for you. Not what's best for the Bureau, nor for the family. What's best for you. Get yourself together. It's time."

"I'll think about it. Thanks, Connor."

"I'm here if you need me."

"You'll be around for a while?"

"I think so," he told her. "I have a few things to work out, too."

"Then I guess I'll see you soon," she told him before hanging up.

"The chief is on line seven," Garland stuck his head through the door, "and he wants to speak with you."

"Thanks," she said and lifted the receiver of the phone on the table behind her. "Beck?"

"You were right," he said tersely. "Lisa was strangled. She was dead before he wrapped her up. At least she didn't have to suffer through that slow suffocation the way the others did."

"So I'm guessing she was not raped, either," Mia said, and silently gave thanks that Lisa had been spared the agony the other victims had been made to endure.

"Right again. Viv found two little marks on the back of her right shoulder. Looks like she'd been stunned, then strangled, then wrapped up when he was sure she was dead."

"Interesting. That tells us something we didn't already know."

"Yeah, what?"

"It tells us his motive wasn't the same. This time he was motivated not by lust or the thrill of the kill, but to get rid of her as quickly as possible. This is a totally different sort of crime. This wasn't about power or pleasure. It was expediency. He needed Lisa out of the way because she knew something he didn't want anyone else to know, or he was afraid she was about to find out something he felt he needed to protect."

"Like his identity."

"That would be my guess. And he knew her well enough to know he'd have to immobilize her if he was going to kill her. And that he'd have to kill her fast or he wouldn't be able to subdue her. She looked like she was in pretty good shape, she would have put up one hell of a good fight."

"Lisa was very strong, and she was in great shape," Beck agreed. "Anyone who knew her would know that. Of course, just about everyone in St. Dennis knew her."

"I think the killer knew Lisa really well. I think he wanted to kill her quickly to get it over with—not just for her sake, but for his. I think this one was a hard kill for him."

"Interesting observation." He fell silent for a moment. "Mickey Forbes would certainly fit."

"He knew Lisa that well?"

"They were engaged, before she met Todd."

"Well, shit. There is no end to the surprises you find in these little towns." She thought that bit of news over for a moment. "You really think he would have killed her?"

"To tell you the truth, I wouldn't have thought he'd have killed anyone, but God knows I could be wrong about that. He sure got ahold of his lawyer fast enough. Ham's lawyer was waiting for them when they arrived over at the Cameron station."

"Why did Hal take him to Cameron?"

"We don't have a holding cell. We have a room we use when we need to keep someone for a very limited time, but we aren't set up to keep a murder suspect. I'm sure they're going to go for bail, and that's going to take a while. I'd feel better if Mickey was in a secure place."

"Is Hal going to stay in Cameron?"

"No need to. Rich Meyer can handle the situation. Right now, Hal's over talking to Christina."

"I imagine she'll have plenty to say."

"She always does."

"Did you tell Vanessa?"

"Yeah." He exhaled loudly. "She had plenty to say, too."

"Guess I'll see you when I see you."

"I shouldn't be too much longer here. I expect to be back within the hour." He paused, then said, "By the way, when was the last time you ate?"

"Last night. The break-in interrupted what had promised to be a great dinner."

"If you can hold off until I get back there, I'll buy."

"You're on," she told him. "I'll be here."

Mia drained the last of the soda from the can, then took it into the kitchen and dropped it in the recycling bin. She poked around the snack tray, one of those cardboard displays that offered snacks on the honor system, and passed over the candy bars for a bag of peanuts. She searched her pockets for coins, came up with a dollar, which she fed into the slot. Once the dollar was in, there was no getting change, so she grabbed a bag of chips and took both back into the conference room. She'd just rounded the corner when Garland called her name.

"Duncan's on the phone. He said he needed to talk to you or the chief right away," he told her.

"Which line?"

"Two. But the connection is poor. I don't know what it is with these cell phones this week . . ."

"Duncan? Mia Shields here. Where are you? The chief's been looking for you all day."

"He told me to check out all the abandoned buildings in St. Dennis, so that's what I've been doing."

"Why didn't you call in sooner?"

"The reception over on this side of town isn't too good."

"Where are you now?"

"I'm in the basement of the old bank building over on Locust," he told her. "I think I've found the place where . . ."

The voice faded out.

"What? You found what? Duncan?"

"I said, I think . . ." The line went dead.

"Damn it." She muttered as she swung her bag over her shoulder and hurried down the hall.

"Garland, do you know where there's an old bank building? I think he said Locust Street?"

"Oh, Locust Lane, sure." He nodded. "Right on Charles for a block, left onto Locust for two. It's a red brick building, only property on that corner. Is that where Duncan was calling from?"

"Yes. He found something, but I couldn't understand what he was saying. I'm going to run over there and see what's what."

"You want some backup?"

She looked around. "What backup? There's no one else to go. I think he might have found the place where Mickey had been keeping his victims. If that's the case, I'll call the techs in from the other scene and have them start processing it.

She left the building and got into her car. She arrived at the old bank in less than three minutes. Duncan's patrol car was parked across the street. Mia parked behind the cruiser, then got out of her SUV and stood on the sidewalk and looked around. The house on the opposite corner had a for sale sign on its over-grown lawn. Across the street was a park with the frame of a swing set but no swings. This must be one of the areas Beck was talking about when he said there were neighborhoods prime for renovation, she thought.

She crossed the street, assessing the old bank. At one time, it must have been an imposing structure. Even now, with the front windows boarded up, it was handsome, all brick with white pillars and faded black shutters. She walked up the front steps and tried the door, which was securely locked. She came back down the steps and followed a path worn into the grass that wound around to the back of the building, trying each door she came upon. As she searched for an opening, she dialed Beck's phone, but the call failed. She tried again, but met with failure each time. Damn dead zones. Finally, she gave up and dropped the phone into her jeans pocket. As she rounded the back of the building, she found a door that stood ajar. She pushed it open, and went inside.

The door opened onto a landing, with steps going straight up, and steps to the left going down. She hesitated, listening for some sound, but the building was silent. He'd told her he was in the basement, so she took the steps leading down.

"Duncan?" she called out. "Duncan?"

The windows alongside of the building shed some bit of light in the room directly at the bottom of the steps, but the long hallway that stretched ahead of her grew darker as it fed into the heart of the building. She waited until her eyes adjusted, then followed the hall, her hand opening her bag and closing on her Sig.

Well, this is certainly creepy, she thought and wondered for a moment if she should have had backup.

I'm the backup, she chided herself. *There was no one else. And the suspect is in custody. Jesus, if you can't handle being in a dark building after nine years in the FBI, you should probably be selling real estate.*

"Duncan?"

She ducked as something white flew at her, causing her heart to all but leap from her chest.

"Pigeons," she grimaced as it flapped past her. "I really don't like pigeons . . ."

Up ahead, at the end of the hall, was a closed door. A hint of light bled out from underneath, and she headed for it.

"Duncan?" she called as she pushed the door open and stepped into the room.

Hands grabbed her from behind and a voice whispered something unintelligible in her ear.

Searing pain, hot and white and sharp as a bolt of lightening, punched her squarely in the back between her shoulders. The last thing she saw before she blacked out was Duncan's body stretched out before her on a bed covered with a bloody sheet.

26

Mia forced her eyes open, then squinted against the blaze of light that blinded her from every direction. She twisted and tried to turn over, but found she could not move. It took several minutes for her foggy brain to figure out that she was flat on her back on a narrow bed against a wall in a small yellow room. Her mind felt like mush. She tried to raise her hands but could not move her arms, tried to pull her legs up but they, too, remained motionless.

Good Lord. Duncan. Had she really seen him . . . ?

"Duncan . . ." she whispered.

"Ah, there you are. Welcome back."

A man sat just a few feet from the side of the bed, but with the harsh light in her eyes, she could not make out his face.

"Duncan . . ." she repeated.

"Duncan had to go," the man told her. "He got in the way."

Her brain was still fogged from the charge she'd taken from the Taser. She wet her lips and attempted to sit up again. She struggled against the leather straps that bound her ankles and wrists to the metal bed frame.

"Feeling vulnerable, Agent Shields?" He leaned in

close and traced a finger from her neck to her navel, and that was when she realized to her horror that she'd been stripped naked.

"I've had my eyes on you from the day you arrived in St. Dennis." His mouth was close to her ear. "And now I have you."

"Todd?" She blinked, still trying to focus.

"Ah, you remember me." He pulled back from her. "I'm flattered."

"Lisa's husband . . ."

"Make that, the grieving widower."

"*You* killed her? How could you have done that?"

"How could I not? After you came up with that profile the other night, she was watching me, I know she was." He pulled his metal folding chair closer. "It fit me like a glove. I'm surprised no one else realized it. Trauma at an early age . . . my parents died in a car accident when I was three, did she tell you that?"

She shook her head.

"Or that our grandparents raised us, me and my sister? That they used to bring us here for the summer? God, I hated it." He got up and began to pace. "A toney boarding school during the school year, then in the summer, they brought me here. You can imagine how well I fit in with all the fishermen's kids. To say they weren't very kind to a boy like me would be an understatement."

"Then why did you move back here?"

He shrugged. "I inherited the big house, the land along the waterfront. I built the marina, the showroom." His smile was pure satisfaction. "I got to be a very big fish in a very small pond. Even the townies who'd made my life a living hell when I was a kid came around."

"Even while you were thinking about ways of getting even with them."

"I'd thought of that a long time ago."

"Lisa . . ."

"Lisa should have stayed home with her children where she belonged," he snapped.

"What happened to the grieving husband?"

"What better way for a grieving husband to get through the pain of losing his beloved wife than to have a handy replacement." He reached over and drew a delicate circle around her right breast with his index finger. "Sort of like getting back on the bike after falling off, if you know what I mean. So we're going to play a little house. I'm going to be the daddy, and you're going to be the mommy . . ."

"You stupid son of a bitch, the FBI is going to be all over you before you can blink." She struggled against the bindings.

"Oh?" He blinked several times, then looked around. "I don't see anyone."

"Duncan told me what he'd found. I told Garland to send the techs here to process . . ."

"Process all they want. I'll be long gone by the time they get here. And so will you, pretty Mia."

"It won't take Beck long to figure out what you've done, Todd."

"Beck's a fool. He's got Mickey Forbes locked up and he's not looking beyond him. Besides, he's too busy mourning my wife." He stared at Mia, then asked, "Do you think they were lovers?"

"Beck and Lisa? Are you crazy?" *Well, duh. What a stupid question.* "They were friends. He liked and respected her. And she adored you."

Mia almost choked on her words. "She told me you were her dream man."

"Yes, well. Of course I was." He looked away from her face. "Don't think killing her was easy for me. She was a very good mother to my children."

"Is that all you can say about her? That she was a good mother to your children?"

"That was all she had to be. That was her function. She did it well. I was sorry to have to kill her, for their sakes. They'll be very unhappy when they find out she's dead."

"They'll be even more unhappy when they find out who killed her."

"You talk too much, you know that?" He took a white cloth out of his pocket, then forced it into her mouth. "There. That's better. Now you truly are the perfect woman."

She cursed behind the gag and he laughed.

"Do you like the water, Mia? I hope so." He ran a hand over her bare arm and her stomach roiled. "I have it all worked out. There's a boat down at the marina all stocked and ready to go. We'll be living and loving on the high seas, won't that be romantic? We can sail to the ends of the earth together. I have it all planned."

She struggled against the restraints and he laughed again.

"Eager to get started, are you?" He glanced at his

watch. "It won't be long now. As soon as it gets dark, my sweet. As soon as it gets dark . . ."

He started whistling a tune it took her a few minutes to place. The chorus from Pink Floyd's "Southern Cross."

Todd rose from the chair and stood over her.

"You really are quite beautiful, you know that?"

He ran his fingers through her hair and fanned it out around her head, and she cringed at his touch. He smiled, then lowered his head, and licked her stomach. She drew away from him, drew into herself, and in spite of the heat, she chilled to the bone.

This cannot be happening to me. This cannot be happening . . .

She thought of all the many victims she'd seen in the past, all of rape victims and the murder victims whose stories she'd heard and then forgotten, as their stories were replaced by those of other victims. They'd been women just like her, just as vulnerable, just as frightened. Their lives just as important as hers, their loves as deep, their dreams just as real. And surely they all had been just as surprised as she was to find themselves a victim.

And soon, she'd be just as dead.

She thought of Colleen Preston's sad good-bye to her parents, Holly Sheridan's sobbing declaration of love, and wondered if she'd be given the chance to leave something for her father, her brothers.

There were so many people she loved, so many who loved her.

The thought occurred to her then that there were those who would go after Todd with a vengeance, who would not rest until he was utterly destroyed. Andy—her brother would go to the ends of the earth to find Todd. Connor—he knew people in every dark corner of the world. There'd be no place on the planet where Todd would be safe, no place Connor could not track him.

And Beck . . . ? She wondered. Would Beck join in the hunt? And if so, would it be revenge or justice he'd be seeking?

It gave her some small measure of comfort—her one small bit of consolation—to know that, in the end, there would not be enough of Todd left to make a positive identification.

27

Beck was beat, hot, and angry by the time he got back to the station. There were circles under his eyes and an air of sadness about him.

"You hear from Duncan yet?" He asked Garland, who held up a hand in gesture to Beck to indicate he was on the phone.

"I'm sorry, but the department has no comment at this time," Garland was telling the caller. "I will tell Chief Beck that, I certainly will. That won't be necessary. I think he knows how to contact your station . . ."

Garland disconnected the call. "Unbelievable. I can't understand how the word got out so fast." He held up a handful of slips of paper. "Here. It isn't that I don't trust voice mail . . ."

"I'd rather have it written down anyway," Beck told him as he scanned the messages.

"Chief, I can't believe that Lisa . . ."

"Neither can I." Beck started toward his office, then turned back and asked, "Where is everyone? Has Duncan turned up yet?"

"He called in a little while ago. He wanted to talk to you or to Agent Shields. She took the call. He said he was over at . . ."

The phone rang and he reached for it.

"Let it go. Duncan was where? We've been looking for him all day." Beck walked back toward him.

"Duncan told her he was over at the old bank building on Locust and he wanted her to meet him there. She said he found something, she thought it might be the place where the killer kept his victims but the connection was bad so she wasn't sure." He shook his head. "Geez, Chief, I still can't believe Mickey . . ."

"What time did she leave?"

"Oh, it couldn't even be a half-hour yet."

"Has she called in?"

"No."

An uneasy feeling clawed at him. If Duncan had found something and Mia was with him, why hadn't one of them called to let him know what they had?

"Get Susan, tell her to meet me there. And Hal. Get Hal over there."

Beck went out the door and started across the parking lot. No car. He'd have to walk. With every step, his anxiety grew. Why hadn't Mia called him?

Why hadn't one of them called in?

He broke into a run. A few short blocks to the corner, one down Charles, a few more to the bank building. He was out of breath by the time he reached Locust Lane.

As he drew closer to the bank, he noticed three vehicles parked opposite the bank. Duncan's patrol car. Mia's Lexus. And another, partly obscured in front of the Lexus. The setting sun cast shadows on both sides of the street, so Beck had to step into the roadway to get a better look. He expected to see Mickey Forbes's black Mercedes parked in front of Mia.

What he saw was Todd Singer's black sedan.

Beck stopped in the middle of the street, piecing it all together.

Why wasn't Todd home with his kids?

Why . . . ?

Jesus God, if he had Mia . . .

"Son of a bitch," he swore as he turned and ran toward the building. "You son of a bitch . . ."

He tried each door, as Mia had done. When he found the door at the back of the building open, he radioed back to the station and told Garland to get any available law enforcement agents—St. Dennis, Cameron or Ballard P.D. or the FBI, he didn't care which—on the scene ASAP. Drawing his gun, he slipped inside the building, and went down the steps.

The door at the end of the hallway was partially open, and bright light spilled out on to the floor. Beck crept along the wall, hugging the shadows, his ears straining against the silence. As he came closer to the light, he heard a voice. He paused to listen. One voice or two?

One voice. Todd's.

Then where was Duncan?

Beck stepped closer, closer. Still against the wall, still in the shadows, until he was close enough to see inside the room.

Mia lay naked on the bed, her wrists and ankles tied with straps that were secured to the bed frame. Todd stood with his back to the door. Beck knew he'd only have one chance to do this right. If Todd had murdered his own wife—if he'd killed the others—taking Mia's life would mean nothing. In that moment, it occurred to Beck that to him, it meant more than he'd realized.

Todd leaned over Mia, and Beck saw his chance. He slipped through the door, his gun raised.

"Why Lisa?" Beck asked. "Why, Todd?"

"She figured it out. I know she did. She spent all morning at The Coffee Counter, someone would have told her." Todd raised his head.

"Told her what?"

"That I knew the girls. That I'd been talking to them. She called me, said she needed to talk to me about something. What else could it have been?"

"I don't know, Todd. What do husbands and wives talk about?"

"She *knew*. And it was her, or me." Todd sneered. "It wasn't going to be me."

"How could you do that to your own wife?"

"Like I said—her or me . . ."

"How'd you do it, Todd?" Beck asked. "How'd you get to them?"

"The girls?" Todd turned to him very slowly. "Have you ever met a young girl who wouldn't jump at the chance for a few days at the beach? Especially when the rent is ridiculously low . . ."

"You met them at The Coffee Counter. Nice friendly atmosphere, easy conversation . . ."

"Non-threatening, that's the key, Beck." Todd smiled. "You go in at the same time every day, you see the same people all the time. You chat a little, you develop a relationship, you understand?"

"So when you mentioned you had a beach house to rent out . . ."

"Like taking candy." He nodded. " 'Gosh, the family we rented to for next week had to cancel, you know anyone who might like to get away for a few days? We kept the deposit, so we'd let them have it cheap if they promise not to tell anyone . . .' "

"And of course they bit."

"Every time. Then it was just a matter of me meeting them someplace to turn over the key. A little Taser . . . a little rope . . ." He smiled. "Let the fantasy begin . . ."

"Fantasy time is over, Todd." Beck took a step toward him. In a flash, Todd's arm shot out, grabbed the chair and swung it at Beck's head. Before Beck could get a shot off, Todd ran through a door in the back of the room.

Beck pulled the cloth from Mia's mouth.

"Are you . . . ?"

"Just get him . . ." she gasped.

Beck took a pen knife from his pocket and slashed the cords that bound Mia's wrists, handed the knife to her, and then took off after Todd.

The hall leading from the room wasn't lit nearly as brightly as the hall that had led into it. Beck paused on the other side of the door and listened. There, from off to his right, he heard a scuffling sound.

Cautiously, Beck proceeded toward the sound, trying to keep his back to the wall and his sight straight ahead while still being aware of either side. He entered another room, and hesitated, perhaps a moment too long. From out of the shadows, Todd lunged at him, slamming Beck against the door, knocking the gun from his hand. By the time Beck scrambled to his feet and found the gun, Todd had escaped through the open door.

From the end of the hall, he could hear the sound of running feet, then of a slamming door.

Then shouts . . . gunshots . . . silence.

Beck rushed back to the room where he'd left Mia. From the end of the hall, he heard voices. Hal, maybe. He prayed it was Hal.

He found Mia sitting up, hunched over on the bed, her knees drawn up to her chest and her head down. She was visibly shaking.

"Mia, it's going to be all right now." Beck unbuttoned his shirt as quickly as he could. "They have him. I'm pretty sure they have him now . . ."

He helped her into the shirt.

"I'm afraid it's a little dirty. Maybe a little sweaty . . ." he told her, "but I don't know where he put your things . . ."

As her arms slid into the sleeves, she looked up and said, "When I told Connor you'd have my back, I never expected you'd give me the shirt off it."

She began to cry softly and tried to work the buttons, but her fingers were shaking too hard. "Get it?

That's cop humor. You gave me the shirt off your back . . ."

"Right. I got it." He finished the buttons for her, then knelt on the floor next to the bed. He eased her head onto his shoulder and wrapped his arms around her, rocking her gently. "I got it . . ."

28

The cemetery had been hot as hell, the July sun unmerciful and the humidity about as high as it could get, but nothing could have kept Beck from standing next to his friend until her casket was lowered into the ground. Even after the other mourners had gone, he'd returned, and stayed by the hole in the ground until it was filled. When the dirt atop the grave had been tampered down, the men assigned to the task had nodded to him, and left him there.

The world was not a good place, it occurred to him, when a woman like Lisa could fall in love with a psychopath like Todd Singer, and be murdered for it. She'd been a great friend, a great cop.

She'd even been a great wife to that murdering bastard.

His thoughts still dark, he walked back to the station. His Jeep had been released, but today he needed to walk off some of the anger. Besides, it was too quiet back at the station, with Duncan and Lisa gone. Mia, too. Her cousin had arrived in St. Dennis within an hour of Beck's rescuing her from the bank, and had taken her away, just like that.

Well, she was a fed. Of course they were going to want to take care of her. Her statement had been

taken and faxed to him. He wouldn't really have
cause to speak with her again until Todd's trial. Assuming there was a trial . . .

He took the long way back, sticking to the side
streets that led close to the river and wound around
behind the municipal building. It seemed that the entire town had turned out for Lisa's funeral, but he had
no desire to bump into anyone right now. He knew
from past experience that those who hadn't gathered
at Captain Walt's to rehash the service and discuss
who gave the most moving memorial would be at
Lola's doing pretty much the same. He'd just as soon
keep to himself for a while. He'd had enough of the
press coverage—the ever-present television cameras
and the print reporters—to last a lifetime.

The frenzy had started at almost the same moment
that he'd brought Mia out of the basement of the
bank. Someone had picked up the radio call for backup, and for the past four days, images of Mia in
Beck's shirt being led to the waiting ambulance were
juxtaposed with pictures of a handcuffed Todd Singer
being led to a waiting cruiser by Hal on one side and
Susan on the other. The papers doled out bits and
pieces of the story in screaming headlines from, *Bay-
side Heir Serial Killer!* to, *FBI Beauty Intended Victim! Bank Chamber of Horrors—Nine Unidentified
Bodies Found in Vault!*

By the time he got back to Kelly's Point Lane, he
was sweating under the collar of his shirt, which he
started to unbutton as soon as he hit the front door.
He waved at Garland and continued on to his office.

"You have a visitor in the conference room," Garland told Beck as he passed.

"Don't you want to know who it is?" Garland called after him.

"Not particularly."

Beck thought he'd just ignore the unannounced visitor, whomever it might be, for as long as possible. He was in no mood for company.

He passed the conference room without looking through the open door, going straight to his office and removing his jacket. From there he went into the kitchen and got a bottle of water from the refrigerator. He wet a paper towel and cooled off his face. Feeling almost human again, he headed for the conference room, the bottle still in his hand.

He walked into the room half expecting another member of the press or another one of the Forbes family lawyers. There'd been several who'd called over the past few days wanting to discuss some proposed legal action against him and the town for the false arrest of Mickey Forbes.

The last person he expected to see when he stepped into the room was Mia.

She was sitting in the same place she'd been when he first saw her, that first day she'd come to St. Dennis to investigate the body that had been left in his Jeep.

"Hey," she said.

"Hey." He walked toward her, smiling broadly. "How are you feeling?"

"Much better, thank you."

"Good, good." He nodded. "I was wondering. I

wasn't sure how to get in touch with you. I guess I could have called the FBI . . ."

"Depending on when you made the call, they may or may not have had a listing for me." She rested her arms on the table. "I've resigned from the Bureau."

"Whoa." His eyes widened. "I wouldn't have expected that."

"It just got to be too much." She sat back as if studying his reaction. "I love law enforcement, it's been my whole life. I don't know anything else. But I can't take the constant parade of psychopaths and serial killers and baby killers and . . . well, you get the idea. It's time I made a change."

"What will you do?" He leaned on the back of the nearest chair unable to take his eyes off her.

"Before I do anything, I have to get my head together. Deal with some issues I had tried to ignore for a while. There are some things I can't handle on my own. I tried, but . . ." She shrugged.

"The situation with your brother . . ."

"That's at the heart of it all." She nodded. "I haven't had to drink myself to sleep in over a week, but that doesn't mean the problem is resolved. Obviously I have some dependency issues. So I'm going to be seeing someone who can help me to sort things out."

"Do you think you'll go back to the Bureau?"

"No." She shook her head.

"Won't you miss it?"

"Honestly, no." A half-smile touched her lips. "Like I said, I love law enforcement, but I've had my fill of the intensity. For the past nine years, I've seen misery and suffering and evil that most people could not even believe exists. I'm ready to move on."

"You ever think about being a small town cop?"

"Actually, I have."

"I'm going to have to replace Lisa and Duncan." His eyes darkened to speak of it aloud. "Not immediately, but soon. For a while, Hal is going to work full time, and his brother, Phil, came back to pitch in. By the end of the summer, I'll be looking for at least one new cop. If you're interested . . ."

"How many serial killers do you normally see in a year?"

"Not counting this one? None."

"Homicides?"

"Two that I remember."

"Rapes? Kidnappings?"

"Again, except for this year . . . maybe one or two rapes in a calendar year."

"What's the most common crime in St. Dennis?"

"Shoplifting."

"Child abductions?"

"We had a few kids get separated from their parents at the Fourth of July fireworks. Does that count?"

"I'll keep your offer in mind. I'll be around for a while."

"You will?"

"I have a room at Sinclair's Cove for the next few weeks. In the main house, this time."

She smiled and added, "Dan Sinclair mentioned that the last time I stayed there, your cruiser was in the parking lot when he went to bed around one in the morning and it was still there when he woke up at five." Her eyes narrowed. "You didn't sleep in your car all night, watching out for me, did you?"

"No." He shook his head. "Actually, I slept in the chair."

"What chair? The lawn chair?"

He nodded.

"Well, that would explain the crabby mood you were in on Tuesday morning."

"Was I crabby?"

"Very." She was smiling. "Thank you."

"You're very welcome."

"And thank you for saving my life."

"That, too." He nodded.

"What do you think was the trigger?" She asked.

"What set Todd off?" He thought it over. "You and Annie both mentioned something in his life that changed. The only thing I know of is that Lisa was spending a lot more time on the job, a lot less at home, and becoming a lot more assertive. A lot more confident, more sure of herself. Did that carry over at home, too? Maybe. I don't know. Todd's the only one who can answer that, and his lawyers aren't letting him talk."

"Sooner or later, he will. They all do. They can't help themselves. Smart of Hal, shooting to wound, not to kill. Shooting would have been too easy a way for Todd to die."

"Agreed." He nodded. "So, you think you'll be around for a while."

"Connor's back and isn't sure how long before his next assignment. He needs his space. It's his house.

Besides, he said something to me about finding a place where I feel at peace. In spite of everything that happened here, I like St. Dennis. I like the people I met here . . . Vanessa, Hal . . . you. I feel at home. I'd like to see if there's something more for me here."

"Besides a job?"

"A job is a good place to start."

"How about ice cream?" He stood up.

"I love ice cream." She pushed out of her chair.

"Soft-shelled crabs?"

"One of my favorites."

"Which would you like first?"

"Oh, ice cream, definitely." She reached out her hand and he took it. "Life's short, Beck. I'm thinking dessert first . . ."

Turn the page for more gripping suspense
from *New York Times* bestselling author
Mariah Stewart

Last Breath

Coming from Ballantine Books in hardcover

October 1908
On a hill in Asia Minor

The sun had not yet risen, but the man climbing the hill was already dressed and warming his hands around a cup of strong Turkish coffee. Under his arm he held a leather folder, and when he reached the top of the hill, he sat on a rock that overlooked the camp and opened the folder. He removed a sheet of pale ivory paper and began to read over the letter he'd written only moments before.

My most darling Iliana,
*   I am praying this letter finds you feeling well and in good spirits, and that our sons are helping to fill the hours until my return. You will be happy to know that I will be home soon, and that in the past few weeks, we have prepared to take our leave of this wondrous place. As much as I long for the warmth and comfort of you and our home, I cannot deny the pangs of sadness I feel at having to leave behind this city where the dreams of my lifetime have been realized. If only I could describe to you*

*the feeling that grows inside me when I stand
and gaze down upon the ruins of this once-grand
city, this city where potters and weavers,
engineers and farmers, glassblowers and jewelers
once plied their trade. There is the temple
where they worshipped their goddess,
Ereshkigal—I believe I have told you that the
people of Shandihar had borrowed bits from
other cultures, not the least of which was
Mesopotamia—and the ancient marketplace
where the merchants offered their wares to the
caravans passing through. This place where
the homes of the wealthy once stood, and now
their tombs, the contents of which I cannot
recount to you. Soon, however, you will see
with your own eyes what your husband has spent
his life in search of . . .*

"Dr. McGowan," a voice called from below.

"Yes, John?" Alistair McGowan turned to the sound.

"We are ready to begin loading the camels. Will you come?"

"Yes. Give me just a moment." He finished reading the letter, then placed it in an envelope. Once back in his tent, he would seal it with wax, then hand it to the member of his team who'd leave the camp before the others to arrange for passage from Constantinople to England, and then from England to America. It would be a long and costly journey, but the expense would be more than worth it. He closed his eyes and tried to imagine the look on the face of his benefactor when he saw what Alistair had found buried in the desert sands, and a thrill of anticipation surged through him from head to toe.

But that moment was months away, and so he took one long last look at the mountains in the distance and the valley below. Over the past nine years, he'd come to love and respect this desolate place, and as thrilled as he was to have found the object of his quest, his leaving was not without some regret, because he knew he'd never return.

He slapped his hands on his thighs, then stood. Time to get his caravan packed and on its way. Time to leave Shandihar with whatever secrets yet remained, and begin the long journey home.

He'd made that journey before—this was his fifth trip to these hills—but this time, unlike in the past, he'd be bringing back a king's ransom. The find of a lifetime. Proof that the legendary city of Shandihar had indeed existed, and vindication of all the years he'd been ridiculed for chasing what others considered nothing more than a wisp of smoke. He'd not only found the city, he'd found its people, its art and its literature, its gods and its treasures. All because he'd refused to give up, refused to believe the skeptics.

It had not been easy.

As a young and promising archaeologist, Alistair McGowan was twenty-seven when he'd first petitioned his university for funding of an expedition to search for the fabled city, but had been denied time and again. Then fate, in the guise of a newly chartered university led by the forward-thinking and very wealthy Benjamin Howe, lured him with the promise of sufficient backing to send his expedition to Turkey to follow his dream. Alistair promptly set out to meet with Howe, and Benjamin Howe had been true to his word. Everything Alistair wanted or needed was supplied, not only that year, but the next, and the next, and the one following that. If Howe was becoming discouraged, he never let on, which had only fueled Alistair's determination to find the city and its treasures, and bring them home.

And this time, he would.

The sun now risen, he finished the last of his coffee and fixed the sight in his memory, mindful of how much he would miss this place once he'd returned home. Finding Shandihar, uncovering its secrets, hidden for centuries, was, in a way, almost bittersweet. Frustrating though it had been at times, in his heart he'd loved the game. He closed his eyes and recalled the day he'd uncovered the the tombs where the treasures of the goddess had all but spilled into his hands. A heart-stopping fantasy of gold and jewels that until that moment, had existed only in his mind. He closed his eyes and relived that moment when he'd glimpsed beyond the stone wall into the interior and knew it was all real. His heart had been pounding, his eyes clouded with a murky mix of dust and tears, the tool shaking in his hand. He'd fought the urge to plow through, choosing instead to painstakingly remove each block of the outer wall, one by one, until there was room enough to pass through.

Once inside, mesmerized by the beauty of the unfathomable riches, he'd stood by patiently while all was carefully photographed. It had taken forever, but he knew that what he'd found was a treasure for the ages, and he was determined to treat the inhabitants of the tomb with the respect they deserved. Here was a find as great as that of Troy, and no one in the archaeological community would be accusing Alistair McGowan of carelessness as they had Heinrich Schliemann.

Yes, Alistair McGowan had loved the game, but the game was now over. It was time to gather the spoils.

From deep in the shadows, a figure watched the foreigner enter the sacred places that the descendants of the Holy Scribes had guarded for more than two thousand years. Below him, the camp was coming alive. Helplessly he watched as sacred artifacts were packed into wooden crates for the journey that would steal his heritage forever.

"Forgive me, Goddess. I have failed you," he murmured into the wind.

"We have all failed." A second figure stepped out from behind the rock. "But what can we do? We are few, and they are many. Their strength is in numbers, and we two are all that remain."

"Then we must increase our numbers until the strength is ours. However long that takes."

He turned to his brother and rested a hand on his shoulder. "It's time to join the others."

"We will be struck down for helping them to commit this abomination."

"The desecration has been done. By accompanying them, we will know for certain the destination. And when the time comes, we will reclaim the sacred icons and return the goddess to her home." His face hardened in the dawn light. "If it takes a millennium. The faithful will remember."

The first man drew his cloak around him against the cool morning breeze and started down the mountain. His brother hesitated before following, whispering aloud, "The faithful will remember. . . ."

April 2007
Northwestern Iran

In the bottom of the earthen pit, a hand of bone lay across a forearm, and boney fingers rested on what had once been the cheek of a beloved. The two skulls lay side by side, their foreheads touching, eyeless sockets gazing eternally into eyeless sockets. From above, faces stared down at the unique find, most definitely unexpected in this part of the world. Here one was more likely to discover swords and knives, perhaps the bronze or silver sidepiece of a horse's bridle. In some graves, a beloved horse had been buried with its rider. But lovers buried together, still locked in an embrace, *that* was a find.

"Have you ever seen anything like this, Dr. McGowan?" Sayyed Kasraian, the excavation director on the dig high in Iran's Zagros Mountains, crouched at the side of the opening.

"Never." Daria McGowan carefully knelt beside the top of the pit, shining a flashlight on the skeletal remains three feet below. "Not just the positioning of the two figures, but the artifacts that were buried with them . . . it takes my breath away."

She moved the light as a pointer.

"Look there, the one is wearing some type of diadem, from here it looks like gold and lapis, see how blue? And the breastplates, also gold . . . rings on the fingers of all four hands, so we're looking at the remains of some very prominent lovers." She looked up at the Kurdish laborers who'd accompanied them, and said, "Gentleman, we may even be in the presence of royalty."

Two of the men smiled, the third shifted uneasily and looked away, afraid, no doubt, of attracting the notice of any spirits that might still be lurking within the grave.

"And over here, see, glass bottles, dozens of them. They must have held water or wine or some type of oil that the dead would have wanted to take with them on their journey into the next world. And there, at the feet, see the bones?" She hopped into the pit, careful to land on the excavated area around the remains. "These appear to be canine."

She directed the light onto the skull, and her companion studied it from above for several minutes.

"It does look like a dog, doesn't it?" He smiled. "Well, that would be something new. I haven't seen that before. Not in this area, at any rate."

She knelt as carefully as she could to more closely examine the human remains.

"These two must have had a long and happy life together," she murmured. "The teeth are quite worn. They were elderly—for their time—when they died. Definitely a man and a woman, judging from the pelvic bones." She glanced up at the man whose face loomed above hers. "We're so accustomed to finding the bones of battle-scarred warriors, that when something like this is uncovered, well, it just melts your heart, wouldn't you say?"

The sound of a car engine drew her attention to the road behind the dig, and as she climbed out of the grave the vehicle pulled up and stopped.

She brushed off her hands on her pants and called to the man who had just arrived by Jeep.

"Dr. Parishan, come look! See what was found while you were back in Tehran at the museum having tea with your friends!" She teased the older man, a long-time friend of her father's.

"I heard there was a find and got here as soon as I could. Daria, thank you for coming." Under other circumstances the elderly man, the project director, would have offered a more gracious greeting to the American, whom he had personally requested join them on the dig, but he was eager to examine the contents of the grave. He reached the edge and stared down. "Oh, look at them . . . look at them . . ." he murmured reverentially. "Perfect . . . they are perfect . . .

"So, Dr. McGowan, what is your feeling?" An obviously pleased Korush Parishan stood and brushed the sand from his knees. "On the site, overall?"

"I concur completely with Dr. Karaian's assessment," Daria said without hesitation. "The artifacts he's already unearthed show such a vast mix of cultures, I can't imagine that these people were anything but nomadic. We've seen the Indian river goddesses on the vases, golden goblets in the style of Bactria.

The pottery bowls with the horned dragon, the god Marduk—definitely Babylonian. So here we have clear influences from India, Afghanistan, Mesopotamia. They all came together here in the mountains." She pointed off to the east, then drew a line across the horizon with her index finger. "The Silk Road passed through this region. You'd have had travelers from China, India, Anatolia, Greece. Their cultures all intermingled through the centuries, which would account for the fact that some of the artifacts are of a different age from the others."

She turned to the others and smiled. "This could be an amazing find. The rise off to your left looks as if it might be a likely spot to start. I cannot wait to see what else you might discover here."

"Unfortunately, Dr. McGowan, you may have to postpone your participation." The older man stood. "As I was leaving the museum, I was handed an urgent fax to deliver to you, and a phone message from a Dr. Burnette. Forgive me, but I could not help but note that the message says it is imperative that you contact her as soon as possible."

He removed a folded sheet of paper from his shirt pocket and handed it to her.

Frowning, she opened it and began to read.

"Dr. Burnette is the president of Howe University back in the States." Daria continued to read, then looked up and asked, "Dr. Kasraian, may I use your computer?"

"Of course. It's on the table in the main tent. Please, whatever you need. . . ." He gestured toward the area where the shelters had been erected.

"Thank you."

Daria went directly to the tent, her mind on the fax and its request that she return to the States immediately. Having to leave soon was not what she'd had in mind when she arrived late last week. That the Iranians had invited a well-regarded foreign authority—and a woman, at that—to this newly discovered site was evidence of their desire to participate in the international archaeological society. It was of particular importance to Dr. Parishan that the rest of the world understood how seriously the Iranian archaeological community was taking its obligation to not only protect but to share and showcase their distinct cultural heritage. Like those of its neighbors Afghanistan and Iraq, Iran's cultural treasures had been finding their way out of the country for years, legally and illegally, and they were determined to not only locate but safeguard whatever remained, and do whatever was necessary to recover those items that had, over the years, been lost due to an active black market in stolen antiquities.

Dr. Parishan had handpicked the team to work on this new find. He'd been unable to secure the services of Daria McGowan, a well-known expert in Middle Eastern archaeology, to participate in the initial excavation, but had been pleased that she offered to come as a consultant as soon as her work in the Gobi Desert had been completed. To Parishan, that she was internationally recognized was the cake; that she was the daughter of Samuel McGowan, an old and esteemed friend and colleague, was the icing.

Daria returned to the others an hour later.

"I'm so terribly sorry," she explained, "but I'm

going to have to leave right away. Dr. Kasraian, could I impose upon you for a car?"

"No imposition at all," he assured her. "I'll have a driver take you wherever you need to go. But your family . . . there is bad news?"

"No, no. Nothing like that." She dropped her duffel bag on the ground and slid a hijab around her shoulders. Once they neared the airport, she would use the scarf to cover her head to conform to Iranian law.

"Dr. Parishan, I feel awful about this."

"As long as everyone is well. When I heard 'doctor,' I feared perhaps . . ."

She smiled to reassure him. "Dr. Burnette apparently has been trying to track me down for several weeks. Dr. Parishan, did my father ever speak to you of his grandfather who was also an archaeologist?"

"Alistair McGowan, of course." He nodded. "Everyone knows of the man who found the city of Shandihar when no one believed it had ever existed. Your father told me his grandfather's journal inspired him to follow in his footsteps to become the great archaeologist that he is."

"Then perhaps he also mentioned that the backing for Alistair's expeditions had come from a university?"

"Yes, I believe so. Your father has lectured there, correct?"

"Yes, Dad lectured often at Howe University before he retired. When my great-grandfather returned to the States following his discovery at Shandihar, he went directly to Howe and brought all the artifacts he'd found with him. The university had supplied the funding, so the spoils belonged to them. At least, that's how it worked at the turn of the century. He spent years cataloging the artifacts to display in the museum that Howe was building. Unfortunately, he died before the construction was completed."

"Yes, yes, this I have heard." Parishan nodded. "But what does this have to do with you?"

"Apparently the university wants to do something to commemorate the hundredth anniversary of Alistair's discovery. They want to put his findings on display, after all these years. Dr. Burnette has asked me to take charge of the entire project."

Parishan's eyes lit up.

"You would be designing the exhibits?"

"Everything, Dr. Parishan." She smiled with dazed pleasure. "They want me to do everything."